carrington cove: book five

SOMEHOW YOU *knew*

HARLOW JAMES

ISBN: 9798991541923

Contents

This one is for my grandma...

The one who I know is cheering me on from the other side...

And the one who said she'd visit me as a hummingbird.

Keep going...

*because that person watching you from heaven
doesn't want you to quit.*

Unknown

Prologue

Hazel

Age Nineteen

I watch the waves roll in toward the shore and back out again as the moonlight shimmers on the water. Swiping away a tear, I barely react to the sound of the lighthouse door opening and closing from below, my father's footsteps echoing on the stairs.

"You found me," I say dryly as he clears the final step and studies me across the small space.

"Wasn't exactly difficult, seeing as the keys to the lighthouse were missing from their hook."

I pull the key ring from my pocket, holding it out to him without taking my eyes off the water. "Sorry."

My father closes the space between us, grabbing the keys before settling next to me on the bench beneath the window. "No need to apologize, Hazelnut."

Another tear falls down my cheek. "I just needed some space."

"No need to apologize for that either." He wraps his arm around my shoulders, pulling me into his chest. "Talk to me."

"I'm pathetic."

"Hey, you're talking crap about one of my favorite people on this planet, so you'd better knock it off."

I scoff through my tears. "I'm serious, Dad. Who the hell thinks her boyfriend at nineteen is the one?"

"Lots of teenagers," he counters. "Hell, I pictured every girlfriend I had back in the day as my future bride."

I look over at him. "Really?"

He winks at me over his shoulder. "Come on, does that really surprise you?"

I attempt a smile before looking back out at the waves. "I guess not."

"Hazel, you are a romantic at heart, just like your old man. There's nothing wrong with that. It just means you have so much love to give, and one day, you'll find the person that deserves it all. But remember, you're only nineteen. Age doesn't mean shit, but the life experience that comes with age will help you know when you've met the right man. Maybe in the meantime, you try to be more selective." He taps his chin. "You need a rule breaker, someone who isn't afraid to push the limits—because if you end up with someone who doesn't push you, you'll be bored."

"Casey *was* getting kind of boring," I admit, even though it pains me. Even though he wasn't the most exciting guy, he had some good qualities about him that made me think we could have had a future.

He nudges me with his shoulder. "See? That's a red flag right there. Be grateful to him for what he's taught you and move forward."

He makes it sound so simple, but we both know it's not.

"Just promise me," he continues, "that no matter how exhausted you may get looking for the right person, you'll never stop fighting for him when you do find him. He'll probably need that from you more than he'll be willing to admit."

I frown. "Why do you say that?"

"Because men have a habit of not seeing what's right in front of them until it's too late."

A heavy sigh leaves my lips. "I just want what you and Mom have."

He huffs out a soft laugh. "You realize your mother and I only have what we do because she never gave up on me, right?"

"You act like your relationship isn't perfect."

He shakes his head. "Oh, Hazelnut. If you think that, then I haven't been doing a very good job of guiding your heart."

I lean my head on his shoulder. "You have, I just..." I trail off, the words caught somewhere between my heart and my throat.

"If it weren't for your mother, I wouldn't be half the man I am today, or the father I strive to be." He clears the emotion from his throat. "She doesn't just love me—she chooses me every single day. Even when it's hard."

I glance back at my father, really looking this time. The wrinkles around his eyes have deepened, and the lines on his face are etched with the weight of a life fully lived. He stares out at the ocean, and for a moment, I wonder what memories the waves are pulling from him.

My father spent ten years in the Marines before coming home, carrying burdens that weren't easily forgotten. My mother never told me the full story, but I know my dad has gone through a lot, both physically and mentally. My brothers joke that I got the best version of him since I'm the youngest of my four siblings. The thought that he wasn't always the loving and caring father he is now makes my heart ache, but more than anything, I feel truly grateful for the relationship we have.

Even though he's the one who plagued me with this hopeless romantic curse, he's also the reason I believe so deeply in love, even when it hurts. And he's the one who helps put me back together every time my heart breaks.

"She really loves you," I say finally, pulling his attention back to me.

"That she does. But loving someone doesn't mean life is easy all the time. It's easy to love someone when things are good. It's the low points—the obstacles and hurdles—that truly test that love. Love is a choice, Hazelnut. And the right person? They'll choose you over and over again."

"I thought Casey had chosen me."

"Casey can't choose between two different kinds of sandwiches," he teases, reminding me of how my ex agonized over his lunch order the other day.

I snort. "This is true."

"Any man who can't make a decision about a sandwich isn't a man worthy of my daughter."

"That's a bizarre standard."

"But it's the truth." He kisses my temple. "Honestly, I feel like no one is good enough for my little hummingbird."

I roll my eyes, but inside, I melt. My father has called me Hazelnut for most of my life, but when I was little, he called me his hummingbird as well. He jokes that I was always running around, never still, so I reminded him of the little bird that flaps its wings at lightning speed. But as I got older, he told me about other things the bird represents—strength, courage, and the zeal for exploring life.

Honestly, hearing the nickname now after so long makes me feel inadequate, like I'll never quite live up to it. But I know my dad loves me no matter what, especially when I don't feel very strong or courageous.

Above us, the lighthouse beam sweeps through the night, cutting through the darkness before vanishing into it again—just like the way

I fall for someone, bright and all-consuming at first, only for the light to fade just as quickly.

"The truth is," he says, "very few people cherish love the way you do. Sadly, that means you'll probably be disappointed more than reciprocated. And I know it sounds cliché, but as soon as you stop looking for love and focus more on loving yourself, the right man will come along."

"That *is* cliché, Dad."

He shrugs. "In the meantime, you know I'll be here anytime you need me, okay?"

I lean my head on his shoulder. "I know." This isn't the first time my father has helped me mend a broken heart or told me not to lose hope for love. And even though I'm still young, he doesn't make me feel childish for believing in soulmates or thinking I could find my person at such a young age.

God, I don't know how other girls handle love and its aftermath without a dad like mine.

"And this place is always here when you need to escape for a while," he says, pulling me from my thoughts.

"I know that too."

Perched on the coast of our small town, the Carrington Cove lighthouse has always been a place of solitude for my dad. It wasn't until last year that he shared it with me. Since then, it's a safe space we retreat to when we need a break from reality—because staring out into the ocean from this vantage point is a reminder of how big our world truly is and how small our problems are by comparison.

"We romantics have to stick together."

I sigh, closing my eyes as I squeeze his arm. "I agree."

"And I can't wait for the day you find the man lucky enough to have you." He kisses the top of my head. "Walking you down the aisle to him will be the highlight of my life."

"Mine too," I whisper, envisioning that day as clearly as I can.

I just didn't yet know *who* would be waiting for me at the end of the aisle.

Or that my father wouldn't be there to walk me down it.

Chapter One

Hazel

Present Day

"Keely, you're a lifesaver." With outstretched hands, I intercept the double-shot espresso from her, eager for the extra boost of caffeine to power through my work.

"Saving the world one cup of coffee at a time." She winks before scurrying back behind the front counter to help a waiting customer.

Most days, I work from my studio or my couch, but when I found myself reaching for my phone for the third time in ten minutes, I knew I needed a change of scenery. So, I came to Keely's Caffeine Kick to push through the last of the wedding photos I shot a few weeks ago. I love my job, capturing the most important moments in my clients' lives, but editing can be a beast.

I lift the mug to my lips and take a cautious sip, smacking my lips together as the sweet nectar of life hits my tongue. I swear, Keely must put a pinch of crack in her coffee because it never tastes this good when I make it at home.

My computer finishes loading the gallery as I take another sip, and I pop my earbuds in, pressing play on the latest album from the one and only queen herself, Taylor Swift. Music hits my ears, and I dial in, ready to tackle these photos so I can stay on track for the rest of my projects.

When I started Hazel Sheppard Photography four years ago, I never dreamed I'd be as busy as I am, but you won't hear me complaining. I know how lucky I am to make a living doing what I love. Some people never get that opportunity, so I practice gratitude often when it comes to my work.

But even my job can't fill some voids that always seem to be lurking under the surface—the doubt, the loneliness, the insecurities that I'm too much, not enough, or just not one of the lucky ones who finds their person like my friends, clients, and even brothers have all managed to do.

The picture of the couple's first kiss as husband and wife pops up on my screen, twisting the knife in my chest even further.

Will I ever find someone who looks at me like that? Like I'm their whole world, universe, and existence all wrapped into one?

Sighing, I pick up my phone and see a message from Derek, the latest guy I matched with on one of the many dating apps I've reluctantly joined. Even though online dating is quickly becoming the bane of my existence, it's how people meet these days.

I swear, if my father knew what I've been through in the past four years, he'd want to throw my phone into the ocean for me.

"What do you call two spiders who just got married?" A voice to my right cuts through my music, startling me.

Plucking out an earbud, I turn, and when I look up to see the man the voice belongs to, a wave of electricity radiates from my chest, freezing me in place.

Holy mother of God. How on earth did DNA configure itself to create this specimen of a man so flawlessly?

The corner of his mouth lifts. "So you *weren't* ignoring me."

"Huh?" I find my voice, grateful my brain is still firing some cylinders since my heart is beating so fast I can barely manage to breathe.

"I've been trying to get your attention for the past few minutes."

Blinking, I glance back at my computer. "Um...Well, I was working."

He slides into the chair across from me, leaning back and resting one hand on his knee, the other draped over the back of the chair. "I can see that, hence the joke," he says, gesturing to the picture of the bride and groom on my screen.

"Joke?"

"Yeah. What do you call two spiders who just got married?" he repeats.

"Oh. Uh, I'm not sure."

"Newly-webs." He smirks, clearly pleased with himself.

I can't help but smile, even though his presence still makes me feel off-balance.

I'd know if I'd seen this guy around town before because there's no way I'd forget *him*. God, he looks like the embodiment of every teenage girl's fantasy—the definition of tall, dark, and dangerous. The epitome of a bad boy, especially given the way his arms are entirely covered in tattoos.

"Did you need something?" I ask, not sure how I'm supposed to react to this perfect stranger interrupting my work, even though my libido isn't complaining. In fact, this is the most alert the button between my legs has been in a long time.

He huffs out a laugh before tilting his head, eyeing me. "Actually, I do." He leans forward now, locking his electric green eyes on me, such a contrast to his jet-black hair and all-black attire. "I wanted to know if I could draw on you?"

My head jerks back slightly, brows knitting together. "What?"

He reaches for my hand, gently laying it on the surface of the table. "I'd like to draw on you, if that's okay with you."

I swallow past the lump in my throat, trying to figure out if this is really happening or if Keely does, in fact, slip something into her coffee.

"You want to draw on me?"

He nods while pulling a marker from his pocket, uncapping it with his teeth.

Jesus. Was that supposed to be that hot?

"I do."

"Why?"

"Let's just say, I have a list of things I'm trying to cross off, and this is one of them."

"A list?"

He nods. "Yup. So, care to help me?"

Watching as he gently takes my hand and places the tip of the marker against my forearm, I debate if this is as harmless as it seems. I mean sure, I don't know this guy, but it's not like he busted out a tattoo gun.

As the heat of his touch sears through my skin, I nod, unable to stop myself even if I wanted to. My mind spins as I wonder how the hell my choice to work at the coffee shop today has turned into the most exhilarating interaction with a stranger I've ever had.

And not just any stranger. A *hot* stranger—the type of man wet dreams are made of.

He flashes me that smirk again, the perfect boyish charm to counterbalance his rough exterior. "Excellent."

I lean forward, studying his every move and memorizing every detail of his face, willing myself not to forget any aspect of this moment. "Wh—what are you going to draw?"

He lifts his eyes to mine just long enough to say, "You'll just have to wait and see."

I roll my eyes. "Well, you're no fun."

He chuckles. "I might have heard that a time or two."

Silence grows between us and butterflies take flight in my stomach as my mystery guy zeroes in on the drawing he's sketching on my skin. The pinch in his brow is so deep that I wonder how he doesn't have wrinkles. But then again, he can't be much older than me. His nails are clean, his hands are remarkably soft, and after he drags the marker over my skin, he goes back over what he drew with his thumb, smoothing and buffing out the lines, like he has far too much experience doing something like this.

A piece of his dark hair falls over his forehead, coming apart from the combed back style he walked in here with. His jaw is covered in black stubble, the kind that offers beard burn in the most delicious way, a way that I'm fantasizing about the longer I sit here and watch this man mark my skin with intense concentration.

But when the marker stops moving and sits back to admire his work, I look back down at my arm to see what he drew—and my stomach drops.

"What do you think?" he asks as I fight to keep my composure, the sting of tears building behind my eyes.

Swallowing past the lump in my throat, I manage to clear it and meet his eyes. "It's beautiful.""Not bad for a marker, huh?"

I drag my finger over the lines. "It's remarkable."

Before I can say anything else, he stands from his chair, staring down at me with that same pinch in his brow, like he's just as confused by this encounter as I am. But all he says is, "Thanks for helping me out."

Then, just as suddenly as he appeared, he's gone, leaving me staring after him in stunned silence.

Chapter Two

Hazel

One Month Later

"No woman is ever going to be good enough for you," I whisper, staring down at my nephew, my heart swelling as his tiny fingers curl around mine. My vision blurs, but I refuse to let the tears fall. Not here. Not today.

My oldest brother, Dallas, steps closer, pride radiating from him as he gazes down at his son. "That's an odd first thing to say to your nephew."

I shrug. "It's true, though."

Willow clears her throat from the hospital bed. "I have to agree with her, babe."

"Goose, he's barely a few hours old and you're already dooming his dating life?"

My brother's nickname for his wife never fails to make me smile, especially given Willow's history with the geese on their property.

"Don't worry. After I tell him all my dating horror stories, he'll have no interest in it anyway," I say, bouncing the baby gently as I pace the room.

"Uh oh. I take it last night didn't go well, then?" Willow asks.

I pin her with a flat look before resuming my enchantment with my nephew. "It was a train wreck."

Willow stifles a yawn. "Oh, come on. It couldn't have been that bad."

This time I glare at her. "Easy for you to say. You found your person. Hell, you just squeezed a kid out of your vagina, and still have hearts in your eyes." She snorts, but I know she knows I'm right. "Dating in this day and age isn't like it used to be."

And I'm beginning to think it's only going to get worse.

"You act like you're ancient, Hazelnut," Dallas says as he sits down on the bed next to his wife, stroking her forehead softly.

I try to ignore the tiny twinge of pain that resonates in my chest from hearing Dallas use the nickname my father gave me. He doesn't know that every time he calls me that, it's a painful reminder of what I lost. But I don't have the heart to ask him to stop, and part of me doesn't want him to, because if he does, it'll feel like losing another piece of my dad.

I know he's gone. I know he's not coming back. But somehow, I still can't fully accept it.

"I'm beginning to feel ancient, especially now that all my brothers are happily in love."

"You're only twenty-eight, Hazel," Willow interjects. "Did you forget that your brother and I met when we were in our early thirties?"

I shake my head as my nephew stirs in my arms. "You just don't get it."

And no one ever does—not how the hope grows with each new guy I talk to, not how my mind spins visions of our future together after just one date, and not how depressing it is each time it doesn't work out.

No one understands it—not like my dad did anyway.

"Tell me more about your date."

I look out the window, watching the white clouds drift across the sky as the breeze pulls them in from the ocean. The hospital is too far inland to see the water, but I know it's out there. It's oddly comforting.

I spin to face the two of them again. "Well, it started with him picking me up and not even bothering to get out of the car. Then, when I got to the car and opened my own door, he pretended he was going to drive off without me, which he found *hilarious*."

My brother growls. "I wanna punch this guy already."

"Oh believe me, I contemplated it. After I finally got in his car—against my better judgment—we drove to the concert while he asked me questions about how I envision the future with my significant other, which I thought was a good sign...until he told me what his vision of *our* future together looked like, and then I had to hold back my vomit."

Willow winces. "I'm afraid to ask."

I adjust my nephew in my arms before continuing. "Oh, it was quite the fantasy. He told me he dreams of me in the kitchen when he comes home from work, ready to serve him dinner. Then after we eat and I clean up, we sit on the couch—correction, I sit on his lap on the couch—while I listen to him tell me about his day. Then he watches television before he goes to sleep. But not before we fuck, of course—in any position he wants me. Because, you know, that's my *job* as a woman."

Dallas's fists grow tighter as Willow's eyes grow wider.

"But that's not the worst part..."

"Oh God, there's more?" Willow asks, shocked.

"Oh yeah. He ignored me the entire concert because he was too busy flirting with the girl next to us. Then he had a few too many beers, and by the time the concert was over, he could barely walk straight. So I ended up driving us home, even though there was a storm in full swing. And as we drove back, he asked me a question I had to think about for so long, it made me wonder if I was the one losing it."

Willow tenses, bracing herself. "What did he ask you?"

I take a deep breath, close my eyes, and say, "He asked me if I could *see* the thunder."

Dallas's eyebrows draw together. "Come again?"

Willow covers her mouth to stifle her laughter. "Oh God."

"I just wanna make sure I heard you correctly," Dallas says, looking at me like I've grown a second head. "You said he asked if you could *see* the thunder?"

"I didn't stutter, Dallas. Yes, that's what he said. And when I calmly explained that thunder is a *sound*, he laughed like I was the idiot and said I just wasn't on his level. Then he launched into some nonsense about how people who are *truly enlightened* can experience reality beyond the constraints of science."

Willow shakes her head. "Okay, you're right. I *don't* get what you're going through."

"What the fuck kind of morons are you dating?" Dallas asks incredulously. "Don't you like...talk to them for a while before going out with them? I mean, seriously, Hazel..."

"Babe..." Willow places her hand on his forearm in warning.

But the damage has already been done.

"Of course I fucking talk to them, Dallas!" I whisper-shout, startling my nephew, but he settles after a few seconds. "This guy seemed great—good career, came from a good family, but meeting him in person was just..." I shudder.

"I'm so sorry, Hazel." Willow reaches for Michael as he stirs again, turning his face toward my chest where there sure as hell isn't a milk supply.

When my brother and his wife told us they were naming their son after Dad, I think I cried the hardest. Not only was it a beautiful tribute to our father, but my dad played a part in bringing the two of them together.

The romantic in him was always at work.

"I'm sorry too, Hazelnut," Dallas says as he watches his son calm down and latch onto Willow's breast.

I let out a heavy sigh after a few moments. "I just can't do this anymore."

Dallas stands from the bed and walks over to me. "What? Date?"

I nod. "It's pointless. I've tried, you know? Given men the benefit of the doubt, been open-minded…but I think I'm just destined to be alone. And without Dad here…"

My brother pulls me into his chest, smoothing my long black hair down my back. "I know you miss him. We all do."

"He would give me some sort of wisdom, some sort of encouragement after last night." Leaning back, I shrug, refusing to let the tears fall. "And seriously? Did this guy fail fourth grade or something? You don't *see* thunder, you moron."

Dallas and Willow both laugh. "Maybe that should be the question you lead with from now on in the get-to-know-you phase," my brother suggests.

"Yeah, because *that* won't make me seem like a crazy person."

"He just wasn't the right person," Willow says as she looks down at Michael resting peacefully in her arms.

"None of them are." I take a step away from my brother, brush my hair from my face, and then declare, "And I don't think I want to keep searching for the right one anymore."

My brother and Willow share a look.

"A break could be good," Willow offers.

Something in my chest shifts as I say my next words. "No. I think I'm done—done trying, done hoping, done being optimistic." I look over at Willow holding her baby and my brother watching them dotingly.

They have the kind of love and life I document with my camera regularly. It's what I've always wanted, what I've always dreamed of.

But that's the thing about dreams—they aren't real.

And they can change.

Maybe it's time I start searching for a new one.

"I'm not meant to have what you two have, what Penn found with Astrid or what Parker found with Cashlynn."

"Hazelnut—" Dallas starts, but I hold up my hand.

"Nope. I'm serious. I'm just gonna be the fun aunt," I say as I hoist my jeans up higher on my waist and smooth down my top, faking a smile. "I'm gonna thrive in my business and take myself on vacation." Dallas's eyebrows draw closer together. "Toys were invented for a reason, right? So I don't need a man for pleasure..."

"For the love of God, please stop," my brother begs.

Willow giggles. "Hazel, I know you're feeling discouraged, honey. But do you honestly think swearing off love is the right decision?"

"Nope." I straighten my spine. "I can't bear the thought of putting myself through another date like that."

Not without Dad here to pick me back up. Not without knowing that he still believes.

Because when he died, I think my hope died with him.

Michael starts to cry again, signaling that it's time for me to go.

"I love you both very much," I say as I bend down and kiss Willow's forehead and then my nephew's. "And I couldn't be happier for you. You did good," I say as I smooth Michael's jet-black wisps of hair.

"We love you too," Willow says with a soft smile.

"I'll come over later this week once you're all settled. Let me know what you want for dinner, and I'll make it. And as soon as my nephew starts to have favorites, let me know so I can spoil the crap out of him."

There's concern in Willow's eyes as she watches me move toward the door. "Are you gonna be okay, Hazel?"

I plaster on the best smile I can muster. "I'll be fine. This is just how things were meant to be," I say with a shrug and then blow a kiss to my brother. "Take care of your family, big brother. You're one lucky son-of-a-bitch."

"Be careful, Hazelnut," he says as I step into the hall.

I can feel the tears just behind my eyes.

But they don't come.

Because I meant what I said in that room.

I'm done.

Being a hopeless romantic doesn't guarantee you love. In fact, it just might mean the opposite.

And for the first time in my life, I think I'm finally accepting that love just isn't meant for me.

***

"Do you need anything else before I go?" I ask as I pack up my camera bag.

Diane settles into her rocker, adjusting the oxygen tubes on her face. "No, dear. But you know you can't leave without having a cup of tea." She gestures toward the couch beside her, where I left her mug, steam still curling from the surface.

I glance down at my watch. All I have left to do is edit this afternoon, but I'm almost done, so it can wait. And Diane is right—our tea tradition can't. "Sure, I guess I can spare you a few minutes of my time," I say with a wink.

She winks back at me as I take my seat. "Well, aren't I the lucky one?"

"Don't you ever forget it either." Just then, Diane's French Bulldog, Blueberry, comes barreling through his dog door and launches onto the couch, his pink cape flowing behind him. "Welcome back, handsome man! Did you take care of business?" I scoop him up onto my lap, as he showers me with kisses.

"His routine is pretty predictable these days," Diane says, gazing lovingly at her pup.

Years ago, when I was just starting my photography business, Diane reached out to see if I would be interested in photographing her dog. At the time, I didn't turn down any type of work, so I agreed, of course. From then on, we set up regular appointments, documenting half-birthdays, all major holidays, and any other excuse Diane could come up with for me to take her dog's picture and dress him up in the latest adorable outfit she found on Etsy. But along the way, between snapping photos of Blueberry in tiny sweaters and superhero capes, Diane became a friend.

Having never married or had kids of her own, Blueberry is her family, her fur baby and pride and joy, and the glue that solidified our friendship. When she was diagnosed with COPD, I made sure to check on her regularly, help her with errands, cook her dinner a few nights a month, and help take Blueberry to the Carrington Cove Animal Hospital for his appointments, which just happens to be where my older brother, Parker, works as a vet.

I know she's much older than me, but in a way, we're kindred spirits—independent, sassy, and confident.

"He's one lucky pup." I stroke the top of his head as he finally begins to settle in my lap.

"I don't know what I would do without that dog." Diane barks out a cough, reminding us both that her health is declining with each passing day.

"Maybe I need to get a dog," I say, trying not to address the elephant in the room. "Since I'm swearing off men, perhaps I just need a fur-boyfriend instead."

Diane lifts a brow. "Well, that's one way to phrase it. Just don't say it in public."

I chuckle as I lean back on the couch. "Noted."

"So you're swearing off men?"

"Oh yeah. After last week, I can officially say the dating world and I have called it quits."

"It's such a shame my nephew doesn't live closer... I know you two would hit it off."

I hold up my hand and roll my eyes simultaneously. "Diane, we've been over this. I know you think he can walk on water, but I'm telling you, I'm done. I have plenty of silicone toys to last me a lifetime, and my business keeps me busy. Love is overrated anyway, don't you think?"

Diane has been single most of her life. She told me the story of how she was engaged once but called it off at the last minute because it just didn't feel right. Lo and behold, her fiancé was cheating with a woman a few towns over, and she found out when the doctor's office called her phone instead of his with an urgent message. Turns out, the call was about his STD test results. Luckily, Diane was in the clear, but it just goes to show you that you can stand at the edge of forever with someone and still realize you never really knew them at all.

And her gut saved her from making one of the biggest mistakes of her life.

I can't help but feel that my gut is doing the same for me.

"No man is perfect, Hazel, but Gage is hardworking and has a creative soul like you. His sense of humor actually reminds me a lot of yours, although lately, due to his—"

My phone rings in my purse, interrupting her. Scrambling to answer it, I say, "I'm sorry, Diane. Hold that thought."

"No worries, dear. Nowadays, it's almost weird if a phone *doesn't* interrupt a conversation." Her smile is genuine, so I know she's truly not bothered by it.

When I see that it's Laney, I wait for the call to end, then shoot her a quick text to let her know I'll call her back shortly.

"Now, where were we?" I look up to see that Diane has started to fall asleep in her chair, with Blueberry now curled up in her lap. Standing from the couch, I grab the blanket off the back and drape it over the two of them, making sure to keep Blueberry's face exposed.

"I'm gonna take off," I whisper.

"Okay, dear. Thank you, as always."

"My pleasure, Diane." I lean down and kiss her forehead, hesitantly reminding myself that each time I see her could be the last.

Because when you've lost people, you start thinking like this—wondering if this time will be the last. Each last is your last before you ever realize it. And then when it hits you, the finality of the moment can make it feel like it's almost too hard to breathe.

"See you on Tuesday," I whisper, gently pulling the front door shut behind me.

I slide into my car, tossing my bag into the passenger seat before sinking into the driver's seat with a sigh.

As I pull onto the road, I tap my screen to call Laney back.

"Hey girl!" Laney's cheery voice bursts through the speakers, instantly lifting my mood.

"What's up? Sorry I couldn't answer. I was with Diane."

"No worries. I just wanted details about your date the other night. You never called me, so I wasn't sure if that was a good or bad sign, you know?"

I let out another sigh. "Oh, Jesus. It was definitely *not* good. But in the chaos of Willow going into labor and giving birth to Michael, I totally spaced on calling you back."

"Oh, don't even worry about it. I totally understand. And, a new little baby to love on? Congrats, auntie! Being an aunt is the best."

"Thank you. He's adorable and hopefully will never treat a woman the way that asshole Derek treated me."

Laney clears her throat. "Well, spill then. Tell me everything."

I spend the next several minutes of my drive home recounting the horrendous details of my date.

"Okay, I don't blame you for giving up on men after that one," she says.

"Right?"

Now it's her turn to sigh. "God, why can't they all be like Hummingbird Guy?"

"Ah, yes...the elusive Hummingbird Guy. I mean, he barely said more than a few sentences to me, but I was already picking out China patterns."

Laney and I share a laugh as I bring up my stranger from over a month ago for the thousandth time. The truth is, the brief encounter plays on a loop in my mind..

"Don't feel too bad. We don't have men like that here in my little town either. But a girl can hope, right?"

Laney lives in Blossom Peak, a small town in the North Carolina mountains, about a seven-hour drive from Carrington Cove. Our mountains might not be as vast as the ones they have out west, but they hold a different kind of magic—the kind that makes you forget where you came from and wonder if you ever want to go back.

A few years ago, Laney reached out to me in need of professional photos for her salon, Blossom Beauty, after she found my photography page on Instagram. As a fellow business owner, I know the importance of the right pictures to portray a brand, so I took care of her and we hit it off instantly. We've remained friends ever since.

Every once in a while, I'll leave town without telling anyone and go visit *her* small town, needing the escape from my own. Not only do we share a love of good wine, 2000s rom-coms, and female empowerment, but she *gets* me. We're both single, both business owners, and both surrounded by married people who have forgotten what it's like to be alone.

I love my friends here, and even though my brothers don't deserve them, they've each married women that I'm proud to call my sisters-in-law. But they're all so happy in their married life bliss bubbles, while I'm sitting on the outside looking in.

And Laney knows exactly how I feel.

"I still can't get over him, though," she says, bringing me back to our conversation and the man who made an impression on me faster than any man has in a long time.

"Girl, you and me both. But I'm almost convinced that I made him up, you know?" I exhale, drumming my fingers on the steering wheel. "I've never seen him again, the hummingbird he drew has long since been washed away, and the whole encounter sounds like something straight out of a romance novel."

"Such a shame. He was tatted too, right?"

I swallow, my mouth watering as the mental image forms. "Oh yeah."

Jet black hair, piercing green eyes, and fully tattooed arms, ink all the way down to his knuckles. The scruff on his chin only added to his sex appeal, and how his rugged demeanor was contrasted by the delicate way he held my arm while he sketched a hummingbird on my skin. He wore all black, but sitting across from him for those twenty minutes felt like being blinded by the sun.

It was the most surreal, out-of-body, orgasmic experience of my life—and then he was gone. Like it never happened.

And the part that unsettles me the most, the part that makes me unable to forget about him, is the *hummingbird*.

Only one person could know the importance of that.

And he's not even alive anymore.

"Maybe it all was a dream," Laney muses as I pull into my parking space in front of my apartment. "Maybe being perpetually single and going on strings of bad dates is making us hallucinate."

"Uh, that doesn't give me much hope, Laney."

She laughs. "I know. Hope is overrated anyway."

"Then let's just vow to be single together."

"Deal...especially given that Seth has pretty much scarred me for life."

"I never met the guy, and I think I might hate him more than you do."

"He's not worth the energy," she says, referencing her ex. "Honestly, I think I knew deep down we weren't meant to be. I just wish he hadn't shaken my confidence so much." She sighs. "But the truth is, he never made me feel anything like what I felt for Fletcher."

"Ugh. Why do older brother's best friends have to be so damn irritating and handsome at the same time?"

I think back to all the times I had a crush on my brothers' friends and how many times I was just written off as the annoying little sister. That is, until one *did* start to notice me. After that, Penn and Dallas ensured none of their friends ever made that mistake again, threatening bodily harm to anyone who so much as looked in my direction.

Let's just say that I didn't have much of a dating life until they both moved out. Even though Parker was still around, he was so focused on school and his own girlfriend that he didn't pay much attention to my dating life.

"Fletcher *is* beyond irritating, especially when I have to see his stupid face on the TV every damn weekend."

"Being a professional football player has only made him cockier, huh?"

"Honestly? I wouldn't know. I've been avoiding him every time he comes to town, which isn't often, but still. Judging by that smug smirk he's perfected for the cameras, I'd say he hasn't changed much. But one of these days, we're going to cross paths again and I'll have to remind myself of how he truly feels about me so I don't do anything stupid...again."

"Well, I wish you luck with that."

"Thank you. I'm gonna need it."

"All right, I better let you go. I just got home and have to catch up on editing. If I don't, I'm going to be drowning in work."

"Life as a business owner never stops, right?"

"Never," I say, unlocking my front door. "But I love it."

I can practically hear the smile in her voice. "Talk to you soon!"

"Bye, Laney."

Once inside my apartment, I grab a glass of wine, change into my pajamas and "wine makes me less murdery" socks, and settle into my favorite spot on the couch. I put my headphones on, push play on my latest romance audiobook, and get to work creating beautiful memories of other people's love stories while quietly wondering if I'll ever have one of my own.

Little did I know that Hummingbird guy and I would cross paths again, and when we did, I'd realize he wasn't such a stranger after all.

Chapter Three

Hazel

One Year Later

"Sorry to keep you waiting," Timothy MacDonald, Carrington Cove's resident attorney, steps out of the hallway leading to his office and greets me in the reception area.

"Not a problem, Tim." I stand from my chair, smooth my shirt, swing my bag over my shoulder, and follow him back to his office.

"Today has just been a little crazy, especially without Mabel here."

Taking a seat across from him at his desk, I put my purse on the floor beside me. "I can imagine. How is she doing? I heard about her knee."

Timothy settles into his chair, resting his clasped hands on his rounded belly. "Luckily, the doctor said nothing is broken or torn, but she definitely angered a ligament. The woman decided to run a marathon and ends up hurting herself." He shakes his head and pats his stomach. "This is why I don't exercise—causes more harm than good."

I hold back an eye roll. "That's one way to look at it."

"Regardless, I can't wait for her to return. She keeps this place running." Timothy leans forward, shuffling papers across his desk. "Well, I would get started, but we need to wait on Gage."

I glance at my watch, noting that it's ten minutes past our scheduled appointment time. Grinding my jaw in irritation, I remind myself to relax. I'm here for Diane, not him. "It's fine. This is the one free day I have this week...but I imagine there's a timeline for handling these things."

"Yes, there is. And Diane was insistent about some of them."

Diane Kingston passed away three weeks ago after her long battle with COPD. Being with her in her final days brought back painful memories of losing my dad to cancer three years ago, but I'm grateful I had that time with her. The friendship that woman gave me, the genuine appreciation and love we shared—it's something I'll cherish forever.

And her precious nephew she boasted about so often was nowhere to be found in her final days... Which probably explains why I'm this irritated with a man I've never even met.

He better have a damn good reason he's keeping us waiting, especially since I hate leaving Blueberry alone for too long. Diane gave me custody of her dog, so now, on top of whatever Timothy tells me today, I am also a new pet owner. That's an unexpected transition I'm still trying to navigate.

"I'm sure he'll be here soon," Timothy says.

As if on cue, the walls begin to tremble with the rumble of a motorcycle outside. Moments later, the front door chimes, and Timothy glances behind me as I twist to see exactly who I'm dealing with.

And the moment I do, my breath stalls.

Holy shit.

Jet-black hair, piercing green eyes, and tattoos snaking down his arms all the way to his knuckles. The air around him crackles with something electric, something that makes my stomach clench.

Hummingbird Guy.

"Hey, there. Sorry I'm late. Traffic on the beach road was a nightmare," he says, stepping past me to shake Timothy's hand across the desk.

"No problem. The traffic always gets crazy in the morning as tourists head toward the beach and everyone else is trying to get to work," Timothy replies.

Gage takes a seat in the chair beside me as my pulse pounds violently. "I'll remember that in the future." He twists to face me, flashing me a lethal grin that shouldn't affect me the way it does, especially now that I know who he is. "I'm Gage."

I clear my throat as I debate how to respond. I'm speechless, truly speechless. And that never happens to me. I *always* have something to say.

"Uh... Hazel."

He gives me a curt nod and then turns back to Timothy.

Jesus, really? He's going to act like he doesn't know me?

And then the realization slams into me.

Oh my God. What if he doesn't remember me?

Did I dream up our interaction? Or does he go around drawing things on random women so often that we all just blur together?

"Hazel, Gage is Diane's nephew, which I'm sure you've put together by now," Timothy says, pulling me from my mental spiral.

I manage a dumbfounded nod in response.

"So what did you need to talk to us about?" Gage asks, not even bothering to glance my way.

Great. He's gorgeous and *an asshole.*

"I thought everything was taken care of with my aunt's estate."

"Most of it was, yes," Timothy says, opening a file folder and pulling out a few papers. "But there was one other matter she wanted settled that just involves the two of you."

I shift in my seat, suddenly uneasy. "The two of us?"

Timothy nods. "Yes. As you know, Diane had no children, no spouse, and therefore no legal beneficiaries of her wealth. So, she chose you two."

I barely have time to process that before he drops the next bombshell. "Diane had amassed a total wealth of 10.2 million dollars."

My eyes threaten to fall out of my head. "Holy shit."

Diane was rich?

Beside me, Gage exhales sharply. "Christ. I knew she had money, but I didn't think we were talking *eight figures.*"

"Yes, well... She made a good living as an engineer and had stock in a little-known software company back in the '90s—before it became one of the biggest names in cybersecurity. She wanted to be sure the people who meant the most to her were taken care of long after she was gone."

But she lived so simply... The most frivolous thing she ever spent money on was Blueberry's endless collection of tiny sweaters and superhero capes. Yet, apparently, she was a millionaire?

"There are a few stipulations to the inheritance, of course," Timothy continues.

"Like what?" Gage asks.

Timothy lets out a heavy sigh. "Let me just say, I was opposed to this idea, but your aunt was insistent."

"So what's the catch?" I ask, trying not to sound insensitive as I process this turn of events. "I mean, even if we split it, that's still life-changing money." I exhale, shaking my head. "I just can't believe she included *me* in this."

"Oh, that was her intention—for the two of you to split the money, but only after you satisfy a set of conditions." Timothy shifts through the stack of papers, avoiding our eyes.

Gage folds his arms across his chest. "What kind of conditions?"

I wait on bated breath, wondering what crazy idea this woman could have possibly come up with. I mean, I know Diane was quirky, but what could she possibly have come up with that's making Timothy look this nervous?

Timothy shakes his head and finally meets our gazes. "In order to inherit the money, the first condition is that you two have to...get married."

I snap my head toward Gage at the exact moment he looks at me, our wide-eyed shock perfectly mirrored.

I whip back to Timothy. "I'm sorry. Did you say...*married*?" My voice comes out strangled, like my brain can't even process the word.

"To *each other*?" Gage asks, his voice dripping with disbelief.

Timothy gives a tight smile, clearly uncomfortable. "That's what she insisted on."

Both Gage and I lean back in our chairs defeatedly as time seems to stand still.

Married? To a complete stranger?

No—scratch that. Married to *him*? The same guy who once held my wrist like I was something delicate, traced soft lines on my skin, and then disappeared from my life without a second thought?

Gage exhales a harsh laugh and drags a hand down his face. "That's not an option," he declares, his voice firm.

Ouch.

I'm no Victoria Secret model, but Jesus, at least pretend to give it some consideration before you straight up reject a girl.

"Yeah, I'm not down for that either," I say quickly, crossing my arms—not out of indignation, but pure self-preservation. Because, despite the absolute absurdity of this moment, my nipples are still peaking against my bra like they didn't get the memo that we're in full crisis mode.

Gage adjusts himself in his chair. "Any alternatives?"

Timothy shakes his head. "No. That was the requirement, and just so you know, she anticipated your reaction." He fishes out another paper from the file folder, his expression softening. "So, she wrote a letter I'm supposed to read to you."

The sight of Diane's familiar handwriting has me fighting back tears.

Timothy clears his throat. "Gage and Hazel. If you're hearing this, then Timothy has just told you about the inheritance I wish to give you and the stipulation that comes with it. Please know that I did not make this decision lightly. Choosing to leave this money to you both was the easy part, but requiring marriage was not. In fact, I almost reversed my decision. But then I remembered how well I know the two of you. You're probably wondering how I could ask you to make this commitment when I was never married myself. The truth is, I wish I had. I wish I had fought harder for love in my life. You've both sworn off love and vowed to be alone—for your own reasons. And I'm telling you that I think your reasons are bullshit."

Gage lets out a sharp, incredulous laugh, but I remain frozen, eyes locked on Timothy.

"Take it from me—we, as humans, aren't meant to be alone. We're meant to have someone to lean on through the good and bad, and that's what both of you provided to me. Now I'm just asking you to provide that to each other."

For the first time since Timothy started reading, I feel Gage's eyes drift in my direction, but I remain focused ahead.

"I'm asking you to give this six months—six months of marriage to see if you might just be perfect for each other. And if you decide you aren't, then get a divorce and walk away with a life-changing amount of money. It's as simple as that. But I've always had a feeling about you two, and if I'm right, then hopefully you'll change your mind by the end of the six months. I love you both so much. You're like the children I never got to have. I know I'm asking a lot of you, but I'm hoping you'll entertain my quirkiness one last time and let me watch from the other side. Don't overthink it. Love, Diane."

When Timothy lifts his head, he appears blurry through the tears building in my eyes. I wipe them away quickly.

Gage clears his throat. "Fuck, my aunt was a piece of work."

Timothy nods. "Yes, she was."

Gage shakes his head. "She's giving us a guilt trip from beyond the grave." He turns to me, and this time, I meet his gaze. "Don't you think?"

When our eyes lock, something in my chest tightens.

How does he not remember me?

How can I still feel this pull toward him now that I know who he is?

And how the hell am I supposed to make this decision right now?

I clear my throat and turn back to face Timothy. "Do we have time to think about it?"

Timothy drops his eyes to the paperwork. "Yes. She said you have one week to decide."

Gage straightens. "And if we don't do it?"

"The money goes to COPD research."

Gage claps his hands once and then throws them up in the air. "Done! Let them have it." He moves to stand, but I reach out and grab his forearm. This money could be life-changing for both of us, and I can't just let the possibility of changing mine and my family's futures slip away that easily.

"Wait!" Our eyes lock again.

"Come on. It's an easy decision, Spitfire."

My nose wrinkles. "Spitfire?"

Gage slowly returns to his seat with a smirk on his lips. "Yeah, that's what my aunt always called you."

I don't get a chance to respond because Timothy cuts me off. "What if you got married, survived the six months, and then still donated to the COPD research?"

I turn back to him. "You honestly think we should do this?"

He shrugs. "Look, like you said, it's life-changing money. Plus, Diane was insistent that you two actually think about this before making a rash decision."

Gage pinches the bridge of his nose. "I swear to God…"

"There's one more condition," Timothy adds hesitantly. "You two would have to live together for the duration of the marriage."

Gage lets out a slow exhale, staring at the ceiling like he's praying for patience.

"I need time," I say quietly. "I know this is crazy, but I really do feel we should think about this."

He turns to me, eyes narrowing slightly. "We're talking about getting married here, Spitfire."

"It's only six months. Hell, I've endured much worse than *you*." I straighten my spine. "I know *I* can handle it for five million dollars, but if you're too scared…"

Gage scoffs. "You think *I'm* the one who's gonna be the pain in the ass?"

Leaning in, I lower my voice, "I'm *positive* that you'll be the worst part of it, especially given this act you're putting on. But we owe it to your aunt."

I sit back, watching how Gage's eyes dip to my lips. Addressing Timothy again, I say, "You're right. We can still donate to COPD research in her honor. That amount of money is insane, Gage..."

"You could open up your own tattoo shop," Timothy interjects, pulling Gage's attention to him.

"Huh?"

Timothy taps the desk in front of him. "I was supposed to say that to help convince you." He winks. "Diane said you've always dreamed of owning your own shop."

She told me he was a tattoo artist, and now our first encounter makes a little more sense. I don't know why I didn't think of it before.

Needing space from him and the enormity of this meeting, I grab my purse from the floor and stand. "Look, I'm going to take the week to think. Can we meet back here then?" I look down at Gage. "Does that sound good to you?"

His eyes narrow, but he nods curtly. "Yeah, I guess."

"Why don't you two exchange phone numbers in case you have questions?" Timothy suggests.

Gage sighs, pulls his phone from his pocket, and opens up to add a new contact, handing it to me.

I quickly type in my number and, just to fuck with him, I save my name as *Spitfire* .

"There. Now you know how to reach me, if you must," I say to Gage with a bit too much snark in my voice.

He glances at the screen, one brow lifting, but doesn't say anything.

I turn back to Timothy and flash him the best smile I can muster. "Thanks, Tim. I know this isn't your fault. You're doing what Diane asked... I just need some time."

"Understandable. Have a good day, Hazel."

I twist, push through the door, and race to my car, reeling from what just happened.

Me? Get married to a perfect stranger? For money?

Well, he's not a complete *stranger, Hazel...*

"Ugh. Stupid Hummingbird Guy," I mutter to myself, racing back to Blueberry and wishing my life wasn't turned upside down by this monumental decision that I now have to make.

***

"5.1 million dollars?!" Laney screeches through the phone.

I wince, pulling it away from my ear. "I know, right? I mean, that's a lot of fucking money." I continue to stroke the top of Blueberry's head as he lies in my lap on the couch, his red cape curled around his back.

"Exactly. Can you imagine how you could expand your business with that? The trips you could go on, the house you could build for yourself..." Her voice trails off. "Why on earth would Gage be so quick to give that up?"

That's the same thought that's been going through my mind all afternoon since the meeting. It's currently after eight, and I'm ready to call it a day, go to sleep, and see if I wake up and convince myself that today was just a dream. But I know better.

I know I tried convincing myself that Hummingbird Guy wasn't real, but after today, I think it's safe to say that my imagination is shit.

I chew my lip, considering. "Maybe he's just one of those men that's afraid of commitment. That would explain why he turned it down without a second thought."

"That's a possibility, but I think there's more to it than that. What exactly had Diane told you about him?"

I think back over the numerous times she brought him up in conversation. "Only that he lived in Florida, was a tattoo artist, and she thought he was the perfect man for me. But after how he acted today? I'm beginning to wonder if Diane was losing it long before she died."

Laney huffs out a laugh. "Don't say that."

"I mean it. You should've seen him in that meeting. He acted like the idea of being married to me was repulsive." I groan. "And he doesn't even remember me, Laney."

"Oh my God! What?" She's offended on my behalf.

"I know. I know." I sigh. "But even if he did remember, there's no way he's agreeing to this. He probably cycles through women like underwear, and this would throw a wrench in his promiscuous lifestyle."

Laney laughs but then grows serious again. "Is the only reason you want to do this is for the money?"

"I mean, it's a huge selling point..."

"What about the fact that Diane thought you two belong together?"

"I've already told you. She was going crazy. That's the only explanation for her thought process. And besides, she knew about my vow of celibacy and life of loneliness. I thought of all people, she would understand why I felt being alone was better than settling for someone not meant for me. But according to her letter, she had some regrets about giving up on love."

"And maybe she doesn't want you to have those same regrets," Laney says, and I hate that her words hit me so hard. "But if you're not interested in him romantically, then convince him to do it for the money. Make a freaking poster board presentation for crying out loud, but don't let this opportunity pass you by. You'll definitely regret *that*."

She's right. I know she's right. But is it possible that Diane could be right too?

I know what I felt that day in the coffee shop when he approached me. I know the dreams my mind has conjured up since that interaction as well.

But if we're going to do this, I have to let that go. I have to accept that this is nothing more than a business transaction. There have to be rules we both agree to. And if I can convince myself of that, perhaps I can convince him too.

"It's worth a shot," I admit.

"Exactly. And I'll be here every step of the way, you know that."

"I do. Thank you."

"Have you told your mom yet?"

I slap a hand to my forehead. "God, no. But she's not the one I'm concerned about. It's my brothers."

"I know if I told my brother I was getting married to a complete stranger, he'd have some choice words, for sure."

"Parker won't have any place to judge, seeing as he was only pretending to be engaged to Cashlynn at first. But Dallas and Penn? They're going to want to drill Gage, probably do a background check, threaten him and…" As I'm speaking, a notification comes through on my phone. I hold the phone away from my ear and see a text message from an unknown number.

Unknown: *I guess you do like the nickname after all.*

Groaning, I put the phone back up to my ear.

"Hello? Hazel?"

"Sorry, I got a text."

"I was wondering why you went silent."

"It's Gage."

Laney's volume increases. "Oh my God! What did he say?"

"Did I tell you that he called me 'Spitfire' in the office today?"

"What? No. He's already giving you a nickname?"

"Apparently Diane used to refer to me that way…"

"Aw, that's kind of cute."

I instantly grow irritated. "No, Laney. It's *not* cute. Nothing Gage does is cute, all right?"

She clears her throat. "Yes ma'am. Sorry. Getting back to hating his guts right this second," she jokes.

"We don't have to *hate* him, but we don't need to *like* him either, okay? I need you on my side in this…"

"You know I am, but—"

Another text comes in before I hear what else she has to say.

Unknown: *I think we should meet up and talk about this.*

I stare at it, my heart pounding. "Oh my God, he wants to meet up."

"That's a good sign!"

"Or it's a setup so he can formally reject me to my face."

"Or," Laney says, "he's actually considering it."

My chest tightens. "Am I really going to do this, Laney?"

Her voice turns gentle. "Hazel, it's only six months…"

"Yeah, but when it ends, I'll be a divorcée. I'll have to tell every man I date that I was married before. And when they ask what happened, I'll have to admit that it was for money." I slap a hand to my forehead. "Oh God. They're going to think I'm a gold digger and—"

"I thought you were going to be alone for the rest of your life? Unless that's not really what you want..." Laney says, calling me on my own slip up.

"You know, I'm beginning to rethink our friendship."

Laney laughs. "Girl, the second you told me you were swearing off men, I knew you were full of shit. There's no way that the girl I've come to know over the years is going to give up on love. And you know your father would have some choice words to say about that if he were still here."

My eyes begin to sting. "Why are you trying to make me cry tonight?"

"It's not my intention, but my duty as one of your best friends is to ask the hard questions, call you out on your bullshit, and make sure that you're thinking this all the way through. If you didn't have reservations, I'd be more concerned."

Laney knows exactly what I can't say—*I'm scared*.

I'm scared to trust this guy. I'm scared to trust myself. I'm scared of what will happen if I go through with this arrangement.

But most of all—I'm scared that Diane could be right. That the two of us could be good for each other. And then what?

I swipe a tear from under my eye and adjust myself on the couch. "I don't want to live with regrets," I finally say.

"So..."

"So, I'm going to do this for Diane, for me, and for Gage. He deserves this money too. If I go into it with that mentality—that I'm *only* doing this for the money—then I think I'll be fine."

"Okay. Then get off the phone with me and set up a time to meet with your future husband."

"Oh God...don't call him that."

"What should I call him? Your future Dom? Daddy? Boy toy?"

"He will be my husband of convenience, Laney. Nothing more than a title. There will be no feelings, sex, or…"

Laney scoffs. "Yeah, okay. Whatever you say, Hazel. Because if he's half as hot as you've made him out to be over the past year, I'm just counting the days until you call me and tell me his dick magically fell into your vagina."

I snort. "Jesus, that sounds like something I would say."

"That's why we're friends. By the way, when's your next passion party?"

I first hosted one a few years ago, and it was such a hit that I've made it a tradition, throwing at least two a year ever since, and Laney always comes into town for them since they're such a blast. The ladies of Carrington Cove love getting to shop for toys without trekking out of town or gambling on a mystery purchase from the internet.

"Next month. Adeline is bringing a few new gadgets she thinks everyone will go nuts over."

"Hell yes. My vibrator is on its last leg. Although I am getting off more now than I was with Seth, so that's something."

"Glad to see you have found the silver lining."

After we hang up, I open Gage's text message, save his number, and text him back.

Me: *I thought you were opposed to this idea. Your reaction sure said so.*

Hummingbird Guy: *When are you available?*

I blink at the screen. *That's it? No snarky comeback?*

Me: *I can meet up tomorrow morning. I have photo shoots the rest of the week.*

Hummingbird Guy: *Tomorrow morning it is then. Meet me at Keely's Caffeine Kick at eight. Don't be late.*

I roll my eyes.

Me: *Says the guy who kept us waiting today.*

Hummingbird Guy: *Don't worry, Spitfire. That was just a fluke. You'll learn soon enough.*

It almost sounds like he's daring me to stick around long enough to find out just how wrong my assumptions about him are.

Which could only mean one thing—he's not as dead set against this as I thought.

I guess I'll find out tomorrow just how much convincing he really needs.

Chapter Four

Gage

Unlocking the front door to my aunt's house feels surreal, knowing she's not on the other side. Grief slams into me—regret and remorse for not being here in her final days, wishing I could have visited her one more time before she passed.

I know she understood. She knew I would have been here if I could, if the doctors had let me. But it doesn't make it sting any less.

I walk further into the house, tossing my keys on the kitchen counter as I look around. The place looks the same as the last time I was here—the familiar stack of books on the coffee table that she'd read through faster than anyone I know, the coffee mug placed right by the coffee pot like she does every night, and her plants in the window, their leaves drooping since she's not here to water them.

She's gone.

She's really fucking gone.

I officially have no family left.

I'm completely alone.

Isn't that what you wanted, Gage?

The wind chimes on her back patio ring out as a breeze passes through. I want to believe that's her, somehow sending me a sign that I'm not alone. As I swipe under my eyes, I remind myself that her presence still remains in other ways—like the stipulation in her will that ties me to Hazel Sheppard.

I glance around the room, gathering myself and wondering how the hell to even start this process. After Hazel left Timothy's office, he told me my aunt's other request—to prepare her house for sale. The proceeds were to be donated to the Carrington Cove Veteran's Center in honor of Hazel's dad.

"Does she know that?" I ask Timothy as he clasps his hands over his chest.

"Not yet. It was one last thing Diane wanted to do to thank her for her friendship."

Hazel.

Fuck.

Seeing her again just piled onto the stress of this entire trip—not only because our interaction last year has played on a loop in my mind more times than I care to admit, but because my aunt has entangled us in a way neither of us could have predicted. A marriage. A small fortune hanging in the balance. And the insane part? I'm actually considering it.

Not only did I not know my aunt was that wealthy, but I never thought she'd be capable of something like this—something so calculated and manipulative.

It's like she knew that kind of money would be the one thing to make me consider something I swore off two years ago when I realized letting someone fall in love with me would be the greatest mistake of my life—and theirs.

Besides, my aunt has told me about Hazel—about her heart, her passion for life.

Aunt Diane never showed me a picture of her, and I never bothered to look her up online. I knew my aunt was delusional if she thought I'd upend my life in Florida to move here for a woman, so I never gave Hazel Sheppard much thought. As far as I knew, she was a photographer, my age, and someone my aunt cherished. That was it.

Little did I know she would be the woman who helped add a checkmark on the bucket list my aunt had all but forced on me after my life imploded thanks to my father and his lies.

The sad part is, that's the only task I completed off that list—because as soon as I touched her, I felt something in me shift, a connection that I couldn't explain that's haunted me ever since, and connection is the last thing I fucking need.

Loneliness.

That is the only avenue for me, and my aunt fucking knew that's what I wanted.

Figures she'd try to fight me on that decision even after she died.

But how do I say no to this opportunity? How do I deny Hazel a life-changing amount of money? And how do I pass up the chance to open my own tattoo shop like I've always wanted?

I venture down the hall and into my aunt's room. I take a seat on her neatly made bed and the scent of her perfume immediately hits my nose. The wind chimes ring again outside, and I stare out the window, trying to convince myself that I can do this—that I can agree to a marriage for six months and come out on the other side unscathed.

I've spent two years perfecting the art of shutting off my feelings. Hell, when women started calling me an asshole instead of charming, I knew my transformation was working. I didn't want to give them the wrong impression—that they would get anything more out of me than the physical connection I was offering.

But even that can't happen with Hazel.

If my aunt thought forcing us to get married was going to change my mind about being alone for the rest of my life, she was sadly mistaken. I have to hand it to her though, dangling a 5.1 million dollar carrot definitely has me considering sacrificing six months of my life.

As long as we can agree to some terms and boundaries, six months will go by in a flash.

So before I can talk myself out of it, I shoot Hazel a text and pray to God—if there is one—that I'm not making the biggest mistake of my life.

***

I twist the ring on my middle finger as I stare out the window of Keely's, waiting for Hazel to arrive. A knot of doubt tightens in my throat, and my stomach twists with nerves. Even though my life down in Florida is calling to me, begging for me to return, I know what I need to do for myself and for Hazel. I'd be stupid to walk away from this opportunity.

The front door chimes, and when I turn in that direction, my eyes instantly lock onto Hazel's long, tan legs peeking out from under the hem of her cutoff jean shorts.

Fuck, those legs would look fantastic wrapped around my shoulders.

I shake off that thought and stand to greet her. "Good morning."

She eyes me curiously. "Is it?"

"Are you going to have a sarcastic reply for everything I say?" I ask as we take our seats.

Keely comes over to take Hazel's order, and once she leaves, Hazel crosses her arms, her gaze sweeping over me like she's debating whether I'm worth the energy. "I'm sorry. Am I supposed to be kind to you after this little turn of events?"

I can't help my smirk. "Please, elaborate."

She rolls her eyes. "You know what? Never mind."

I lean forward in my chair. "No, Spitfire. Tell me. Tell me why you're pissed at me."

"I'm not pissed," she starts, glancing away. "*Annoyed* is more appropriate."

"Because..."

Her eyes narrow, and I can't deny that her irritation is only making her more attractive.

Focus, Gage. Thoughts like that are exactly what you need to avoid.

"Are you honestly going to play dumb with me?"

"I just want to hear you say it."

She just glares at me, and I have to fight the grin tugging at my lips.

"Is it because you think I don't remember you?" I ask, throwing her a bone since she seems to be just as stubborn as I expected.

She tilts her head to the side. "So you *do* remember me?"

I huff out a laugh, leaning back in my chair as I lift my coffee cup to my lips. "Yeah, Hazel. I remember you, babe."

"Ugh. Don't call me babe. You don't even know me."

"I know you better than you think."

She rolls her eyes again. "Just because your aunt talked about me does *not* mean you know me. You only know the version of me she wanted you to."

"Well, based on your reaction to me, I'm guessing the version she painted of *me* wasn't the best?"

She shakes her head. "The opposite, actually. She spoke very highly of you, but I'm having a hard time seeing it, given how you're behaving."

The corner of my mouth lifts. "And how exactly am I behaving?"

"Like an immature man who can't have an adult conversation with a woman because he's afraid she'll see right through his tough guy act and force him to be honest for once in his life."

Jesus, Gage. She just figured you out in record time, and it barely took five minutes.

"Funny. You didn't seem to have a problem with me when I had my hands on you last year."

Hazel's eyes widen, and she stumbles over her words. "I—I honestly was in such shock during that experience, I barely registered what was happening."

"Uh-huh." I tilt my head, my grin growing. "I'm calling bullshit. You wouldn't be so pissed off if you hadn't thought about it."

We stare at each other for so long that I'm wondering if her heart is hammering as hard as mine is right now. Those hazel eyes of hers are hypnotizing, deep and soulful, highlighting the disposition I'm getting to know. This woman has stories. She's lived a life in her twenty-nine short years, and I hate that I want to know more about it, that I want to know more about *her—just as much as I did when I left her the first time.*

Keely comes over with Hazel's coffee, breaking our standoff, and part of me is relieved because I have a feeling Hazel could have kept going.

Yeah, my aunt was right. One hell of a spitfire she is.

Hazel takes a sip of her coffee, then crosses her legs and leans back in her chair, drawing my eyes back to her legs before I catch myself.

Unfortunately, she catches it too.

"Can we move on and talk about why we're really here, please?" she asks pointedly.

"Fine," I agree. "Probably a good idea."

"You'll come to learn that I'm full of them." She smirks as she takes another drink, her full lips a deep pink that distract me all over again.

Snapping out of it, I clear my throat. "Well, I think we both have a lot to learn about each other if we're going to get married."

Her eyes widen slightly, but she recovers quickly and studies me with a mix of curiosity and skepticism. "Does that mean you're agreeing to this?"

I brush a hand through my hair and release a breath. "I'd be stupid to pass up 5.1 million dollars."

Hazel scoffs. "Right? That's how I feel."

"But I'm serious when I say, that's the *only* reason I'm doing this, Hazel." I lean forward again so she can see how serious I am. "Timothy was right. I have always wanted to open my own tattoo shop, and this money would make that happen very easily. But love? Feelings? They have to stay out of it. I don't do that shit."

Hazel rolls her eyes. "Shocker," she says, lifting her coffee and taking a slow sip before setting it back down with a quiet clink. A beat passes before she continues. "Look, I have things I want to do with this money too. Expand my business, travel like I've always wanted. So I get it, and I agree—feelings have to stay out of this."

I scratch my jaw, drawing Hazel's eyes to the sight. "I loved my aunt. That woman was more of a mother to me than my own, so I guess in some way, yeah I am doing this for her too. I know she thought we'd be good for each other. Believe me, I've lost track of how many times she tried to set us up. But it's like I told her—love isn't an option for me. It's more trouble than it's worth."

"You sound... very cynical about the idea."

"Not cynical. Just realistic."

She sits there, studying me, and something passes behind her eyes that I can't pinpoint. Challenge? Determination? Understanding?

"You can try to figure me out all you want, Spitfire, but you'll never get just how serious I am about this."

"Who says I want to figure you out?"

"Your body is saying it." I drop my eyes down her torso, watching her nipples pebble beneath her skintight pink shirt.

She crosses her arms over her chest, trying to hide the way I affect her. And hell, if this weren't already complicated, I might just focus on the physical attraction between us and explore that connection—how those legs would feel wrapped around my shoulders and hips, how those lips would look wrapped around my cock, her reaction when she finds out *all* the places I have tattoos and piercings...

"So we agree then," she says, bringing me back from my dirty thoughts. "We're just marrying for the money?"

I reach across the table with an outstretched hand. "Marrying for money, not love."

She hesitates for a moment but eventually shakes my hand. "And Diane," she adds. "I'm going to give half a million of my share to COPD research because I know that would make her happy."

"Suit yourself." I lean back again in my chair. Truthfully, I was already planning to donate some too. Weird that we both landed on the same number.

"And even though I think she was insane to think you and I would be a good match, going through with this is a way to show her just how much she meant to me."

"You believe in life after death? That she's gonna sit back with a bowl of popcorn and watch us try not to kill each other?"

Her eyes widen. "You don't?"

I shrug. "I don't know what I think, but I do know that my life is being put on hold while we take care of this, and I'm not exactly thrilled about it."

Hazel tilts her head. "It's only six months. That's nothing in the grand scheme of things."

"I have a life down in Florida, okay? A job, friends, an apartment. Having to move here is going to put a wrench in all of that."

She sighs. "Well, I guess that answers my next question about where we will live given that we *have* to live together."

"Contrary to what you might think of me, I'm not a complete asshole. I know you have a life and business here. It's easier for me to come up to Carrington Cove because my job is flexible with relocation, so that's what I'll do. Plus, I have some things to take care of with my aunt's estate, including selling her house."

"Oh. You're selling it?"

"Yes. That's what she wanted."

She clears her throat and actually flashes me a tiny smile. "I guess you can live in my apartment with me, then."

"Better than sleeping on the street."

Hazel studies me again. "You know, for how close you two were, I wondered where you were those final days. I mean, I thought you of all people would have dropped everything to be here."

Fuck. It's already starting—the inquisition, and now the lies.

But that's just how it has to be.

"Something came up and I couldn't be here."

"Like what?"

I clench my jaw. "It's personal."

She crosses her arms over her chest again. "You know, if we're going to get married, there are certain things I should probably know about you."

"Our relationship will be on a need-to-know basis, Hazel, okay? And that detail is something you do *not* need to know."

She looks as though she wants to argue but, thankfully, she drops it. "Fine. So, do we still wait until next week to tell Timothy about our decision?"

"Well, you said you're busy, and I need to get back down to Florida—talk to my boss, my landlord, and pack my shit. So, I think waiting is the best option."

"You're not going to change your mind, are you, Gage?" Her voice is softer than it was before. She places her hands on the table, leaning forward slightly.

"Scared I'll go back on my word?"

She exhales. "I mean..."

"Again, I'd be stupid to pass up this kind of money." Without thinking, I reach across the table and place my hand over hers. The second we touch, it's just as electric as I remember it—her skin just as soft. I retract my hand almost instantly. "I promise, I won't change my mind."

"Okay." Her eyes drop from mine and she pulls her hands back to her lap. "I mean, I'd just hate to start planning how I'm going to spend my new fortune and then you take it all away from me."

I arch a brow. "You thinking of leaving Carrington Cove and starting somewhere new with that kind of cash?"

She shakes her head. "I'd never leave Carrington Cove. This is where my family is."

I shrug. "Yeah, family isn't my thing, so..."

Her eyes snap back to mine. "You know you'll have to meet them at some point if we go through with this."

I hate the way nerves crawl up my spine. Meeting families is something people in relationships do, not two people who are only entering into a marriage of convenience. "Do you *want* me to meet them?"

"I just don't think we'll be able to avoid it. My brothers especially are going to have questions." She lets out a groan. "Honestly, their reactions are the only reason I contemplated not going through with this. But again..."

"We'd be stupid to pass up millions of dollars."

She nods. "Exactly."

"How many brothers do you have?"

"Three, and they're all older. And just so you know, the stereotype of the overprotective older brother is real with them."

"Great," I mutter under my breath, growing more annoyed by all the details of this arrangement I've overlooked. All I can see right now are dollar signs, but this is going to be much more complicated than just signing a piece of paper and trying not to kill each other for six months. "So you don't have family for me to meet then?" she asks, pulling me back to the conversation.

"Diane was the last of them."

She places a hand to her chest. "Oh my God. I'm so sorry, Gage."

I hold up a hand. "I don't need your pity."

Her brows draw together. "It's not pity, it's compassion. Losing your family is..."

"A blessing when they're selfish human beings, Hazel." She blinks, taken aback by my response. "Look, just consider yourself lucky we don't have to worry about my family being around to offer judgment too, okay?"

She stands from her chair, shaking her head and sighing audibly. "Okay then. Well, this has been fun. Gosh, I can't wait for the next six months." She rolls her eyes, and I get the feeling that will be a common occurrence moving forward. "But I have work to do, and you obviously need some space, so..." She moves to turn away but I reach out and grab her hand before she can get too far.

Standing from the chair, I hover over her, her face so close to mine that I would only need to close a few inches to taste her lips.

Fuck. Don't think about shit like that, Gage.

"Look. I meant what I said, Hazel. Feelings have to stay out of this, okay? I don't do that shit, and I know that women say they can handle it, but—"

"I heard you, Gage," she cuts me off, voice firm. "And trust me, the last thing I want from you is any type of feelings. But for the sake of the next six months, I will tell you this: I don't put up with assholes. You might have some anger you need to deal with, or a shitty past that continues to haunt you, but you're sure as hell not going to take it out on me."

My eyes widen in surprise.

Damn. Why does hearing her lay down the law like that make me hard?

Relenting to her intent to stand up for herself, I nod. "You're right. I'm sorry. You don't deserve that. I guess I just don't know what to think about all of this still."

She chuckles nervously. "Yeah, you and me both."

"Look, I think the next few days will be critical for us both to get our heads on straight, then once we talk to Timothy, we can get this going. Because the sooner we do, the sooner we get our payday and can move on with our lives."

She rolls her eyes again before taking a step back. "Just text me if you think of anything between now and then."

"Okay."

She heads toward the door, and for a second, watching her leave does something to me. An ache builds in my chest and my heart starts to race, but then I remember that my heart tends to do that for other reasons—reasons Hazel can never find out about.

Six months.

That's all I have to get through, and then I can open up my own tattoo shop down in Florida, have financial freedom I could have only dreamed of thanks to my aunt, and get back to my life of solitude the way I like it—the way it has to be.

Because even though Hazel does something to me—makes my body react and my heart feel things I've pushed away for years—she can't ever be a permanent part of my life.

I gave up on that idea a long time ago, and even a girl like her can't change that.

Chapter Five

Hazel

"I'm sorry. You're getting *married*?" My mother blinks at me from her place at the stove, where she's making dinner.

"Yes."

She exhales sharply, shaking her head, then returns to stirring the pasta. "Care to explain how this came to be? The last I heard, you were swearing off all men forever." She flashes me a teasing grin.

"I still am."

"Then how—"

"It's Diane's nephew," I reply before she can get any further, and then launch into the meeting with Timothy MacDonald and what has transpired since.

"Well, I can't deny that's a lot of money, but are you sure about this, Hazel?" My mother's eyes are laced with concern. "We're talking about marriage here. At the end of the six months, the only way out is through a divorce."

I stare down at the counter, hating that she's right. I know this decision comes with consequences—I've accepted that. But it's still a hard pill to swallow. "I'm aware, Mom. I just need you to trust me on this, okay?"

It's the first Sunday of the month, which means family dinner Sunday with Mom, our once-a-month tradition. My brothers and their significant others haven't arrived yet, which is why I'm having this conversation now. I wanted to break the news to her before facing the inevitable inquisition from my brothers.

She sighs. "Of course I trust you, Hazel. But it's my job as your mother to question you. Ultimately, you're a grown woman and you're going to do what you're going to do, regardless of how I feel about it."

"I'm scared, Mom," I admit. "But I also know that if I pass up this opportunity out of fear, I'll regret it. Diane wanted us to have this money, obviously, but she was also hell-bent on setting us up. She has been for years. Gage and I agreed to keep this strictly a business arrangement. We both will benefit from it, change the trajectory of our lives, and then move on to our own paths. Simple as that." I brush my hands together, hoping that the next six months do in fact go that smoothly.

But after our meeting a few days ago, I'm doubtful that will be the case.

Sitting across from the man who's about to be my husband and truly engaging with him for the first time was quite the experience. My body betrayed me—forgetting that we're not allowed to give in to our attraction to him—while my mind kept buzzing with so many questions that half the time, all I could do was stare at him blankly.

Gage is jaded about love—that was clear from a few of his declarations on the matter. But he's also full of contradictions. He loved his aunt, but wasn't there at the end? He claimed he doesn't do feelings, yet seemed to care about mine—especially after I called him out on his behavior. I don't know how he usually communicates with women, but the last thing I'm going to put up with is his surly attitude. If we have to live together and endure this timeline, I want it to be as painless as possible.

And denying that you find him incredibly attractive is painful enough, isn't it, Hazel?

"So, are you planning on telling your brothers tonight?" my mother asks, pulling me from my thoughts.

"Yes. No sense in delaying the inevitable. But I wanted you to hear it from me first, and the truth about why."

My mother rounds the counter and places her hands on my shoulders. "I'm not sure what to think about this." She folds her lips in as tears well in her eyes. "I always imagined your wedding day and what that would be like. And this certainly isn't it."

I swallow past the lump in my throat. "I know. But my vision always included Dad walking me down the aisle, and that's not going to happen now, so..."

My mom pulls me in for a hug. "I'm so sorry that was taken from you, Hazel."

A tear slips down my cheek. "Me too, Mom. But maybe since I won't get the fairy-tale wedding, it makes sense that I don't get the fairy-tale marriage either."

When my mother releases me, she brushes my hair from my face. "No marriage is a fairy tale, Hazel. But I think as long as you go into this with the right expectations, you'll come out as unscathed as possible."

"Believe me, that's all I want. I'm still swearing off men, Mom. Gage isn't going to change that."

The corner of her mouth lifts as if she doesn't believe me, and I hate that it makes me doubt myself as well. "So when do I get to meet him?"

"I'm thinking about introducing him to everyone at Michael's birthday party."

Her eyebrows raise. "That's a big day."

"Well, that way I can get introductions over with all at once."

"And when are you getting married?"

"Gage and I texted about that last night. When he gets back from Florida in a few days, we're going to the courthouse. The sooner we get married, the faster the six months will end."

Mom purses her lips. "Well, can I at least be there?"

"Of course, Mom. But that's it. I don't want to make a big spectacle of it."

As soon as the words leave my lips, a crack fissures across my heart. All of my dreams as a little girl, all of the visions of wearing the perfect dress and walking toward the perfect man vanish like a cloud of dust in my mind.

"So, what are you going to tell your brothers?"

I take a seat on the stool next to the counter as my mother returns to the stove. "The truth. There's no point in pretending it's real."

She nods, unsurprised. "Probably for the best. Parker's fake engagement was exhausting enough for everyone involved. At least this way, you don't have to keep up appearances." I roll my eyes. "God, I just can't wait to hear their thoughts about it."

Mom chuckles. "I think they might be more understanding than you think. It is a lot of money to inherit. Do you think any of them would pass up that opportunity? Money makes people do crazy things, Hazel."

"Are you saying I'm crazy, Mom?"

She eyes me over her shoulder. "No, honey. But I do think that this is affecting you more than you care to admit."

I stare out the window to the deck on the back of my parents' house. Even though my dad is gone, it will always be *their* place. "I'm hoping once the wedding part is over, I won't feel so torn up about it."

"You can always back out."

I shake my head. "No. Gage deserves this money too. I just wish Diane had spoken to us about this beforehand."

My mother turns to me and places her hands on her hips. "Right...because when she tried to set y'all up all those other times, you were so receptive to the idea," she says, sarcasm lacing her words. Then, her expression softens. "I think this was just Diane's way of taking care of the two people who meant the most to her."

I nod, blinking back tears.

She sets the spoon down and crosses the kitchen to where I sit. Gently, she squeezes my shoulders, her gaze meeting mine. "I know this isn't what you pictured for yourself—"

Before she can finish, the front door swings open and Penn, Astrid, Bentley, and Lilly scramble through, their voices filling the quiet space.

"Guess our private time is over," Mom says, kissing me on the cheek before greeting my second oldest brother, his wife, and their two kids.

"You're here early," Penn says as he walks into the kitchen and over to me, pulling me in for a side hug as I remain perched on the stool.

"Yeah. I finished editing early today, so I figured I'd come help Mom."

"What was the photo shoot?" Astrid asks as she grabs a cucumber from the veggie tray my mother set out, dunks it in the ranch dressing, and pops it into her mouth.

"A family. They schedule a shoot every year as their kids grow."

Astrid turns to Penn, nudging him with her elbow. "We need to do one soon. Bentley and Lilly have changed so much over the past year."

Bentley is thirteen now and Lilly is nine. I've known these two since they were babies, and Astrid is right, they've both grown a lot in the past year, especially Bentley.

"Well, your photographer is sitting right in front of you. Schedule something, babe." Penn presses a kiss to Astrid's temple and then heads toward the fridge.

"Remind me before you leave, and I'll put you on my calendar," I tell my sister-in-law just as Parker and Cashlynn stride through the door, looking tanner and more in love than ever.

"It's the newly engaged again couple!" Astrid teases as she walks over to them, pulling Cashlynn in for a hug.

Parker and Cashlynn, his boss's daughter, faked an engagement last year after she convinced him to go along with the ruse. But when the truth came out, so did their real feelings. They decided to take their time dating before making it official, and Parker finally proposed for real on their trip to Greece, celebrating the one-year anniversary of Cashlynn's art gallery here in Carrington Cove.

Parker rolls his eyes but leans down to kiss his fiancée. "Yes, the ring is back on her finger, but it won't be alone for long. The wedding is going to happen before the end of the summer."

All of us whip our heads in his direction.

"Is that so?" my mother asks, arching a brow.

"Shotgun wedding?" Penn asks, smirking over the rim of his beer can.

Parker shrugs. "We can work on making it one between now and then."

Cashlynn groans and swats at Parker. "No! Jesus, babe. We are *not* adding a surprise pregnancy to the equation."

I stand from the stool and walk over to hug my brother—and whack him on the back of the head at the same time.

"The fuck?" He jerks away, rubbing at the spot.

"Don't piss off your fiancée now that she's agreed to marry you for real, dummy."

"Hey! No one asked for your advice, especially after the last advice you gave."

I smirk, basking in my own brilliance. "Oh, you mean when I told Cashlynn to intentionally mess with you in your own home so you'd have an existential crisis and admit you had feelings for her?"

Parker glares. "Yes. That."

Cashlynn leans into him, grinning. "To be fair, it worked."

Parker mutters something under his breath about never being safe in his own home, and I beam like the evil genius I am.

"Just remember that payback is a bitch, little sister," he grumbles.

I raise my hands in mock fear. "Ooooh... I'm *so* scared."

Before Parker can retaliate, the front door swings open and Willow enters, with Dallas trailing behind her, carrying my sleeping nephew on his chest.

"Sorry we're late," Willow announces as everyone turns in their direction. "Did Hazel make her announcement yet?"

All eyes drift toward me. Shit. When we were texting earlier, Willow alluded to not coming because she wasn't feeling well. I told her she kind of needed to be here since I had to tell the family something important. Now I'm regretting that decision as I can feel the inquisition beginning to brew.

"What announcement?" Dallas asks, his eyes bouncing back and forth between me and his wife.

Willow winces. "Sorry. I wasn't sure—"

"It's fine," I cut in quickly. "And it's not that big of a deal, so..."

My mother huffs out a laugh as she takes Michael from Dallas and rubs his back while he stirs awake. "Oh, don't try to pass it off as nothing, Hazel," she says, with a warning look directed at me.

"What's going on?" Penn chimes in.

I exhale sharply. "Let's eat first, and then I'll tell you what's going on, okay?"

Parker eyes me suspiciously. "Now I'm nervous. If Hazel has something important to say, I'm afraid it might involve throwing dildos at our heads if we don't like it."

Penn barks out a laugh, shoving Parker's shoulder.

I roll my eyes but smile at the memory. The time I hurled a very realistic-looking dildo at my brothers during a Carrington Cove Passion Party? Legendary. They're never letting that one go.

"Just remember what I'm capable of before you react, then," I warn, even though my stomach churns as I think about having to announce my impending nuptials to my family.

As we settle in to dinner, Dallas eyes me curiously across the table.

"What? Do I have food on my face or something?"

He continues to chew as he stares. "I'm just trying to figure out what this announcement is and how my wife knew about it before I did."

Willow shoves his shoulder. "Oh calm down, you big ogre. All I know is that she has something to tell us, not what it is, okay?"

His eyes soften as he looks at her. "I don't like secrets, Goose. You know that."

I groan. "You act like I'm about to tell you that I'm secretly a stripper who fell for a mafia boss or something." I pause, then shrug. "Not that there's anything wrong with that..."

Cashlynn giggles from across the table. "Sounds like the plot of a romance novel."

"It was, but my life isn't that dramatic, okay?"

Dallas grunts. "Then what is this big announcement, Hazelnut?"

I glance over at my mother, hoping she can sense my need for her support right now. She gives me an encouraging nod.

I take a deep breath. "Fine. I do have some news, but your criticism isn't necessary and just know, no matter what you think, I'm not changing my mind."

"Not gonna lie, I'm a little scared," Penn mutters.

Astrid rubs his shoulder but locks eyes with me. "We're not going anywhere, Hazel. Now, what's going on?"

"I'm…" The words are on the tip of my tongue, ready to spill out. But I let myself soak in the last moment before this decision actually becomes reality.

"I'm getting married."

Silence descends upon the table, eyes moving around the table with unspoken questions.

"His name is Gage," I continue. "He's Diane's nephew. We just met and I know it's fast, but—"

"I'm sorry." Dallas leans forward, planting his hands on the table as he stares at me like I've just lost my damn mind. "Did you say *married*?"

"Do you need a hearing aid already, older brother?"

He flips me off before settling back into his chair. "Sorry for being concerned, but—"

My mother interrupts him, waving a hand. "Oh, please. Don't act so surprised, Dallas. You know your sister, and if she says she knows, well then, we need to trust her judgment."

Dallas stares at her as if she's grown two heads. "You're really okay with this?"

She shrugs. "Even if I weren't, I can't control what Hazel does. And neither can you. Hell, all four of you have made questionable decisions over the years, but did I interfere?" She glances between Dallas, Penn, Parker, and me. "If there's one thing I've learned as a parent, it's that telling you my opinion, especially if it isn't what you want to hear, isn't going to change anything."

"But—" Dallas starts, but Mom cuts him off again.

"When you joined the Marines, even though your father didn't agree with it, did I stop you?"

"No…"

She directs her gaze to my second oldest brother. "And when Penn took years to finally go after what he wanted with his business and Astrid, did I butt in?"

"Nope," Penn replies.

"And when Parker told us all that he was engaged to his boss's daughter—even though it was fake—did I add my two cents?"

"I mean, you *did* yell at me after," Parker interjects. "But you didn't tell me what to do."

She points at him. "Exactly. And it worked out in the end. Now, Hazel's getting married to a man she just met. Instead of questioning it, we should all be celebrating!" She smiles and stands from her chair, heading toward the kitchen.

Parker leans toward Dallas and lowers his voice. "Is Mom drunk?"

"I heard that!" Mom calls out. "And no, I'm not!"

Not wanting this back and forth to continue, I finally stand from my chair. "Look, I know y'all still think of me as a little kid, but I'm a grown woman. And this is what I want."

"Well, when do we get to meet him?" Willow asks, bouncing Michael up and down on her lap from her seat next to Dallas.

"I was thinking Michael's birthday party, actually."

"You're going to introduce us to your husband-to-be at my son's first birthday party?" Dallas glances back at his wife. "Are you okay with that?"

"As long as there's no drama, *Dallas*." She eyes him warily. "Can you be on your best behavior?"

He points a finger to his chest. "Me?"

"Yup. *And* you two." Willow jerks her chin at Penn and Parker.

"What did I do?" Penn asks.

"Nothing yet. But I know you three. You're going to go all big brother on this guy and try to intimidate him." She hands a dinner roll to my nephew as he settles onto her lap. "If I have to wrangle you three instead of focus on my baby turning one, you will regret the days you were born."

"I second that!" my mother calls out from the kitchen.

"Looks like I don't have a say in the matter," Dallas grumbles.

I cross my arms. "No, you don't. I told you I've already made up my mind."

"I didn't even know you were dating anyone." He looks at my other brothers. "Did you guys know?"

Penn and Parker both shake their heads.

"We weren't dating," I explain. "In fact, we just met this past week."

Dallas stares at me like I'm a puzzle he can't figure out. "And now you're *marrying* him?"

Sighing, I sit back down in my chair and prepare to tell my brother about the wealth I stand to inherit through this ordeal, but my nephew chooses that moment to throw his dinner rolls at his father's head. The entire table bursts into laughter.

"I think that was your son's way of telling you to lay off," Willow says through a laugh. Then she turns to me. "Hazel, I just want to say that I'm happy for you since my husband clearly can't."

"Thank you."

"Of course. Besides, you know you'll get your own inquisition from me, Astrid, and Cashlynn later without the boys around," she says with a wink. Astrid and Cashlynn nod in agreement.

Rolling my eyes, I stand and take my plate to the sink, knowing my confession could have gone much worse. I didn't even get a chance to tell them about the money, but maybe that's for the best. If I wait until it's already a done deal, they can't try to talk me out of it.

It's going to be okay. Six months is nothing. Time keeps ticking no matter what, and it will be over before I know it...

So why does it feel like I'm walking into something I won't be able to come back from?

***

"You look beautiful, Hazel," my mother says, dabbing under her eyes with a tissue.

I smooth my hands down the front of my dress, offering her a small smile. "Thank you, Mom."

We're standing at the back of the courtroom, waiting for Gage. He's not late this time—we're just uncharacteristically early because she insisted on driving me over as soon as I finished getting ready.

Even though this wedding isn't the extravagant affair I once imagined, Mom still tried to make it feel special. We got manis and pedis, did our hair and makeup together, and even had my assistant, Stacy, take photos of everything.

A part of me appreciates it. But the part that knows this isn't real almost wishes she hadn't.

The white silk dress I chose is simple, a far cry from the lace-and-tulle fantasy I pictured as a kid.

But what's the point of pretending?

This isn't a real wedding.

Obviously, I know that the legality of it is, but if I'm wasting my one marriage on Gage and this arrangement, I didn't want it to look anything like the wedding I once dreamed about. Especially since my father isn't here to walk me down the aisle.

"I still can't believe my little girl is getting married," she says with a sniffle.

"Not *really...*"

She cuts me a look. "This is real, Hazel. If you want to back out, I won't blame you, but—"

"For the hundredth time, I'm not changing my mind."

She arches a brow. "Then let me bask in this moment since it's the only one I might get. You've made it very clear—"

A throat clears behind us, interrupting her, and honestly? I'm grateful. Her support is appreciated, but her guilt trips are not.

I turn—and forget how to breathe.

Gage stands there dressed in his signature look—all black from head to toe. But this time he's in slacks, a crisp button-down shirt, and a silk tie. His hair is slicked back and he has a faint dusting of scruff along his jaw.

He looks...sinful.

For a brief second, I wish this marriage was real with real feelings. I can almost imagine what I'd have to look forward to tonight when he—

Nope. Don't go there, Hazel.

We're marrying for money, not love or lust...remember?

"You must be Gage," my mother says, breaking the awkward silence as I stand there, gawking.

Gage blinks a few times before coming back to the present himself, turning to face my mom and reaching out to shake her hand. "Nice to meet you, Mrs. Sheppard."

"Oh please. Call me Catherine." She swats his hand away and pulls him in for a hug. His eyes widen with a flash of panic. I fold in my lips to hide my smile because seeing him this uncomfortable pleases me a little too much.

When they part, my mother pats his tie and shirt, returning him to his unruffled state. "How are you feeling?"

"Uh..."

"My mom knows everything," I say, saving him from whatever fake sentiment he was about to conjure up.

"Oh." His shoulders relax. "Well, this is uh..." He rubs the back of his neck. "It's a lot to process."

"I'm sure you two have a lot of feelings about all this," Mom says, "but I believe Diane's heart was in the right place. Though I *am* worried about how it will affect you two when this is all said and done."

"So you knew nothing about this?" Gage asks my mom.

"Oh, heavens, no." She glances at me for a second before returning her attention to Gage. "But I trust my daughter, and I know this money could change both of your lives. If she feels this is what she should do, and you agree, then you have my support."

Gage swallows hard. "She's lucky for that."

Placing a hand on his shoulder, Mom lowers her voice. "You're a part of our family now, Gage. Don't be afraid to ask for anything if you need it, okay?"

My soon-to-be-husband glances away from her and right at me, like the reality of us being married is finally hitting him.

"You look like you're about to pass out," I tell him.

He shakes his head and looks back at my mom. "Thank you."

Her motherly smile offers him comfort. "My pleasure, Gage."

"Hazel Sheppard and Gage Kingston!" Judge Carlson calls out from the front of the room, beckoning us forward.

Adrenaline races through me as I take one step forward, but my mom tugs me back. "Wait. They're going to play the wedding music so I can walk you down the aisle."

Gage, already near the judge's bench, turns when he realizes I haven't followed. "Hazel?"

"Mom...it's really not necessary."

She cups the side of my face, tears filling her eyes. "Yes, it is. It's what your father would have wanted."

I try not to let my emotions overwhelm me, but it's hard. Turning my back to Gage, I take a few moments to gather myself.

It's not too late to run, Hazel. You don't have to do this.

But then the logical part of my brain kicks in.

5.1 million dollars. Suck it up. It's just six months.

I inhale deeply then turn back to my mother. "Okay."

Mom gives me a nod then snaps her fingers in the air, cueing the music.

From the front of the room, the bailiff pulls out a Bluetooth speaker and starts fiddling with his phone.

After a few seconds, he mutters, "Hang on, it's being finicky."

Mom starts tapping her foot impatiently.

Finally, a loud *pop* crackles through the room, followed by a burst of static.

Then, suddenly, the unmistakable disco beat of a breakup anthem blares through the speaker.

I blink. *Is... Is that "I Will Survive"?*

The judge sighs. "Dammit, Ray. Wrong playlist."

The bailiff frowns down at his phone, and a few awkward beats later, the right song finally starts playing.

Mom beams, and then she weaves her arm through mine and leads me toward the front of the room, to the man who's about to be my new roommate, among other things.

Oh my God. I'm about to be someone's wife.

When we reach Gage and the judge, my mother kisses me on the cheek and whispers in my ear. "I love you, Hazel Marie Sheppard."

"I love you too, Mom."

She places my hand in Gage's. "She's your responsibility now."

Fighting the urge to roll my eyes, I look up at a wide-eyed Gage and murmur, "Last chance to back out."

He huffs out a laugh and leans closer to me, giving me a whiff of his cologne that instantly puts me under some type of spell. "5.1 million dollars, Hazel."

I can't help but smile back at him. "Marrying for money, not love."

"Let us begin," Judge Carlson says, and he starts to go through his spiel. I try not to focus too much on the words, instead studying the man standing much taller than me.

Gage holds his gaze on our hands, stroking the top of mine with his thumb. I don't even think he's aware he's doing it, but it's oddly calming. For a second, I feel safe with him, almost grateful that he's the man I'm going through this with.

Then I remember how much he irritates me and snap myself out of it.

"Do you take Hazel to be your lawfully wedded wife?" Judge Carlson asks Gage.

Gage clears his throat. "Yeah, I do."

"And do you take Gage to be your lawfully wedded husband?"

"I do," I answer softly.

"Well then, by the power vested in me by the state of North Carolina, I now pronounce you husband and wife." Judge Carlson turns to Gage. "You may now kiss your bride."

Gage locks his eyes on mine, and then he shrugs. He steps closer and leans in, his lips hovering just above mine.

My pulse stutters as I brace myself, barely breathing as he…veers at the last second, placing a kiss on my cheek.

A sharp pang of disappointment rushes through me, and I try not to think about why that is.

"Oh, come on now, Gage. That's no way to seal a marriage!" my mother admonishes from beside us.

I glare at her over my shoulder. "Mom…"

"I have to agree with Mrs. Sheppard," Judge Carlson adds.

I roll my eyes. "It's fine."

Gage clenches his jaw and releases my hands. "No, they're right."

Before I can process what's happening, he leans in again and frames my face in his hands. My breath catches.

This time, his lips *do* touch mine, and the contact feels like a spark to dry kindling.

A mixture of shock and warmth courses through me, the softness of his lips moving over mine. When I feel Gage's tongue slide against my mouth, I almost push him away. My body has other ideas, though, and my tongue darts out to meet his.

That's when I lose all control.

Gage doesn't rush as he deepens our kiss. No. In fact, he seems nervous to push too hard, too fast, but my body sure as hell wishes he would.

Then, a small metal ball flicks against my tongue, and I realize his tongue is pierced.

Holy mother of God. Why is that so hot?

Can you imagine what that would feel like against your clit, Hazel?

With one last pass of his tongue over mine he pulls back, still holding my face in his hands, staring down at me as my eyes drift open.

"Hey there, wifey," he says, a teasing lilt to his voice.

"Um, yeah."

Yup. That's all my brain can come up with at the moment.

My mother squeals beside us, clapping her hands. "Now that was much better! Aw, my little girl is married!"

I spin to face her. "I'm beginning to wonder if my brothers were right. Have you been drinking more than usual, Mom?"

She narrows her eyes at me. "You know, any other daughter would be grateful their mother isn't trying to talk her out of this ordeal, Hazel Marie."

"Yeah, you should be grateful," Gage adds, the smirk on his lips indicating how amusing he's finding this now.

"Thank you, Gage."

"My pleasure, Catherine."

Huffing out my frustration, I start toward the exit. "Well, good to know my husband and mother are already ganging up on me. Looks like the next six months are going to be *loads* of fun."

✳✳✳

"Why were you acting like my mom was going to give you an infectious disease when she hugged you earlier?"

"What are you talking about?" Gage comes out of the kitchen with a plate of Chinese food in hand, headed toward the couch where I'm currently parked, eating my own dinner while Blueberry snores in my lap.

After our wedding, we immediately stopped by Timothy's office to provide the appropriate documentation of our nuptials and officially start the clock on our marriage. Now, we're finally home after the crazy day and I, myself, can't wait to go to sleep.

Home.

Yup, my apartment is now Gage's home too.

"You looked like her touching you made you uncomfortable," I press.

Gage takes a seat on the other end of the couch. "It's not that. It's just..." He twirls a bite of chow mein onto his fork, considering his words before finally saying, "I'm not used to people being that nice. Plus, she's your mom."

"What does that have to do with anything?"

"I told you. I don't do family, Spitfire. And honestly, I'm surprised your mother was so cool about this."

My heart aches for him. "Yeah, well, she's the best. But my family is big and they're touchy, Gage. You might just have to get used to it for the next six months."

Gage shrugs as he stares down at his plate. "I can't make any promises." Then he flicks his chin toward my feet. "Nice socks, by the way."

I wiggle my toes. "Thanks. They're one of my favorite pairs."

Gage leans down to read the bottom of them. "Leave me alone, unless you have wine." His eyes lift to mine. "I take it you're a wino then?"

"That's a little fun fact you should know about me, yes. There's always a bottle in my kitchen. Also, I have plenty more pairs of ridiculous socks—just an FYI."

Gage huffs out a laugh. "Can't wait to see what else I'll get to learn about you from your feet."

I ignore his sarcasm and change the subject. "Do you have anything else you need to get from Diane's house?"

He brought several bags of clothes and things from his place in Florida and unloaded them in my spare room when we got here. Lucky for him, I have the space. Though, I'm still worried he won't be entirely comfortable here.

"I never unpacked anything there, so no."

"Oh."

"I do have to go over there tomorrow, though, so I can start cleaning out her things in preparation to sell the place."

I sit up straighter. "You're selling her house, right?"

"Yeah, that's what she wanted."

"She never told me that."

"Me either. Timothy did after you left the day we found out about..." He doesn't have to finish the sentence because we both know how life-changing that day was for both of us.

I settle back in my seat. "Wow. I assumed she'd leave it to you."

"Well, I made it pretty clear that I wasn't interested in living here long term, so I probably would have sold it anyway."

I nod, understanding yet again just how temporary this move was for him. And that's what we agreed on, so I'm not sure why it's making my chest ache. "So, what are you planning on doing for work while you're here?"

The corner of Gage's mouth tips up. "Not sure I'm going to be able to foot my half of the bills, wifey?"

"Please don't call me that."

"You didn't seem to mind after I kissed you earlier."

Yeah, my body sure as hell didn't mind that kiss—every single second of it.

"That's because I was too focused on trying not to throw up afterward."

Gage barks out a laugh. "That's not what your nipples were saying."

I glance down at my chest as if they're betraying me now.

"Nice piercing by the way," he adds casually. "Only could handle the one side, huh?"

I cross my arms over my chest, not realizing my piercing was that obvious through this shirt. "That's inappropriate, even coming from you"

"Oh, but my kiss was vomit-worthy?" He arches a brow. "Don't dish out the shit-talking if you can't take it, Spitfire."

"Oh, I can take it."

Gage's eyes darken as if we're both thinking of something else I could take.

Oh, God. It's only been five hours since we've been married and I'm already feeling my defenses weakening against this man.

Gage clears his throat. "Back to your question—I saw there's a tattoo shop down on the boardwalk. Figured I'd stop in this week and see if they could use some help. I'm not one to just sit on my ass, Hazel."

"I get that. I rarely take time off...and when I do, I feel guilty about it."

"I guess that's one thing we have in common." He gestures toward the coffee table. "Looks like you make time to read, though."

My eyes find the stack of books he's referring to. "Sometimes. If I don't feel like I can concentrate on reading, I'll listen to an audiobook and color instead."

His brows rise toward his hairline. "You color?"

Carefully, I reach for the adult coloring book sitting on top of the stack and hand it to him. "I'm not coloring Disney Princess pictures. Not that there's anything wrong with that."

Gage flips through the pages, reading off some of the designs. "*Fuck this. Kiss my ass. Is there alcohol involved?*" He looks back at me, one brow raised.

I shrug. "Being an adult sucks sometimes, so I try to find the humor in it when I can."

"That's one way to handle things, I guess."

"The responsibilities never end. In fact, I was thinking...since you're here now, I could use your help with Blueberry."

His gaze drops to the dog on my lap. "With what?"

"Well, sometimes I work late, especially on weekends. He needs to be taken for walks, fed dinner, loved on. My neighbor's daughter has been coming by to check on him, but since you're here, that'd be a big help."

Gage scratches Blueberry's head. "Yeah, I guess I can help with the little man. How's he been doing since..."

I stroke the dog's back. "He's doing better now. He whined for the first few days, scratching at the door as if he wanted to leave my apartment and go back home."

"She really loved this dog," he says, his voice tight.

"I know." I sigh. "He was lucky to have her."

"Guess he's lucky to have you now, huh?" Our eyes meet and the solemn mood from this conversation now rests between us.

A sharp knock at the front door startles us both.

Gage frowns. "Are you expecting someone?"

Blueberry jumps off my lap and runs to the door— not to guard it, but to wag his entire body in anticipation of whoever might be on the other side. He used to do the same thing at Diane's house, always eager to greet a visitor.

I glance at the clock on the wall. "Oh yeah! The male stripper I ordered is right on time."

Gage's laugh fills the room, warm and deep.

Placing my plate on the coffee table, I stand from the couch and cross the room, opening the door to find...no one. I look around for a sign of anyone, and my eyes land on a pink envelope lying on the doormat.

"What is it?"

I jump at Gage's closeness, spinning to find him standing right behind me.

"Some space would be nice." I scoop up the envelope and slide around him, heading toward the kitchen. I lay the envelope on the counter, eyeing it cautiously.

Gage is right on my heels. "Forgive me for wanting to know why the hell you're getting a letter mysteriously dropped off at six o'clock on a Wednesday."

"Sometimes the mail comes late," I argue, trying to convince myself as much as him.

"To your *front porch*?" He looks at the envelope. "And there's no address, Hazel."

"Well aren't you just a modern-day detective..."

Gage gives me a deadpan look. "Are you going to open the fucking letter or not?"

I swipe the pink envelope from the counter and slide my finger under the seal. "No need for profanity, dickhead."

He rolls his eyes. "Man, this marriage is off to a *great* fucking start," he mutters as I pull a piece of paper from the envelope and instantly feel goosebumps prickle over my skin.

"It's a letter from Diane."

Gage moves closer, peering over my shoulder. "What?"

Neither of us speaks as we read the letter.

Gage and Hazel,

Congratulations, newlyweds! I have to say, as I write this letter, I'm hoping it's not for nothing. But, if you're reading it, then that means my proposition was persuading enough to make you go through with the marriage. Selfishly, I'm ecstatic about that prospect. But I also know you'll need more incentive to give this a real shot, so there are a few more stipulations to the inheritance.

In the coming months, you'll receive more letters from me. Each one will designate an activity you must complete in order to receive the money at the end of the six-month timeline. Documentation is a must, and everything must be submitted to Timothy upon completion. Don't worry, I'm not going to make you do anything crazy like skydiving.

But I do believe that in order to make a marriage work, you should be able to have fun with each other, speak candidly, and put trust in one another. After all, my hope is that the two of you realize how perfect you are for one another. Remember?

Don't worry. This letter doesn't contain anything for you to do yet. I figured I'd give you time to acclimate to your new normal before springing anything else on you just yet.

Love you both. Here's to a lasting marriage.

Love,

Diane

Gage lets out a low groan, dragging a hand down his face. "This is just fucking perfect," he mutters as he stalks to the fridge and yanks it open. "I need a drink."

"All I have is wine."

"I don't even care right now." He finds the bottle of chardonnay that I haven't opened yet and shuts the fridge, immediately searching for a way to open it and finding the corkscrew in a nearby drawer.

I lean against the counter, arms crossed, watching him struggle to get the cork out of the bottle. "Do you need some help?"

He tosses the corkscrew on the counter and peers up at me, defeat written on his face. "Please."

I pop the cork in two smooth moves and pour us each a glass. After Gage chugs his, he wipes his mouth, grimacing. "Fuck. How do you drink that shit?"

"First of all, wine is *not* meant to be chugged. And second, you don't get to complain when I warned you this is all I have."

I tap my glass against his empty one. "To Diane and her matchmaking schemes."

Gage exhales through his nose, eyes flicking down to his drink. "She really wasn't joking around, was she?"

"Nope. We should've known she had something else up her sleeve."

He huffs out a laugh. "I can only imagine what she's going to make us do."

I tilt my head, considering. "Do you think it will be bad?"

Gage shrugs. "All I know is, if the money wasn't on the line, I'd ask for an annulment right now."

I scoff as I take another sip of wine. "Yeah, you and me both."

Neither of us says anything for a few seconds, both still processing.

Gage exhales and rubs a hand over the back of his neck. "Well...guess I should go unpack."

I nod, still caught up in my own thoughts. Diane's letter just made one thing painfully clear—this isn't going to be as easy as we thought. But the part I can't stop wondering about?

Why was she so convinced we'd fall for each other?

It's safe to say that whatever connection she believed we'd have was all in her head. Based on the way we already argue, there's no way in hell any type of relationship between the two of us would ever work.

"Married for money, not love," I repeat out loud to myself as I pour myself another glass of wine, remembering that the man freaking out in the other room is now my *husband*, and there's no going back from the choices that we made today.

The only way to get through this is to just keep pushing forward.

Chapter Six

Gage

"That's the last box we can take right now." One of the Salvation Army workers shuts the door on the moving truck, wiping his hands on his jeans.

"No problem."

"We'll come back tomorrow to get the big stuff. Furniture is always in high demand."

"Sounds good."

With a nod, the guy hops into the truck, fires it up, and slowly pulls out of the driveway, leaving me alone at my aunt's house yet again.

I look back at the home that holds a lot of memories for me, especially from when I was a kid. My aunt took me in every summer for a few weeks so I wasn't alone while my father worked. I'd help her in the yard, pulling weeds and planting flowers. She'd take me to the beach so I could build sand castles, use a metal detector to hunt for treasure, and boogie board on the waves. And she taught me how to cook. Hell, if it weren't for her, I'd probably still be surviving off of TV dinners.

It's memories like those that haunt me more than I care to admit, reminding me of how alone I truly am in this world now.

Well...except for Hazel. But that's temporary, which I have to keep reminding myself of.

A car door slamming shut behind me pulls me from my thoughts. I turn—and immediately size up the tower of a man walking toward me, a tool belt slung around his hips.

"You must be Gage."

I eye him warily. "Do I know you?"

The man steps toward me with an outstretched hand. "Penn Sheppard. I believe you know my sister," he says with a laugh.

Realization clicks into place, and my guard instantly goes up. "You're one of Hazel's brothers, huh?"

"Did the last name give me away?" There's a joking tone in his voice before he shoves his hands in his pockets, resting his weight on his heels.

"That, and I can see the family resemblance."

"Don't tell her that or she'll rip your head off. She hates being told she looks like her brothers." He chuckles. "Something about not wanting to be 'built like a linebacker.'"

An amused grin stretches across my lips, but I think I'll keep that bit of knowledge tucked away for later—just in case.

"Sorry to drop in unannounced, but when I saw the 'For Sale' sign out front, I had to stop by. I own a contracting business and turn homes into rentals for tourists. I'd be a fool not to see if you've found a buyer yet."

I glance behind me at the house. "Not yet. The sign just went up this morning. Pam at Cove Realty said it wouldn't take long for the place to sell, though."

"Normally, Pam gives me a heads-up about houses coming on the market, but I guess she forgot about me this time."

"In her defense, I only found out about it last week and just got the paperwork going a few days ago."

Penn nods in understanding. "I'm sorry for your loss, by the way. Diane was a wonderful person. I know she meant a lot to my sister, too."

Just the mention of Hazel makes my pulse spike. "Thanks. And yeah, Diane never stopped talking about Hazel and how amazing she is...and was always trying to set us up." I huff out a dry laugh, knowing my reluctance to take her up on that is what got us in this mess.

He laughs. "Yeah, so I guess you'll be a part of the family now, huh?"

"As of yesterday, yes."

Penn's brows draw together. "Wait, you two already got married?"

Fuck. "Um, yeah."

Penn shakes his head in disbelief.

"Hazel didn't tell you guys about the wedding?"

He pushes a hand through his hair. "We knew you were getting married, but not this fast. But honestly, it doesn't surprise me we weren't invited, given how Dallas reacted when she told us about you two." Before I can reply, he continues. "I guess that makes you my brother-in-law now, doesn't it?"

I shrug, hating the label since I know this marriage is only temporary, and any relationship I have with her family will be too. "Yeah, it does."

He clasps a hand on my shoulder. "Well, hopefully that means you'll be willing to consider my offer for this house when the time comes."

"I'm sure we can discuss it."

Knowing that her brothers don't know the true reason we're married doesn't sit well with me. Penn thinks I'm in love with his sister.

He thinks we fell madly in love and couldn't wait to spend the rest of our lives together.

With each passing day, I'm hating the arrangement we agreed to more and more.

"I appreciate that," Penn says, taking a step closer to me, his size suddenly feeling a whole lot more intimidating. Then he lowers his voice and I see the nice guy demeanor slip away.

Here we go.

"Now that the pleasantries are out of the way, let me be clear about something." His jaw clenches. "My little sister is one of the best fucking people on this planet. She may be outspoken, stubborn, and a little crazy, but that girl loves hard. If you do anything to hurt her, you'll not only have me to answer to, but her two other brothers as well." His eyes narrow. "I have a hard time believing that my sister—who swore off love last year—met some guy and decided to marry him within a week. It's not like her at all. So, if I find out that you're hiding something, that your motives are anything but pure, just know that I have many power tools at my disposal." He holds my gaze, unblinking. "Have I made myself clear?"

I swallow around a lump in my throat but straighten my spine. "Crystal. Though, if you have questions about anybody's motives, *she's* the one you should be speaking to. I'm just going along with what she wanted."

Penn grunts. "She can be a difficult person to say no to."

"Believe me, I'm discovering that myself."

We hold eye contact for a beat before he finally takes a step back. With a dip of his chin, he says, "Pleasure to meet you, Gage."

And just like that, he turns and heads back to his truck, leaving me standing there, realizing how much more complicated this marriage is getting by the hour.

***

"So, Axel said you could work there for now?" Hazel flicks the blinker on and waits for traffic to clear before turning.

We're headed to her brother Dallas's house for her nephew's first birthday party. I offered to drive, but she said arriving on my motorcycle would only add fuel to the interrogation waiting for us.

"He did. He was happy to have an extra set of hands. And once I showed him my portfolio, including work I did on Fletcher Adams, he was more than eager to hire me."

"Wait... Fletcher Adams, the receiver for the Carolina Thunder?"

"The one and only."

She lets out a low whistle. "Oh, how the plot thickens."

I raise an eyebrow. "What's that supposed to mean?"

"Nothing," she says too quickly.

Yeah, okay. I make a mental note to return to this topic later.

"By the way, I met Penn yesterday."

Her grip on the wheel tightens and she darts a glance my way. "And you're just now telling me this?"

I wasn't exactly eager to bring it up, and last night she got home late from a wedding shoot, so we barely got a chance to talk. But now that we're almost at our destination, I figure I should give her a heads-up so she isn't blindsided like I was when Penn showed up and delivered his big brother spiel. He clearly assumes real feelings are involved, and Hazel and I agreed there'd be none of those—no matter how hard my heart beats around her, which isn't a great thing for me for multiple reasons.

"He stopped by my aunt's house while I was packing up the first load of stuff to donate. Saw the 'For Sale' sign and asked if I had a buyer yet."

Hazel rolls her eyes. "Of course he did. He buys houses and turns them into rentals."

"That's what he explained to me...before he threatened me."

She scoffs. "God, of course he did. Let me guess—fishing accident? Power tools?"

"Bingo." I clear my throat. "So, I'm guessing your brothers don't know the real reason we got married?"

She's quiet as she turns onto Bayshore Drive, a road I recognize from when I was here as a kid. The houses on this street are the type you see in Hallmark movies—grandiose, picture-perfect dream houses with wraparound porches and ocean views.

"They don't," she admits, swallowing hard. "I was debating whether I should tell them the truth, but I guess Penn's behavior made that decision for me."

"Yeah, I mean, I'd love to avoid all of them threatening to chop my balls off if I break your heart. Although, I've gotta say, Penn's power tools threat was both creative and terrifying."

Hazel groans. "It's Dallas you should really be worried about."

I try to recall everything Hazel told me about her siblings and their significant others, plus their children...and something about geese? I actually made an effort to keep track because, for some reason, I care what these people think about me.

And that's not sitting well.

Penn's big brother speech and meeting Hazel's mom made one thing perfectly clear—this marriage won't just affect the two of us. Her entire family is going to be a part of this, too. And since I've never really had to worry about family opinions, I'm not too bothered by it. But I can tell that it's bothering Hazel, and for reasons unbeknownst to me, I want to make this as easy on her as I can.

After all, we both agreed to this. We both stand to benefit. She shouldn't have to take all the judgment alone.

"I can handle Dallas," I say.

Hazel snorts. "Okay." Patting me on the shoulder, she says, "Just let me know when your balls have fully retreated into your body after you've endured his big brother death glare for too long, and we'll call it a night."

"I'm sure my balls will be fine." As the car comes to a stop, I take a look at the back of the house she just pulled up to. "Holy shit."

"Yeah."

"This place is incredible."

Hazel turns to me. "It is, but there aren't many places to hide, just so you know. And remember, the geese are territorial. Watch your back." She takes a deep breath. "You sure you're ready for this?"

I wipe my sweaty palms on my shorts. "As ready as I'm going to be."

"I'm serious about leaving early if it gets to be too much, okay?"

"I'll be fine, Spitfire. You sure *you're* going to be able to handle this?"

She turns back to look at the house. "Honestly, I don't know."

Her lack of confidence doesn't do anything to build my own, so I reach over and take her hand, lifting it to my lips and pressing a kiss to the back of it.

And fuck, was that a mistake.

When our eyes meet, Hazel's appear darker than they were before. Her red painted lips are parted just slightly, and I swear I can see her pulse fire in her neck.

My dick sure likes the sight, and suddenly the issue I'm facing isn't the inquisition looming from her brothers, it's getting through this birthday party without a perpetual hard-on.

I can't deny that there's chemistry between us. Hell, I felt it that day in the coffee shop and even more so when I kissed her at our wedding. But we're only a little more than forty-eight hours into this marriage, and I'm already fighting for control of the way my body reacts to this woman.

"We've got this," I manage to croak out. "We're a team, remember?"

Hazel laughs. "Since when?"

"Since we got married. That's how it's supposed to be, right?"

She eyes me suspiciously. "Yes, but our marriage isn't exactly traditional."

"Not romantically, no," I interject, making sure I'm being clear. "But we're the only ones who need to be okay with our choices. Fuck what anyone else thinks, okay? If they can't support us and understand where we're coming from, then we don't owe them an explanation. Right?"

Her lips spread into a soft smile. "Yeah. You're right." As her shoulders drop, she tilts her head to the side. "Besides, it's not like my brothers haven't gotten themselves into some interesting situations over the years."

"Oh, do I hear potential blackmail?" I cup my hand around my ear, making her laugh again.

"Plenty of it, if necessary."

Laughing, I open my door and round the car to catch Hazel's door before she can step out.

She looks up at me, surprised. "You don't need to do that."

"Look, I may not be looking for romance here, but I'm still a gentleman when it counts." I hold out my hand, and Hazel hesitates for half a second before sliding hers into mine. She climbs out of the car, and I shut her door behind her before leading her toward the side of the house, where sounds of the party draw us out of our bubble and into the chaos.

I don't miss the way Hazel squeezes my hand as soon as the crowd comes into view.

"Oh my God, it's true!" a short brunette shouts from the front yard, racing over to us in the sand. "There *is* a man, and you actually brought him!"

Hazel studies the woman with narrowed eyes. "Did you think I was lying?"

The woman's eyes bounce back and forth between Hazel and me. "No, but…"

"But what?"

Before she can respond, Penn comes over and wraps his arms around the woman. I realize this must be his wife. Astrid, I think it was.

The woman leans in toward Hazel. "Well, I was a little bummed when Penn told me you already married the guy. I thought for sure we'd at least have a little girls' night to send you off into wedded bliss."

I can feel Hazel tense up again, so I reach out to shake her sister-in-law's hand. "Hi, I'm Gage."

"Astrid." *Good, I was right.* She shakes my hand before Penn pulls her back into his arms. "Penn told me he met you yesterday," she adds.

I slide my gaze over to Penn. "That he did. How's it going?" I reach out to shake his hand, and he reciprocates, but there's scrutiny in his gaze.

"It's going. Surprised you two are late. Hazel is never late to anything."

"Well, forgive us for not wanting to rush into the inevitable interrogation." She places a hand on my shoulder, peering up at me. "Come on. Let's go get something to drink."

"It was nice to meet you," I say to Astrid as Hazel leads me toward the porch like her pants are on fire. "Hey, slow down there, Spitfire."

"I need alcohol if I'm going to get through this."

As we enter the house, Catherine sees us and her face lights up. She immediately makes her way over, holding a little boy I can only assume is the guest of honor.

"Well, hello there!"

"Hi, Mom," Hazel says, kissing her mom on her cheek and then turning her attention to the child, her whole demeanor softening. "And how is the birthday boy doing today?"

The baby lets out a string of babbles, completely unintelligible, but Hazel nods like she understands every word. "Is that right?"

Catherine kisses the boy's cheek. "He's actually doing quite well, considering it's past his nap time."

Hazel looks around the room. "Where's Dallas and..." She stops mid-sentence when her eyes land on a man headed our way. "Well, speak of the devil."

A tall, rugged-looking guy, who I assume must be Hazel's oldest brother, moves over to us with a beautiful blonde woman at his side, her hand tucked in his.

"Hello there, Hazelnut." As quick as lightning, his gaze slides over to me. "And you must be her fiancé."

"Uh, husband, actually," Hazel mutters, barely audible.

Dallas's eyes go wide. "I'm sorry, what?"

He, however, is so loud that several partygoers' heads turn in our direction.

Hazel exhales sharply, then straightens, crossing her arms over her chest. "We got married this week, big brother," she says, chin raised in defiance. Seeing as how Hazel's father isn't around anymore, I imagine her oldest brother has tried to take on that role.

Dallas looks to his mother. "Did you know about this?"

Catherine nods, smiling down at the baby. "Yep. I was there."

Concern is etched in every line of Dallas's face, but before he erupts, or worse, causes Hazel to, I step forward and offer him my hand. "I'm Gage. Nice to meet you."

Dallas remains stiff but, thankfully, his wife steps in. "It's nice to meet you, Gage. I'm…"

"Willow," I finish for her. "Hazel gave me the rundown on everyone before we got here to help me keep track."

Willow laughs. "Smart. We are a pretty big bunch now, aren't we?" She rubs Dallas's arm, smiling through the awkwardness, but his eyes remain locked on me.

"Newsflash, Dallas," Hazel says dryly. "Staring at Gage isn't going to make him vanish into thin air."

His gaze snaps to her. "Listen, Hazelnut—"

"No, you listen for once. I am not some incompetent little girl. I didn't fall in love with a stranger overnight like a lovesick teenager. Diane left us over ten million dollars to split if we got married for six months—which I would have told you last week at Sunday dinner, if you'd ever listen instead of just assuming you know what's best."

Dallas and Willow's eyes widen in shock just as another couple approaches—a man wearing glasses holding the hand of a petite blonde. "Oh shit," the guy says, popping the last bite of his sandwich into his mouth. "Did I hear that right—you married some random guy for *money?*"

"Shut up, Parker," Hazel snaps.

"Oh, please," Catherine interjects. "Are you telling me that if you had the chance to inherit over five million dollars if you got married for six months, you wouldn't do it?"

Parker and Dallas share a look just as Astrid and Penn enter the house.

"Hey, Penn!" Parker calls out to the other Sheppard sibling. "Did you know that Hazel married this guy for money?"

Penn stomps over to where we're standing, eyes narrowed in anger. Even though I know she's not the one in danger here, I pull Hazel to my side. When her arm wraps around my waist, this insane need to protect her overwhelms me.

Now I can see why she was so nervous about this.

Penn stands next to Dallas, his eyes moving between Hazel and me. "Tell me he's joking."

Hazel presses a palm to her forehead. "Jesus..."

Before this one-year-old's birthday party gets out of hand, I decide to take control of the conversation. "Look, I know everyone has questions, but let's just take a second to calm down, all right?"

Dallas pins his gaze on me again. "You have a lot of nerve acting like the peacemaker when you're clearly taking advantage of our sister."

My jaw tightens. "Look, buddy, I didn't take advantage of anyone—"

Hazel steps in, shielding me from her brother and pressing a palm to his chest. "Just stop it, Dallas. Gage didn't lure me or force me to do anything I didn't want to do. He didn't trick me or pressure me or whatever insane scenario you've cooked up in your head. We both agreed to this."

She turns back to me and that fire in her eyes that I've come to appreciate is alive and well. I give her an encouraging nod before she turns to Penn and Parker.

"And before either of you start, let me save you the trouble. This is happening. It's done. So you can either get on board, or you can keep acting like overbearing assholes. But if you do the latter, just know I'm not going to sit here and take it."

Fuck, she's sexy when she stands her ground.

Jesus. There goes my dick again.

"You boys need to knock it off," Catherine interjects.

As if her voice doused the flames coming off the top of Dallas's head, his shoulders drop and he blows out a breath. "I'm sorry. I just—"

"I get it. She's your little sister," I interrupt. "But trust me when I say we knew what we were getting into. This is just temporary and we'll go our separate ways when the time comes. I respect her and the life she has here, which is why she wanted to be honest with you guys. You don't need to worry about me, though. I have every intention of returning to Florida when this is all over."

Willow clears her throat, a tight-lipped smile on her face showcasing her frustration even though she's trying to keep the peace. "Well, now that the introductions have been made, would you all mind if we got back to the reason we're here, please? To celebrate Michael turning one, yeah?"

Hazel turns back to her sister-in-law. "Yes, please."

Catherine bounces the birthday boy in her arms. "Yes, let's do it! Maybe all of the men need to take a turn in the bounce house to let out some of their aggressive energy," she suggests as Penn, Dallas, and Parker grumble.

Hazel's brothers follow their mother outside, but not before shooting more warning looks at me over their shoulders.

"Well, that went well," I say sarcastically.

Hazel huffs out a laugh. "Sure. Yeah. We'll go with that."

I look down at her. "Was that as bad as you thought it was going to be?"

"Honestly, I thought there would be more yelling. But I think we put them in their place before they could start." Peering up at me, she says, "Thanks for having my back."

"I told you I would." Our eyes remain locked as a wave of determination rolls through me. "Why don't you go get that drink you were after?"

Hazel blinks, then nods. "Yes. Alcohol. I definitely need some of that."

Leaning down, I whisper in her ear, "Don't get too tipsy, Spitfire. I'd hate for the alcohol to give you the courage to tell me what you *really* think of me."

Her eyes darken when I lean back, but I don't wait for a reaction before I head toward the front door.

"What...where are you going?" she asks, stumbling over her words.

Glancing back at her, I say, "To show your brothers that I'm not the bad guy."

With that, I head outside and make my way toward the bounce house, feeling this innate need to ease the tension with Hazel's brothers. And I don't dare let myself question why I care so damn much.

Chapter Seven

Hazel

"You all right?"

Astrid comes up behind me as I fill my wine glass to the rim, resting my hip against the counter in the kitchen. Thank God my brother and his wife decided to serve alcohol at their one-year-old's birthday party.

I take a large drink from my glass, smacking my lips together before sighing. "Now I am."

"That was intense," Cashlynn says, joining us. Like clockwork, Willow darts around the corner a second later and reaches for my hand.

Before she can say anything, words spill from my lips. "Oh my God, Willow. I'm so sorry we—"

"Nonsense. You have nothing to apologize for. Your brother is the one who will be dealing with the heat of my wrath later," she says, her jaw clenching. But then her proud, motherly smile is back in a flash. "I just wanted to make sure you're okay."

My hands are still shaking from the interaction with my brothers, but at least the hard part is over. They all know the truth now.

And Gage sure had your back during that whole debacle, didn't he, Hazel?

Why was that so hot?

"I'm fine," I mutter around my wine glass, taking another large drink.

Cashlynn scoffs. "Yeah, you seem just *fine.*"

"Well now everyone in my family thinks I've lost it..."

Willow rubs my shoulder. "I think we're all just wondering how the hell this happened and, more importantly, how you're feeling about it."

I look between my sisters-in-law, the three women I'm so grateful to call my family now. My older brothers may be giant pains in the ass, but at least they're with women I genuinely love.

I blow out a breath and lower my voice. "It's been a lot. Of course this isn't the way I envisioned getting married... But I couldn't pass up that much money."

Astrid nods. "I don't blame you. But..." She hesitates, biting her bottom lip. "I just have to ask..."

I narrow my eyes. "What?"

Her eyes scan the room before she leans in and whispers, "Do you realize how *hot* your husband is?"

The four of us dissolve into giggles, but then I let out a groan. "Oh, yes. I'm aware. But he's also off-limits. We don't want to make this any messier than it already is."

There's a collective groan of disappointment among the group.

Cashlynn huffs. "Well, that's no fun."

Nodding, I add, "And what's even more unfair about the entire thing is that I met him before I knew he was Diane's nephew, and we really hit it off." I inhale deeply before continuing. "He's Humming-bird Guy."

Their jaws all drop open.

"No way," Cashlynn says, breaking the silence.

"Way," I say before taking down a few more gulps of my wine. "When we met at Timothy's office, I thought he didn't remember me. It made for a less-than-cordial reunion."

Willow laughs. "I can imagine."

"And now we're married and living together for the next six months so we can both walk away with a life-changing amount of money. Only...it's not going to be as easy as we initially thought."

Cashlynn leans forward. "What do you mean?"

"We got a letter the other night from Diane."

Astrid's eyes bug out. "Uh, isn't she dead?"

I shake my head. "And here I thought you were keeping up."

She swats at me playfully as we all laugh. "You know what I mean."

"Apparently, she planned out a series of tasks we have to complete while we're married. If we don't, the inheritance goes out the window."

Willow tsks. "Smart woman."

"What do you mean?" Cashlynn asks.

Willow turns to me. "Diane always wanted the two of you to date, right?" I nod. "So of course she wouldn't be satisfied with just the paperwork. She wanted you to fall for each other."

I snort. "Ha. That's not going to happen. We barely tolerate each other."

The deflection rolls right off my tongue because in the back of my mind, I'm thinking of all the things Diane could possibly have us do.

There's no telling... I thought I knew her well, but these past few weeks have proven otherwise.

And perhaps I don't know as much about her nephew as I thought either.

I gaze out the front window to find Gage talking to one of the servers from Catch & Release. He's moving his arm around as they stare down at it, so I can only assume they're discussing his tattoos—the miles of ink on his skin that I have a hard time not staring at.

I seriously wonder about all the other places that man has tattoos—and how many of them are lick-able.

"Earth to Hazel." Astrid waves her hand in front of my face.

I blink myself back to reality. "Yeah?"

"We lost you there for a minute. You okay?"

Staring down into my almost-empty wine glass, I feel the alcohol settle warmly in my veins. "I'm no longer sober, if that answers your question."

Astrid grins. "How does it make you feel to have lusted after this guy for a year and now suddenly be married to him?"

"I actually forgot all about him," I say, trying to sound convincing.

Cashlynn snorts. "Yeah, okay. Did you forget that I was at your apartment the day after you met him? You looked like you slept with a hanger in your mouth as you recounted the incident. You couldn't stop smiling."

"Personally, I'd find a man who looks like that hard to resist," Willow adds.

"Need I remind you all that you're taken...by my brothers?"

"And need we remind *you* that you're Hazel Sheppard, the same girl who spent years dreaming about what her future husband would be like?" Astrid says, lowering her voice. "I just want to make sure you're doing okay because even though I totally understand why you agreed to this, I also know *you*, Hazel." She reaches down and squeezes my hand. "I know your heart and what you wanted for your life."

I swallow hard, because Astrid isn't wrong. But if I acknowledge that—if I let myself want something I know I can't have—it'll only hurt worse when this is over.

I take my hand back and bring my wine glass up to my lips. "Well, not everyone gets what they want."

Willow and Astrid share a look as Cashlynn frowns.

"Don't feel sorry for me, okay?" I say, forcing a smile. "I'm going to be a millionaire in six months. Who needs love when you have that amount of money?"

But as the words leave my lips, I'm not even sure I believe them.

***

"Uh, what's going on here?"

Standing on the sand, I watch nervously as my brothers and Gage square off in an intense game of cornhole, their competitive energy rolling off them like the salty breeze coming in from the shore.

The birthday song has been sung, the cake served, and the presents opened, now Willow is putting Michael down for a nap, signaling that the party is coming to an end. I came outside to collect Gage, fully expecting him to be eager to leave, only to find him laughing and talking shit with my brothers like old friends.

How much wine did I drink in there?

I begin ticking off the number of glasses on my fingers before Dallas's shouting pulls me from my focus.

"Fuck yeah!"

"Shit!" Penn yells from the other side as Dallas races across the sand and high-fives Gage.

Uh...I'm seeing things, right?

"That's game!" Gage declares before shaking hands with Penn then Parker.

Just a few hours ago, all three of my brothers looked like they were about to murder my new husband, and now they're slapping him on the back like he's one of them?

"Will someone please explain what's going on here?"

Dallas steps up to me first, catching me off guard. But judging by his lopsided grin, he's either feeling the effects of the couple of drinks he's had since the day started or—against all odds—Gage has somehow managed to charm him.

"What's going on is that your husband completed the even number we needed to play cornhole, Hazelnut. And after the way he sunk those bean bags, I'm ordering you not to divorce him. Ever."

Laughing, I grip my older brother by the shoulders. "You're drunk."

Dallas waves me off. "I am not. Just riding a winner's high, is all."

Parker comes up beside me and mumbles in my ear. "He always loses to Penn and me when he plays with Grady."

"The man used to play professional baseball but can't play cornhole for shit," Dallas says, referring to our family friend, Grady Reynolds, who left earlier with his wife Scottie, which explains why Gage was recruited to play this game.

I turn to the man I haven't seen in a few hours, checking him for injuries or a façade that he's perfected while spending time with my brothers. But all I find is that annoying smirk plastered on his lips as he shoves his hands in his pockets. "What can I say, Spitfire? Guess your brothers don't hate me after all."

Penn turns to him and leans in slightly. "Let's not get ahead of ourselves, man. But after today, I think it's safe to say it won't be horrible having you around for the next six months." He extends his hand, and they shake.

I blink in disbelief. "So you guys are cool with this now?"

"Oh no," Dallas interjects quickly. "I still have some concerns…"

"Of course you do," I mumble.

"But we can talk about those later."

My eyes shift to Gage. "Apparently we can leave now since my oldest brother has given us his blessing."

As we turn to go, Dallas grabs me by the hand, leading me to a secluded spot by the side of the house. "Hazelnut—"

"I'm a grown woman, Dallas," I interrupt, ready to defend myself, but my brother presses a finger to my lips, silencing me.

"I know that. Just…let me say something, okay?"

I nod, relenting to his request but crossing my arms over my chest in preparation for a battle.

"The moment you told us you were getting married, I knew something was off. My little sister, the girl who used to dress up as a bride every Halloween, wouldn't be getting married out of the blue like this. And even though I understand why you agreed, I'm worried about how this is going to affect you long term."

Hearing the concern in his voice, the protectiveness morphing to worry, has tears building in my eyes. "I know what I signed myself up for. I've had many emotions about it over the past week, but I'm managing."

"And Gage? He's on the same page?"

I turn back to look at the man in question. "Yeah, he is."

"You sound disappointed about that."

Spinning back to my brother, I say, "Believe me. There is nothing more than irritation between Gage and me regarding this situation."

"He seems like a decent guy, Hazel." He shrugs. "Granted, I've only been able to assess his cornhole skills, but..."

I chuckle. "I'm sure he is a good guy, but earlier this week he acted like marrying me was worse than getting a root canal."

Dallas glares at him over my head. "Maybe I should put him through a few tests, then."

I smack his chest. "Please, no. Just let me get through the next six months unscathed."

He flashes me a sad smile. "Fine. But if at any point he treats you poorly, you tell me. Husband or not, I'll set him straight."

My defenses soften just a little bit. "I appreciate that."

He pulls me into his chest. "I love you, Hazelnut."

"Love you too."

"Part of me is glad that Dad isn't here to see this, though. Not sure how he'd feel about this type of marriage for his baby girl."

One tear slips down my cheek at those words.

***

"Well, I guess we can leave for real now," I say, making my way to where Gage is now standing with my whole family. The rest of the party guests have left by now, and after everything we've endured today, I'm more than ready for some space from them.

"Nonsense. Your mother was just about to tell us what happened during your senior year of high school," Gage says, an all-too-pleased grin on his stupid, sexy lips.

I twist my head in my mother's direction so fast that I momentarily see stars. "What?"

"Your brothers think this is the craziest thing you've ever done in your life, but I think that night I got called down to the school and found you in a room with half-naked teenage boys was worse than this."

The air shifts.

Three heads snap toward me.

"What the fuck, Hazel?" Dallas practically shrieks. "Is this what Mom's been talking about when she tells us you weren't a saint growing up? Naked boys in a classroom?"

"Oh, get your mind out of the gutter!" I fire back. "Jesus, Mom. You had to lead with that?"

She shrugs, completely unbothered. For a moment, I wonder if she's beginning to go crazy as well. "That was the wild part, in my opinion."

Astrid raises her hand. "Please tell us there is more to this story before my husband has a heart attack." She rubs Penn's chest as I catch how tense his entire body is.

Pinching the bridge of my nose, I explain, "It was nothing like what I'm sure all of your dirty minds are thinking, all right?"

"So what happened then?" Willow asks, looking both entertained and horrified.

I lift my chin. "The reason all the boys were in their underwear was because I beat them at strip poker."

Cashlynn wheezes. "Oh, Jesus. That's great!"

"Wait, why were you playing strip poker at the high school?" Dallas demands, pulling my attention back to him.

"Corey Johnson was talking about how good he was at poker during English class." I roll my eyes at the memory. "He was so cocky, and all I wanted to do was shut him up. Well, Dad taught me how to play when I was the last kid living at home, so I knew I could beat him. I challenged Corey to a game, but he was too afraid to lose, so instead of just him, I challenged the entire baseball team. Turns out none of them could resist the opportunity to exercise their misogyny and said they'd only play if we played strip poker." I shrug. "Didn't work out that well for them."

Willow slow claps. "Damn, girl. I'm impressed."

Astrid giggles. "That's the Hazel Sheppard I know and love."

Standing proud, I take a bow. "Thank you."

Gage lets out a low whistle. "Damn, Spitfire."

"So why were you called down to the school?" Penn asks our mom.

"Sheriff Thompson had to go check on things because someone reported 'unusual activity,'" she says, using air quotes.

"It was the trespassing that almost got me arrested," I admit, even though this secret has been kept for so long that the idea of it coming out now is making me want to run right into the ocean. "But when he walked in and found the entire baseball team in nothing but their boxers, looking humiliated, while I was fully clothed and grinning like a damn champion...he decided to let our parents handle it."

"You almost got arrested?" Parker asks, clearly pleased with this information. "I don't know why that makes me so happy."

"'Cause you're a dickhead," I reply.

"I thought that was your nickname for me," Gage chimes in, pulling my attention to him.

"That was just the most PG one I could think of for you," I fire back at him.

Willow and Astrid snicker from the side. "Oh Jesus, these next six months are going to be entertaining as hell," Astrid says.

Parker nods. "Agreed." Then he sniffs the air. "Do I smell some meddling lurking on the horizon?"

Cashlynn smacks his chest. "Oh, behave."

"Um, excuse me. Do you not remember how she meddled in *our* relationship?"

She leans in closer to my brother. "I do, and I believe you benefited from her meddling, did you not?"

Parker squeezes her ass, grinning. "I did. But there's something you need to understand about siblings, baby. All's fair in making the other one pay for any minor inconvenience they cause."

"Is that how the saying goes?" Gage asks, reaching for my hand. And even though I should protest, I don't. The heat of his palm feels too good against mine.

It's not about the fact that I actually have a person that's on my side for once.

Nope. That's not it at all.

"Speaking of minor inconveniences," Cashlynn says, turning back to all of us. "Don't make any plans the second weekend in August." She looks back up at my brother with love shining in her eyes. "You all have a wedding to attend."

"Ah!!" Willow, Astrid, and I scream in unison.

"Not wasting any time, huh?" Penn asks, patting Parker on the back.

"Nope, I told you it was happening this summer. It's time to make this official." Parker turns back to me and winks. "Hell, even Hazel beat us down the aisle."

I roll my eyes. "Ha, ha."

Gage clears his throat. "Congratulations, Parker," he says, reaching out to shake his hand before facing my family again. "I have to say, today has been entertaining and a relief. It was a pleasure to meet you all, and I appreciate you for supporting Hazel and me throughout this journey. However, I can tell by the look on my wife's face, that if I don't get her out of here soon, she's going to erupt like a volcano."

Willow and Astrid giggle and my mother clasps Gage on the shoulder. "You're getting to know her quite well already, it seems."

"That glare of hers isn't exactly subtle, Catherine." Winking, he pulls me toward the house, keeping my hand in his as he waves to everyone. "See y'all next time."

"Be prepared for a rematch!" Parker calls out as Gage leads me along the side of the house and back to my car, my mind reeling from everything that transpired since we arrived.

"I don't know whether to thank you or be mad at you," I say once we settle in and Gage turns out onto Bayshore Drive, the warmth of his hand fading quicker than I expected. Since I had a few glasses of wine and Gage didn't drink at all, he insisted he drive us home.

"A simple thanks will suffice."

"You're good, I'll give you that."

"Good at what?"

"Putting on a show."

Gage peers over at me for a split second before staring out the front window. "It wasn't a show." He huffs out a laugh. "Your family is something else, though."

I sigh dramatically. "They're a nuisance."

"Nah. They're just protective of you."

Staring out the windshield, I swallow down my usual sarcastic reply. "Yeah, you're right. We always look out for each other."

And in that split second, it dawns on me—Gage will never have that.

Diane was his last living family member, and after these six months, when this is all over...

He'll be completely alone.

Chapter Eight

"Who's that for?"

Axel hovers over my shoulder as I finish a sketch for a client that's coming in later tonight.

"The guy's name is Tucker."

"Ah, yeah. Harold's boy. Didn't know he was in town."

I shade in the branches of the tree he asked me to design, a symbol of his growing family. "Oh, he doesn't live here?"

Axel shakes his head, leaning his forearms against the top of my desk. "Last I heard, he was in West Virginia with his wife and kids, but Harold is turning seventy this week, so Tucker must be here for the occasion."

I try not to focus on the fact that everyone in this small town seems to know everything about each other and, instead, dial in on the finishing touches of this design.

Axel nods toward the trunk of the tree. "Now the dartboard on the trunk makes sense. Harold is always playing darts with Baron and Thompson at Catch & Release."

"That's Dallas's restaurant, right?"

"Yup. I figured you'd know that place pretty well by now."

Shaking my head, I pick up the brown pencil and darken a few branches. "Haven't been there yet, actually."

"Really? Aren't you married to his sister?"

Fuck. I was hoping to avoid this topic a little longer.

I set down my pencil and twist to face my new boss. I've been working at CC Ink for three weeks now, and except for the occasional small talk, Axel has left me alone. I've had several walk-in clients leave happy, and I've paid my booth rent on time. We never got into specifics about why I needed a job, but I guess word's finally spread about the youngest Sheppard sibling tying the knot.

"I am."

Axel crosses his arms over his chest. "Then I figured you'd have enjoyed the family discount ten times over by now."

The truth is, ever since the birthday party, I've been avoiding her family. That day did something to me, made me yearn for that life when I know it's not a possibility. Big families are foreign to me, and meeting hers just confirmed that it's better if I keep my distance. That way, it'll be easier to say my goodbyes when the time comes.

I shrug, turning back to my design. "Just haven't gotten around to it, I guess."

"That Hazel is quite the catch. How'd you trick her into marrying you?" The teasing lilt in his voice is easy to detect, but something about those words makes my stomach turn, like she would need convincing to marry me.

Forcing a grin, I say, "She couldn't resist the ink, Axel."

His boisterous laughter echoes in the small room. "If I had a dollar for every jackass who's come in here getting inked because he thought he'd attract more women." Shaking his head, he says, "Hell, I could retire now instead of in a few years."

I glance around the tattoo shop. It's small, but honestly the perfect size for a town like Carrington Cove. I didn't even know this shop existed until a year ago, but back then I never dreamed I'd actually be living here, needing a new place of employment. "How long have you owned this place?"

"Twenty years," he says, running a hand through his short, gray hair. Axel is covered in tattoos himself, though time has softened the ink on his skin. "My wife's been on me about trying to sell the place. She wants to travel, but there's not much time for that when you own a business, you know?"

"No, I don't," I admit. "But I can imagine."

Owning my own shop has always been the end goal, but the last place I would want to set up shop is Carrington Cove. I have clients and friends back in Orlando that I know would support me. That's where my life is.

Definitely not here.

"I'll find a buyer one of these days. The other guys here have no interest in being the boss, and regardless, I don't trust them not to run this place into the ground."

"I'm sure you'll find someone," I say, picking up my pencil again—half to get back to work, half to signal that I don't want to be recruited as his retirement plan.

He claps me on the back. "Only time will tell. Well, I'll let you get back to it. Make sure to lock up when you're done."

My appointment with Tucker is the last one for the day, which means I'm responsible for closing up the shop when I'm done.

"Sure thing, Axel."

With a nod, he walks back to his office, leaving me alone with my work—and my thoughts.

Thoughts of Hazel and her family... And Axel's not-so-subtle hint about selling the shop.

I never expected Carrington Cove to pull me in, but with each passing day, keeping my distance gets harder.

***

"Say cheese?"

Hazel's eyes pop up from her computer as she grins, wiggling her sock-covered feet at me. "Cute, huh?"

I arch a brow. Her socks are covered in little cartoon wedges of cheese with bold lettering across the bottoms.

"Is it a photographer thing, or are you really passionate about dairy products?"

She just shakes her head as I walk past her into the apartment.

I have to admit, this woman's zany sock collection is extensive. From slogans about pickles to puns about wine, I don't think I've seen her wear the same pair of socks since I moved in three weeks ago.

And I hate that I look forward to discovering what pair she'll have on each night as she lounges on the couch editing photos or coloring.

"Did you have a good day?" she asks as I grab a soda and join her on the couch, sinking into the cushions as my back protests from hours of leaning over clients. After chugging wine that first night out of desperation, I had to remind myself that alcohol is the last thing I should be reaching for right now. Yet another change in my life I've had to get used to.

"Yeah. I made good progress on the design for Tucker, and we got half of it done. I'm finishing the other half tomorrow so he can surprise his dad with it at his party on Saturday."

"Gosh, I can't wait to capture the look on his face when he sees it."

"You're going to Harold's birthday party?"

Hazel tilts her head. "Uh, yeah. Who else do you think would be taking the pictures?"

I shrug. "I don't know. I just figured people would snap some on their phones or disposable cameras. Those are making a comeback, aren't they?"

Hazel scoffs. "They are, but the quality is horrible. Besides, I'm the resident photographer for all major milestones in this town. I made it a law when I opened my business."

I blink a few times. "You're joking, right?"

"Sure, but you know what I mean. I almost feel like it's my duty to capture the memories of my friends and neighbors."

I study her for a beat. "Why?"

Hazel stares down at her computer before quietly saying, "Because when someone's gone, all you have left are the pictures. And I, for one, want to make sure that the people I love get to have those memories." Her eyes lift back up to mine. "I know I wish I'd taken more pictures with my dad."

I swallow past the lump in my throat and turn back to my soda.

We haven't spoken much about my aunt since the first letter came. After Michael's party, we slipped back into our own lives, only interacting when necessary. There've been a few nights like this where we've talked on the couch after a long day of work, but for the most part, I've been avoiding Hazel just as much as her family.

I swear, everywhere I turn there's somebody who knows someone in the Sheppard brood and questions quickly follow about how I'm now married to the youngest sibling. Then, without fail, those are followed by mentions of my aunt and how much she's missed in the community.

Fuck, I miss her, and just as Hazel said it, I realize I don't have many pictures with her to reminisce on—yet another regret I'm forced to live with now.

I haven't let myself dwell on her absence too much though, opting to only push forward—selling her house to Penn and checking days off the calendar until my time in Carrington Cove is over.

Right now, I feel like it can't come fast enough.

"Would you like to see some of the last ones I took of Diane?" Hazel asks, pulling me back to our conversation.

My heart starts beating wildly, but I do want to see what she captured. "Uh, yeah. Sure."

She rearranges herself on the couch, scooting next to me and clicking through a few files on her computer before opening a folder that contains hundreds of pictures of my aunt, her dog, and Hazel.

Fuck. They really were close.

"I love this one," Hazel says, pointing to a shot of Blueberry staring up at my aunt, a big, toothy smile on his face as his tongue hangs out the side of his mouth.

As if sensing that we are talking about him, Blueberry sighs from his bed in the corner of the living room.

"Yeah, that's a good shot."

"This one's great too." Hazel clicks through to a photo of my aunt in her motorized scooter, her eyes closed as the wind whips through her hair. Her oxygen line hangs off her face, but I barely notice it because she looks so enraptured by the feel of the breeze on her skin.

"She looks so frail in this one." I point to another picture on the screen. Hazel opens it with a click, and my chest tightens. My aunt is sleeping in her recliner, Blueberry curled up in her lap. She looks smaller compared to the other pictures Hazel and I just looked at.

"That was a few weeks before she died," Hazel explains, emotion thick in her voice.

Before I lose it in front of her or smash my soda bottle against the wall, I stand from the couch and drain the rest of the bottle, heading into the kitchen for another.

Just then, the doorbell rings.

Saved by the fucking bell. A trip down memory lane, complete with the guilt that comes with it is not how I wanted to spend my evening after a long day.

It's something I don't want to deal with at all, if I'm being honest.

I hear the front door opening and closing, but Hazel doesn't say anything when she steps into the kitchen a few moments later.

She doesn't have to—because she's holding a pink envelope in her hands.

"Shit," I mutter.

"I was wondering when this was going to come," she says.

"Did you happen to see who dropped it off?"

She shakes her head. "Nope. Whoever was tasked with this is stealthy, that's for sure."

"Fuck." I push a hand through my hair and then pop the cap on my new soda. "Part of me wants to know what's inside, and part of me doesn't. Can't we just ignore it and wait until the end of the six months to do everything?"

"I don't know, but I don't *want* to do that. I'm sure there's a reason Diane wanted these delivered at a certain time, you know?"

I glance back at the computer where my aunt's face is still on the screen. If I didn't know any better, I'd think she knew we were talking about her and that's why this letter arrived right now. "Yeah, you're probably right."

Hazel holds the envelope out to me. "Do you want to open it this time?"

"I really don't fucking care, Hazel."

Her brows draw together. "No need to get testy. I was just offering..."

"I'm not *testy*," I counter—a tad too defensively.

She rolls her eyes as she slides her finger under the seal and pulls out a piece of notebook paper with my aunt's handwriting on it. The sting of her loss radiates through me once more, and I wonder if that will ever diminish.

I peer over Hazel's shoulder as we both begin to read.

Gage and Hazel,

I hope wedded bliss has been treating you well. If you're reading this, then you're coming up on your one-month anniversary! Congrats!

Hazel snorts and I shake my head, but I'm fully aware that one month of our arrangement is almost over, inching us closer to the finish line. Not that I'm counting or anything.

To celebrate this momentous occasion, I'm writing to inform you of your first task. This one is fairly easy, in my opinion.

I want you to go on a date. All the bells and whistles included: hold hands, dress up for each other, share a favorite meal. And Gage, you need to open Hazel's car door and pull out her chair. Be a gentleman.

BUT, the key component of the date will require you to go thrift shopping. While at the store (Judy will be expecting you), you have to choose outfits for each other and then have a photo shoot in your new get-ups. (Hazel, I know you know your way around a camera, but for this, let Gage take a few pictures, honey. If he breaks your camera, just know you'll have enough money in five months to replace whatever you need, okay? Relinquish the control.)

I huff out a laugh. "Clearly, my aunt anticipated every argument that was about to come out of your mouth."

She elbows me in the ribs, making me fold over with a grunt. "Too bad she didn't anticipate *that*."

I stand tall again and put a bit more space between us, but the grin on my lips won't go away.

Fuck, this girl is something else.

When you're done with your photo shoot, you need to pick out and purchase something for your home. I assume you're living at Hazel's place, but part of living together means making the space yours—together. Find a new chair or piece of art to hang on the walls. Buy a new set of dishes and toss the old ones out. Buy a used board game that you can play on quiet nights at home. Whatever it is, make sure it's something you agree on.

You have one week to complete the task and submit your proof to Timothy.

I love you both and hope this date night brings you closer.

Love,

Diane

Hazel folds the letter and sets it on the counter. "I just got a little nauseous, did you?"

"I've been nauseous since this started, Spitfire." I chug down half of my soda as we stand there, processing what we just read.

"Honestly, this doesn't sound too bad. I was expecting worse," Hazel says.

"I think she's just easing us into this."

Hazel shrugs. "Well, whatever comes next, I know I can handle it." Crossing her arms over her chest, she glares up at me. "Can you?"

I take a step closer to her. "You know, now that I think about it, I'm going to thoroughly enjoy picking out something ridiculous for you to wear."

"Right back at you, dickhead."

"There's that pet name again."

"It suits you," she says, her eyes dipping down to my mouth.

Instinctively, I mirror her, watching the way her tongue darts out to wet her lips, leaving them glistening under the kitchen lights. "When shall we commence this torture?"

"As soon as possible."

"How about Thursday since that's technically our one-month anniversary?"

She shrugs. "Sure. Makes it all the more poetic."

"I'll tell you one thing—don't expect flowers or poetry from me on our date," I say, dipping my eyes down to Hazel's cleavage just long enough to catch a glimpse of her nipples hardening right before my eyes. If I didn't know any better, I'd think every time we spar like this, it turns her on.

Well, that makes two of us.

I feel my cock begin to swell against the zipper of my jeans as Hazel glares at me harder.

"I wouldn't dream of it." She takes a step back, shaking her head. "Well, this night just took a turn, and I don't have the mental capacity to deal with it. I'm going to bed."

"Suit yourself."

I finish the rest of my soda before tossing the bottle into the trash. When I spin around, I run into the woman I was sure had just left the room.

Reaching out to steady us before we both go crashing to the floor, I grip her shoulders, teetering on my feet as I regain my balance.

"Fuck."

"Sorry. I just..." Hazel's eyes dart to the counter. "I was just coming back for the letter."

"Why?"

She shrugs, but her eyes are full of emotion. "I was going to keep it with the other one. I figured we might need to refer back to them at some point, you know?"

"Oh. Yeah, good idea."

Hazel's breasts rise and fall with labored breaths, and with each one, her nipples graze my chest.

She's so much shorter than the women I usually pursue. Hell, I feel like that's part of the reason her nickname suits her so well. Tiny but mighty. Stubborn but sharp. With each new argument, I feel like I discover a new wrinkle in her brow, another corner of her mind I want to explore.

What the fuck am I even thinking right now?

Holding my breath, I twist to grab the envelope off the counter and hand it to her.

"Thank you."

"No problem. Good night, Hazel."

"Good night."

But before she gets too far, I call out to her. "Could you send me those pictures of my aunt, please?"

She stops in her tracks and turns back to me, a sad smile on her lips. "Sure."

"Thank you."

With a tight-lipped smile, she walks back down the hallway to her room.

And I don't miss the way her ass sways as she does.

Chapter Nine

Hazel

"But you're supposed to open my car door."

I flick my gaze between Gage and the motorcycle.

"Well, if we take this, then I don't have to."

I cross my arms over my chest. "I'm not sure I trust you not to get us both killed on this thing. Plus, if we find something at the thrift store for the apartment, how are we supposed to bring it home?"

He steps closer to me, tipping my chin up with his fingers so I have no choice but to look into his striking green eyes—the same ones that shamelessly took in every inch of my body when I walked out of my room in my black romper, ready for our date.

"I would never let anything happen to you on my bike, all right, Spitfire?"

The sound of that nickname coming off his lips is beginning to do sinful things to my lady bits, along with the way he's commanding my attention right now. If any other man had tried what he just did, I'd be punching him in the junk, but it seems I'm out of my element around Gage—something I'm becoming increasingly aware of.

"I'm sure you say that to all the girls," I mutter.

He chuckles. "Not that it's any of your business, but you'd be the first girl to ride on the back of this bike."

"Wh-what?" That news has me stuttering.

He hands me a helmet. "Just trust me. This is going to be a lot more fun than taking your car. And I've technically already opened a car door for you when we went to your nephew's birthday party, so..."

Trying not to overthink his confession, I slowly slide the helmet on, silently cursing the time it took to get my hair to look like this before messing it up. Gage swings his leg over the bike and motions for me to get on behind him.

As I slide up against his back and wrap my arms around his waist, I immediately regret every life choice that led me here.

I can feel his rock-hard abs contracting beneath my grip, and the heat of his body burns through his simple black T-shirt.

God, I want to count the ridges of his stomach with my tongue.

I have yet to even see him shirtless, and I hate how disappointed I am by that.

"Hold on tight," he says before revving the bike to life, the sound roaring in the parking lot of my apartment complex. I can already hear Ms. Higgins complaining about the noise at next week's tenant meeting, but I push that thought aside and tighten my grip on Gage.

My breasts are pressed against his back and my nails are digging into his stomach, but as soon as he pulls out onto the road and we begin to coast, the anxiety begins to melt away.

The past month with Gage has been...uneventful.

After Michael's birthday party, I could tell he retreated a bit, preferring solitude to spending time with me...which is fine. The less we have to see each other, the better.

Although, those nights when it's just the two of us in the apartment, talking on the couch after long days have started to become something I look forward to.

For years it's just been me, alone in that apartment, day in and day out. I barely had a chance to adjust to having Blueberry around before Gage entered the space. But having him there, having someone else to think about, has been interesting.

I catch myself noticing things. What food he likes, what soda he drinks, whether he's changed his laundry over or not. It's a shift I didn't expect to get used to so quickly.

I knew this second letter was coming, though. And as Gage cruises toward Catch & Release, I prepare myself to be cordial to this man for the next few hours. Our repartee has been lively, which I enjoy more than I should. Selfishly, I'm glad he's not one of those men that just lays down, rolls over, and does everything I say. I don't want a pushover for a husband. I need someone who will push me back.

But he's not your real husband, remember, Hazel?

"Ugh," I groan out loud. Luckily, Gage can't hear it over the bike.

I hate how these convoluted thoughts slip into my mind at the most inappropriate times. I hate that I have to remind myself that this whole relationship isn't real. And I really hate that, even though I can tell Gage is trying to keep his distance, there's a part of me that doesn't want him to—a part of me that wants to get to know him better.

That part of me needs to be smothered with a pillow.

Gage pulls into the parking lot of Catch & Release, finding a spot with ease before shutting off the engine. He pats my hands, silently directing me to climb off first.

After I whip off the helmet and fluff my hair, I catch him watching me.

"What?"

He clears his throat, eyes flicking away as he removes his helmet as well. "Nothing." When he lifts his gaze to mine again, he asks, "So, how'd you like it?"

"The breeze flowing through my romper was nice. Helped air everything out, you know?" I joke.

He laughs. "Glad to help you out with that."

"It wasn't too bad, actually."

Gage rubs his hand over the body of the machine that was just purring between my legs. "When you're on a long ride, and it's just you and the open road, there's no feeling like it."

I take a step back and arch a brow. "Would you like me to leave you alone with your bike for a minute so you can write it a love poem?"

Gage shakes his head, reaching for my helmet and putting them both in the satchel on the side of the bike. "I told you, Hazel. There will be no poetry on this date."

"Fair enough." I start to head toward the restaurant, but he tugs me back by the hand. "What are you doing?"

"Holding your hand," he says like it's the most obvious thing in the world.

"Why?"

"Because that's what the letter said to do." He takes his phone out of his pocket and snaps a picture of our hands clasped together before slipping it back into his jeans.

"Did you need the memory so you don't forget it happened, or what?"

Gage begins to lead me to the restaurant. "I'm documenting, Hazel. You did read the letters, didn't you?"

"Yes..."

"Well, I don't want to take any chances on us missing something. So, we need to take pictures of everything. The last thing I want is to get to our six-month anniversary and find out we didn't check all the right boxes to get our money, all right?"

"Good point," I concede. Though, I'm not complaining—I forgot just how much my body enjoys having a man take the lead.

When we make it to the entrance, Gage pulls the door open for me, guiding me through with his hand on the small of my back, making a shiver race down my spine and right to the juncture between my legs.

Dear God. I have a problem.

"Table for two, please," Gage tells the hostess, who then turns to me.

"Hazel? Oh my gosh, how are you?" Sally steps around the podium, pulling me in for a hug.

"I'm great. How are you?"

Her eyes slide over to Gage and then back to me. "I heard you got married! Is this your husband?"

Plastering on a fake smile, I look up at Gage. "Yup, this is the old ball and chain, Gage."

He leans forward to shake Sally's hand. "And the wifey here sure does love being chained up, if you catch my drift." He flashes her a wink and her cheeks instantly bloom with pink.

I swat at Gage's chest. "Seriously?"

Sally regains her composure quickly and grabs two menus, leading us to a table near the back.

"That was a bit too far, don't you think?" I mutter to Gage as we walk through the restaurant.

He shrugs. "Oh, come on. I thought it was funny."

Sally leaves us the menus and scurries away. Poor thing is probably traumatized for life.

I slide into my side of the booth, still irritated. "Not that it's any of your business, but I'm actually a fairly adventurous person...sexually, that is."

Gage's eyes lift from the table, the intensity of the green hue catching me off guard. "It was just a joke, Hazel."

"Still. I'd appreciate it if you didn't make comments like that. They would allude to..."

"Us having sex?" he finishes for me, putting the menu down and smirking at me. "You do realize people already assume that, given that we're married."

"True, but—"

"I hate that this is the conversation I chose to interrupt."

My head snaps up to find Dallas standing there, a look of disgust on his face.

"Well, that was your own fault," I say dryly.

"Good to see you too, Hazelnut." He turns to Gage, tone clipped. "Gage."

Gage nods. "Dallas."

Seems their friendly repertoire from my nephew's birthday party can be pushed aside when sex enters the conversation.

"What are you two doing here tonight?" Dallas asks, flicking his eyes between us.

"Word on the street is that you serve food here, and we're hungry, so..."

Gage chimes in before I can piss off my brother more. "We're on a date."

Dallas's brows shoot up. "A date?"

"Yeah. Newlywed stuff, you know?" I force a smile, already exhausted and we haven't even ordered yet.

"Okay. Well, if you're in the mood for—"

I cut my brother off. "I know the menu, Dallas. I'll give Gage the rundown."

My brother nods, seeming to accept that response. "Suit yourself. Good to see you both." He leans down and presses a quick kiss to my cheek. "Love you, Hazelnut."

"Love you too."

After Dallas walks away, Gage blows out a long breath, like he'd been holding it in.

"You okay?" I ask.

"Fine." He picks the menu back up. "So, what's good here?"

After I spend several minutes going over the best items on the menu while trying not to dwell on Gage's obvious irritation, we place our order, then sit there in silence until I can't take it anymore.

"You know, I never asked you why you became a tattoo artist."

He shrugs. "Same reason most people do. I used to sketch all the time, so much so that I got in trouble in school for drawing instead of paying attention to what the teacher was saying. But my art teacher encouraged me to harness my talent and find a way to make money with it, so I learned how to tattoo."

"That's it?"

"Were you looking for something more meaningful? Something more...poetic?" he arches a brow.

I roll my eyes. "I mean, I'm sure the job has to have affected you in some ways by now."

"What do you mean?"

"Well, like Tucker's tattoo, for example. You get to design art that lives on people's bodies, pictures that mean something to them. Have you ever done a tattoo that really stuck with you?"

Gage stares down at his beer, and I realize this is first time I've seen him drink a beer. "The ones that hit me hardest are done in memory of someone. The worst are baby footprints with angel wings, or portraits of a child that someone lost."

I reach out and cover his hand with mine. "I can't imagine."

"I try not to think about it too much. Loss is part of life, you know?" He pulls his hand back and adjusts himself in his seat. "Man, I'm starving. Hope the food gets here soon."

I can tell that my question rattled him, so I don't push further. "It usually comes out pretty fast." Reaching for my iced tea, I take a sip before changing the subject. "So what do you think we should find for the apartment?"

"I don't care."

I sigh. "Oh, come on. We're supposed to find something we both agree on."

Gage's eyes meet mine. "It's *your* apartment. What do *you* want?"

"You live there now too, so..."

"But I don't plan on being there long term." He taps the table in front of him. "It'd be best if you picked something you'd still want when I'm gone."

Something in my stomach twists. "Well, forgive me for trying to make the best of the situation and follow the rules, like the letter said." I take my phone from my purse and snap a picture of his grumpy ass sitting across the table.

He frowns. "What was that for?"

"Just documenting, you know...for the letters."

Gage sighs, looking out over the bustling restaurant. He stays silent for a moment before surprising me. "I know we brought my bike, so we'd have to pick it up later, but an ottoman would be nice. Something to put my feet up on when I'm sitting on the couch."

His suggestion momentarily stuns me. "Okay..."

"I had a recliner back at my place in Florida, and I like being able to put my feet up. You sprawl across the whole damn couch when you're editing or coloring, so it'd be nice to have somewhere to put my feet."

Suddenly, I realize how hard this probably is for him. He left his home, his things—his entire life—to be here. He probably feels like a stranger in my space.

"Okay then," I say, nodding. "We will find one."

Gage stares down at his beer. "If they even have one."

I reach across and grab his hand again, taking him by surprise. "If we don't find one today, I'll order one. I want you to be comfortable at my place."

That smirk of his returns. "You sure you're not just trying to butter me up so I'll enjoy this date a little more?"

I yank my hand back, rolling my eyes. "I'm going to have fun with this, Gage, because that's the type of person I am. You're stuck along for the ride either way. Might as well make the best of it."

***

"This place smells like ocean air and asshole," Gage whispers in my ear as we step into Thrifty Finds, the thrift store on the boardwalk.

I wrinkle my nose. "It's concerning that you know what that combination smells like, Gage."

We finished up our dinner at Catch & Release and made it here just before closing. And sure enough, when we walked in, Judy knew exactly why we were there.

Diane must have gone to great lengths to set all of this up...and just thinking about that makes my chest ache. God, I miss her.

Pushing the thought aside, I force myself to focus on the task at hand—finding the most ridiculous outfit possible for Gage and capturing evidence for future blackmail, if necessary. The ironic thing is, I bet he's thinking the same thing.

"Where the hell are the clothes?" Gage grumbles as we walk deeper into the store, past shelves of mismatched kitchenware and old bakeware.

"Calm down, we're almost there."

"I am calm."

"Really? Because you're hovering so close I half expect you to jump on my back for a piggyback ride." I glance back over my shoulder to find Gage practically glued to my side.

"I hate clutter, Spitfire." He visibly shudders, and I can't help but laugh. This store is brimming with clutter, tons of unnecessary items that people have discarded over the years because they no longer served a purpose in their lives.

"Well, that makes two of us," I say as we finally come to a stop in front of dozens of clothing racks. "But remember why we're here."

Gage's eyes widen in disbelief at the sheer volume of clothes there is to sort through, but he quickly recovers. "All right. Let's get this over with."

"No need to remind me how badly you're itching to get away from me," I say, turning toward a rack of absurdly patterned blazers.

But before I can take a step, Gage grabs my hand and spins me into his chest. I let out a small squeak of surprise, my palm pressed against his solid frame. When our eyes meet, I see sincerity in his. "Clutter makes me anxious, Spitfire. That's all, okay?"

Nodding, I simply accept his truth. "Okay."

His grip lingers for a second longer before he releases me, then turns and walks in the opposite direction, leaving me standing there, trying to get my racing heart under control.

That's the third time he's intentionally touched me. And each time, it leaves me completely rattled.

Luckily, I have a mission to keep me busy—finding the most ridiculous outfit possible. I take a deep breath, hoist my purse higher on my shoulder, and get to work.

I just hope he's not going to be as mean as I am.

***

About fifteen minutes later, we meet each other at the dressing rooms, hiding our selections behind our backs.

"You sure about your pick?" I ask him, taking a moment to appreciate the way his biceps strain against his shirt, flexing slightly as he hides his choice from view. Not distracting at all.

"Oh, I'm sure. You?"

"Dead set."

"Reveal on three?" he asks, his smile building.

"One..."

"Two..."

"Three," we say in unison, and I hold up my pick just as Gage does the same, and when I see what he's chosen, I burst out laughing.

"Oh, God. That's the worst you could do?" I ask as I take in the Grinch pajama onesie that looks about five sizes too big.

"Don't worry. We're going to stuff it full of pillows to give you the belly too."

Laughing, I say, "Fair enough." Then I hold up the outfit I picked for him.

His smile vanishes. "What the hell is that?"

"It's a dress, Gage."

His eyes narrow. "It looks like a torture device."

To be fair, it kind of is. The hot pink sequined gown I found has so many straps that Gage may very well get trapped in it, but when I saw it, I knew it was the winner.

"Don't forget the heels and blonde wig," I say, holding up the other two items I found to complete the look.

Gage lets out a whistle. "I underestimated you, Spitfire."

I shove the dress into his chest. "Let this be your lesson to never make that mistake again."

After I change into the ridiculous Grinch onesie, I step out of the dressing room to find Judy helping Gage into the gown. "Oh God..."

"This dress feels like being stuffed into a tube sock," Gage mutters as I take in the entirety of him.

The dress is about two sizes too small, but he managed to squeeze his body into it, and my, oh my—what a body it is. Tattoos cover his back and chest, but his abs are still bare. The halter top neckline of the dress strains against his broad back and the tight fit does nothing to conceal the bulge between his legs and his muscular thighs.

And now, I'm being forced to process the fact that my husband is absurdly hot in a dress.

"There." Judy ties the strings in the back of the dress as best she can before handing Gage the wig. "Don't forget this."

Gage glares at her. "Gee, thanks."

Chuckling, I grab a few pillows from the basket by the dressing rooms and stuff them into my Grinch suit, rounding out my belly.

"The sight of you two right now sure is something," Judy says.

I take my camera out of my bag, adjusting the settings. "Blame Diane for this."

Judy smiles, but it's a sad one. "If she were here, she'd be laughing right along with you two."

Gage and I share a look but before either of us can respond, his phone starts ringing from inside his dressing room.

He rushes in to grab it and comes out looking concerned "Shit. I need to take this."

I nod. "Sure."

He walks back toward the front of the store to take the call outside, but not before I hear him answer. "Hey, Miranda..."

My stomach clenches.

Who the hell is Miranda?

I quickly turn back to Judy, forcing a smile. "Sorry. I'm sure he won't be long."

Judy waves a hand. "No problem, dear."

A few minutes later, Gage returns.

"Sorry about that," he says, running a hand over the stiff blonde wig. "But you should have seen some of the looks I was getting from people walking by."

Even though my mind is still spinning with questions, I force a laugh. "Serves you right for interrupting our photo shoot."

I try to pretend I'm not affected and go back to prepping my camera. Once I'm happy with the settings, I direct Gage to stand in front of the empty wall to our right.

"All right, Gage. Strike a pose."

He just stands there, arms limp and his expression blank. I lower the camera, unimpressed. "Come on, at least try to have some fun with it."

He rolls his eyes, but eventually purses his lips, juts his hip out, and tosses a hand in the air.

"Yes! Work it!" Laughing behind the camera, I take a few more shots and then hand it to him. "All right. My turn. But for the love of God, please be careful."

Gage takes my camera from my hands—and immediately pretends to drop it.

He laughs, but I do not.

My face is flat as stone when I tell him, "Just remember that you're in a vulnerable position right now, dickhead. It would be very easy for me to sucker punch you in the balls."

"Oh relax, Hazel, and go stand in front of the wall."

I do as I'm told, holding my fake belly and grimacing, trying to channel my inner Grinch. Judy giggles from the side, and my husband even cracks a smile or two.

My husband.

I hate how easily that thought slips in.

"This is fucking great," he says, snapping a few more shots.

Judy walks over and takes the camera from Gage, motioning for him to join me. "Now let's get a couple of you together."

Reluctantly, he awkwardly clomps over to me in his heels and too-tight dress.

"For the record," I say, peering up at him, "you're the prettiest wife I could have asked for."

His eyes narrow playfully. "Careful, Spitfire, or you'll *really* get people talking."

I throw my head back with laughter.

Once Judy takes a few shots, Gage walks over to the dressing room, grabs his phone, and returns.

"Might as well get a selfie while we're here."

Then, without hesitation, he hooks an arm around my waist, pulling me snug against his chest before lifting his phone and snapping a few pictures.

As he lowers his arm, I glance at the screen.

We're both grinning broadly—and looking far too happy for my comfort.

Chapter Ten

Gage

"Fucking hell," I mutter to myself as I pull the pink sequin dress over my head and stare at myself in the mirror. My skin might be red and irritated from the itchy fabric, but I'm still grinning like an idiot. I can't believe I expected anything less than that from Hazel, but she still managed to surprise me.

I can hear the woman in question moving around in the dressing room next to me, slipping back into her original outfit, and I can't stop thinking about how much fun that actually was—or what her body looks like underneath that Grinch onesie.

The moment Hazel stepped out of her room today, wearing that sexy little black outfit, I had to fight to keep my reaction in check. Not only did my dick enjoy the sight of her tan legs and petite body encased in black—my favorite color—but the anxiety about going on a date with her went right out the window.

In fact, the only thing I could think about was getting her on the back of my bike. And I wasn't lying when I said no other woman has been on the back of my bike. *Ever*.

As irritated as I was about this ridiculous task, the evening has been fun—a breath of fresh air in the monotony that my life has become these past few years.

But laughing with Hazel and verbally sparring with her, seeing that fire in her eyes? I like it.

And that's a problem.

As well as the phone call from Miranda that came at the worst time possible.

I pull my shirt over my head and button my jeans before sitting to lace up my shoes.

"I'm ready when you are," Hazel calls out to me from outside the dressing room.

When I open the door, Hazel is dressed in her hot outfit again, and you'd never know she was just channeling her inner Grinch. She's also sporting a smile that matches my own.

"Ready to look for an ottoman?"

I blink. "Oh yeah. I forgot about that."

She eyes me curiously. "Well, I didn't."

I follow her to the front counter to return our clothes to Judy, and then we head to the furniture section, tiptoeing through the cluttered aisles.

I swear, I've never seen so much junk in my life, and I wasn't exaggerating earlier—clutter makes my anxiety go through the roof.

When we reach the furniture, it's immediately obvious there are no ottomans to be found.

"I was optimistic, but I'm not surprised."

I scan the selection—two small couches and a handful of dated dressers. "Yeah, looks like slim pickings."

She turns and looks up at me. "Well, what should we get now?"

I shove my hands in my pockets, shrugging. "Beats the hell out of me. You choose."

"We're supposed to find something together, remember?"

"Why does it matter? It's *your* place."

The irritation on her face returns, but I'm doing everything I can to give her the control here. If I'm leaving five months from now, why should I have a say in decisions that will impact her later?

"Whatever." Hazel huffs and stalks off toward the kitchenware.

I let her go and casually stroll around, trying not to let my anxiety get the best of me as I navigate the chaos.

Then something catches my eye.

When I pick it up, goosebumps spread over my skin.

For a moment, I debate if I should show this to Hazel, but as I see her assessing shelves of bakeware, I know without a doubt that she'll treasure this long after I'm gone.

"Hey, wifey…"

She spins around at that, scowling. "Don't call me that."

Chuckling, I say, "Well now I definitely can't stop because I know it irritates you."

I hold up the wind chime so she can see it. "I think I found what we should buy."

Hazel's eyes grow wide and her lips part. "Oh my gosh…"

"My aunt had a million of these," I say, trying not to let my own emotion show. But for some reason, I almost feel like seeing this was kismet.

"I know." Hazel reaches out to stroke the stained glass humming-birds and umbrella piece at the top holding it all together. "And it has hummingbirds…"

"Couldn't be more perfect, right?"

Her gaze lifts to mine, and there's a faraway look in her eyes. "It's perfect."

"All right then. Let's pay for it and get out of here."

Hazel follows me up to the register in silence. Even as Judy tries to make small talk while wrapping it up for us, she doesn't say a word.

If there's one thing I've learned about this woman, it's that she *always* has something to say. Her silence is unnerving.

We walk to my bike, where I stash the wind chime in the side bag before turning to her. She's gazing absently into the night sky.

"You okay, Spitfire?"

"Uh-huh," she murmurs, but my gut knows better.

The entire drive home, I dwell on what could have happened to make the night shift. I mean, I know I was less than enthusiastic about finding something to take back to the apartment, but Hazel didn't seem that put off by my suggestion. And up until that point, I thought we were having a good time. Dinner was fucking delicious, dressing each other up was surprisingly entertaining, and I thought I hit the jackpot on the perfect item to purchase in completion of our task.

So what the fuck happened in the last fifteen minutes?

As I pull into the parking space at her complex, she practically jumps off the bike, tosses the helmet at me, and heads inside without waiting for me.

When I make it to the apartment, I find her in the kitchen, pouring herself a glass of wine.

"What the hell is going on, Hazel?"

Her eyes meet mine and there's a fire there that I've seen before. But something else is lurking there too—and I'm inclined to say it's pain. That's something I recognize all too well.

"Nothing," she says curtly, replacing the cork before putting the bottle back in the fridge.

"You sure? Because you've been weird ever since we picked out that wind chime."

She shakes her head. "I'm fine."

I toss my keys on the kitchen counter, crossing my arms over my chest. "I may not have much experience in relationships, but I do know that when a woman says she's fine, it means she's not."

Hazel scoffs. "Why do you care?"

"Why do I—" I drag a hand down my face. "Because you flipped a fucking switch on me!"

She shakes her head again, lifting her glass to her lips and taking several gulps before dropping the glass back down to the counter, studying the liquid like it holds all of the answers to every question flowing through her brain right now.

I exhale sharply. "If I did something, tell me. I can't fix it if I don't know what I did."

Silence.

I want to bring her smile back, but what am I supposed to do if she won't talk to me?

"Fine. I'll leave you alone." Dropping my arms, I turn to leave the kitchen, but stop dead in my tracks when she speaks.

"Why didn't you tell me who you were that day?"

I freeze.

Shit.

I close my eyes and let my head fall. I knew this conversation was coming at some point, but I didn't expect it to be *now.*

Twisting to face her, I find her only a few feet away, her hands hanging at her sides and tears in her eyes.

"I didn't know who you were," I say carefully. "So it didn't make sense to tell you who *I* was." I shrug.

"So you just go around drawing on random women for the thrill?" Her brow furrows as she waits for my reply.

How do I explain this to her without revealing too much?

I push a hand through my hair and blow out a breath. "It's something I started doing a few years ago. Art is like this universal language and some people just give off this energy that I can't ignore. When I saw you sitting in the coffee shop that day, I *felt* something. So, I followed my gut, and the first thing that came to me when I touched you was a hummingbird."

Her eyes well with tears. I take a step closer to her, but she takes a step back, turning away from me.

"Fuck. Why are you crying?"

"It's nothing."

I place my hand on her shoulder. "It's obviously not fucking nothing, Hazel. Talk to me."

She gathers herself and turns to face me again, inhaling shakily. "Before my dad died, he told me that when he visited me, he would come to me as a hummingbird."

My chest aches from her admission. "Holy shit."

"Yeah. So that wasn't just some meaningless interaction for me, Gage. It felt like it was a message from my dad." She wipes under her eyes again. "And then you came up to me with that wind chime today, and all I could do was think about your aunt and all of the wind chimes she had on her porch."

"I know," I reply, hating how seeing her cry is affecting me.

This pull toward her is growing stronger by the day. No matter how detached I try to remain, I can't deny that we are connected somehow, and all of these little coincidences are getting hard to ignore.

"Nobody knew about that conversation except him and me." A tear slips down her cheek. "I told my mom eventually too, but that day when we met at the coffee shop...it meant something to me."

"I'm sorry, Hazel. If I would have known—"

She cuts me off. "But that's the thing, you couldn't have, right?"

We stand there, eyes locked, and I can hear my heart hammering in my ears. I place my hand over my chest, willing it to calm down. But when I'm around this woman, it never does. Somehow, in four short weeks, I've grown to care about her.

And I don't know what the fuck to do with that.

She sighs. "Whatever. I get it, Gage. I was just some random girl, and this whole thing is just an inconvenience for you."

She starts to walk away, but I grab her hand, pulling her back to face me. Before I can think better of it, I reach out and cup the side of her face. Red blotches cover her cheeks and her eyes are still brimming with tears, but right now I have an insane desire to kiss her, to make her feel better, to taste those lips that have been haunting my memories for weeks.

What the fuck?

"Maybe your dad was with you in that moment. Maybe that's why I felt the hummingbird when I started talking to you..."

Her eyes bounce back and forth between mine. "Yeah. Maybe..."

"And today? Maybe my aunt was with me today when I found that chime..."

"I thought you didn't believe in that stuff?"

My eyes drop to her lips as her tongue peeks out to lick them. "I don't know what I believe anymore, Spitfire."

She holds my gaze, something charged building between us. Before I can stop myself, I'm leaning in.

Her lips part, her breath catching as her gaze flicks from my mouth back to my eyes. "Gage..."

I stroke her cheek with my thumb, loving how her breath hitches when I do.

And then I snap back to reality.

Before I do anything stupid, I jerk my hand away and take a step back.

Her expression falters. It's quick—just a flicker of hurt—but I see it. And I hate that I put it there. It's enough to warn me that I'm playing with fire, and if I'm not careful, we'll both get burned.

"We should get some sleep. It's been a long day," I say, turning away from her and hating myself for it.

She's funny, yet serious. Kind, but doesn't take shit. Loves her family and holds strong in what she believes in. She values her relationships with people, which is exactly why she shouldn't be wasting her time with me.

Hazel scoffs. "Yeah. I agree. Wouldn't want you to miss your beauty rest, although"—her gaze rakes over me as she folds her arms—"I'm not sure it's helping much."

There she is.

A smirk tugs at my lips. She's back to giving me hell, and honestly, I'm relieved.

I could fire back with something snarky. Hell, I could be a top-notch ass right now if I wanted to. But instead, I chuckle and walk down the hall toward my room. "Good night, Spitfire."

"Yeah, whatever," she mutters, turning back to the kitchen.

"Fuck." I close my door and lean back against it, my heart pounding so hard in my chest that I need to get it under control before this night turns into an even bigger shit show.

I force a slow inhale, then let it out through my nose. Deep breath in. Deep breath out.

It doesn't help.

With a low curse, I walk over to my nightstand, twist the cap off my medication, and toss a pill into my mouth.

"Lock it up," I mutter to myself, continuing to focus on my breathing. "Don't let her in."

But even as I say those words, I know it's already too late.

Hazel Sheppard has officially gotten under my skin.

Chapter Eleven

Gage

"Great. Keep smiling. Now look at each other."

Dressed in a black cotton sundress, Hazel bends her knees, angling her camera at the couple and their newborn, nestled tightly in the mother's arms. She pulls the camera away from her face, checking the shots she just took, and smiles proudly. "Perfect."

The baby stirs, a soft whimper escalating into a full-blown wail, the cries bouncing off the studio walls.

"I think it's time for a feeding," the mother says, adjusting the swaddled bundle in her arms as she steps away from the backdrop.

"Of course. Feel free to use the lounge in the back. Make yourselves comfortable and just let me know when you're ready for the last round." Hazel's voice is about two octaves higher than normal as she speaks to her clients, but the smile plastered on her face drops the second she spins around and sees me standing there watching her.

"Gage? What are you doing here?"

"Damn. Not the warm welcome I expected for surprising my wife in the middle of the day."

She sighs, setting her camera down on a table with more force than necessary before crossing her arms. "Am I supposed to be happy you're interrupting me at work?"

My eyes drift around her studio, taking in every detail that reflects Hazel and her warmth—the warmth she hasn't shown me much of, but I guess that's warranted given our dynamic.

Photos line the walls, showcasing her talent. Most are black and white, but others are rich with color. The walls are a soft white, but her logo is painted in pink and black on the wall behind the front counter—her business name, *Hazel Sheppard Photography*, with a pink hummingbird nestled in the corner.

This girl really does love hummingbirds, doesn't she?

"Interrupting you wasn't my intention," I say, suddenly second-guessing stopping by. But this weight living in my chest for the past five days is what led me here.

Guilt.

It's been gnawing at me from every angle—guilt over not being here when Diane died, guilt over agreeing to this marriage for money, and guilt over caring about how Hazel feels—because that's one thing I promised myself I *wouldn't* do.

Maybe that's why I'm standing in her photography studio right now with a gift for her. The second I saw these socks, I knew she had to have them.

Also, it was one of the only things I could think of to show her I'm not a complete ass—aside from actually telling her how guilty I feel about the whole hummingbird drawing incident.

But I meant what I said—something pulled me to her in the coffee shop that morning. She wasn't just some random girl. She captured my attention the second I saw her and my gut told me to talk to her, and when my idea to draw on her came to me, I went with it.

I just didn't realize I was being pulled toward my future wife.

Hazel lets out a loud sigh. "What do you need, Gage? As you can see, I have clients." She waves one hand in the direction the family went.

I close the distance between us and hold out the small bag I'm carrying. "I brought you something. It's no big deal. I just saw them and thought of you."

She eyes me suspiciously, taking the bag from my hand at a glacial pace. "Okay..."

Shoving my hands in my pockets, I fight the urge to run out of the building. "I know you have a million pairs, but..."

She pulls the socks from the bag and reads the bottom of them. "*I just want to drink wine and pet my dog.*" Pictures of a French Bulldog are printed on the burgundy socks, along with wine glasses. When her eyes lift, I can't read what she's thinking, which scares the shit out of me.

Fuck.

What the hell was I thinking buying her a gift? I crossed a line. That's the kind of shit real husbands do...

"Wow. I, uh..."

"Look, it was stupid," I say, pushing a hand through my hair and turning to make a break for it.

But then—Hazel reaches out, fingers wrapping around my arm, stopping me in my tracks.

"Gage..."

I twist back around to meet her gaze, heart pounding.

"Thank you. This was..." She holds up the socks as the corner of her mouth lifts, hinting at a smile. "This was really sweet. My first pair of dog mom socks since I got Blueberry." She shrugs as her mouth forms a full smile now. "They're perfect."

Relief punches through my chest. "Well, I know your first love is wine, but Blueberry is…"

Hazel laughs. "Yeah, he's definitely up there now." She sets the socks on the counter and then directs her attention back to me. "Is that the only reason you came in? To give me socks?"

I blow out a breath. "Yeah, I guess. I just feel like things have been weird since our date last week and I wasn't sure how to…"

"Apologize?"

I shrug. "Sure."

She drops her eyes to the socks again. "Well, socks are one way to say you're sorry."

"Better than flowers, right?"

"I mean, they're definitely more practical. Perhaps sock companies should adopt that as their new marketing slogan—socks last longer than flowers." She smiles back up at me and then says something I wasn't expecting, "I'm sorry too."

I blink. "What do you have to be sorry for?"

"For unloading on you like that." She wraps her arms around her body, almost caving in on herself. And shit, I hate that look on her. It's so different than the confident, sharp-tongued woman I've come to know.

I take a step closer to her. "Don't you dare fucking apologize. In fact, I'm glad you told me. It explains why you hated me so much in the beginning."

"I didn't hate you, but…"

I hold up a hand. "Hey, I get it. Let's just move forward, okay?"

She nods. "Yeah. Okay."

When I realize how much better I feel, I shift my focus back to her. "I didn't mean to interrupt you, but it's kinda cool seeing you in action." Her smile builds again. "Uh, do you photograph many babies? I imagine that's hard." I nod in the direction of the backdrop.

She drops her arms and straightens her spine, her confidence returning like flipping a switch. "I do. It has its challenges, but they're some of my favorite photos to take."

"How come?"

She grabs her camera from the table, walking over to where I'm standing and turning it so we can both see the small display screen. "It's all about the little details." She flicks through a few pictures of the family together, but then there are some of just the baby. "The wrinkles, the tiny fingers and toes..."

Her smile is electric, and before I realize it, I'm staring at her instead of the pictures—her details, the little things about her that I'm trying like hell not to notice but know I won't ever forget. The dimple in her right cheek. The tiny mole on her earlobe. The slope of her neck and the pout of her lips.

I clear my throat, snapping myself out of it. "They look like little aliens to me."

She gapes at me. "Haven't you ever seen a baby before?"

"I mean, sure. Out in public, but not this close-up."

She looks back down at her camera. "It's incredible, huh? How an entire person can be that tiny?"

"It's a trip, for sure."

"Do you want kids someday?" she asks, peering at me from the side before looking back at her camera. My chest tightens, the question hitting harder than I expected.

"I used to." The words slip out before I can think about what they imply.

Shit. Why did I fucking say that?

"Used to?" She turns fully toward me, her brows knitting together. "What changed?"

Regret and anger race through me simultaneously. "It's just not in the cards for me, Spitfire."

"How come?"

Thankfully, before I can come up with a safe response, the door to the studio chimes, pulling Hazel's attention away from me as someone walks in.

"Nathan?" The shock in Hazel's voice is the first red flag. The second? The way she shifts closer to me —like the man who just walked in isn't just a surprise, but a problem.

I slide my arm around her waist so she knows I'm here if she needs me.

"Hey, Hazel."

I take in the man standing a few feet away from us—blond, muscular but not more so than me, and dressed in a khaki suit that looks like it belongs in a corporate boardroom rather than Hazel's studio.

"Wow. It's been a while," she says, her voice laced with something between wariness and forced politeness. "What...what are you doing here?"

His smile morphs from hesitant to slimy. "I'm in town visiting my folks. Just thought I'd stop by." He looks around the studio. "You're still working out of this tiny space, huh?"

My grip on Hazel's waist tightens. *Who the fuck is this guy?*

Hazel doesn't miss a beat, though. "I sure am. Lower overhead, higher profit margins. Most of my shoots are on location anyway."

Nathan scoffs. "Glad to hear your little photo hobby is paying the bills, at least." His eyes land on my hand around her waist and then flick back up to her. "And who's this?"

Taking a step forward, I flash a wide smile and say, with an overwhelming amount of pleasure, "Her husband."

His gaze snaps back to Hazel. "You're married?"

"Uh, yeah. This is—"

"Gage Kingston." I extend a hand for him to shake, even though I'd much rather punch him in the face with it. "And you are?"

Slowly, he places his hand in mine. "Nathan Smith. Hazel and I go way back," he says with a smirk.

Hazel clears her throat. "Yeah, to a time I wouldn't exactly call my finest era."

I bark out a laugh. "Damn. I guess some memories are meant to stay buried, huh?"

His smirk falters. "Yeah..."

"Looks like the little man is sleeping again if you wanna get some more shots in."

The voice behind us has all three of our heads spinning. Hazel's clients are standing there, the mother cradling her now-sleeping baby, their expressions caught somewhere between amused and politely uncomfortable.

"Great! I'll be right there!" Hazel practically shouts, moving out of my grasp while smoothing down her jet-black hair. Turning to Nathan, she says, "Well, this has been fun. Nathan, good to see you. And Gage..."

I place my hand on her waist again. "Yeah, baby?"

Her lips part. For a second, she looks completely thrown—like she doesn't know how to respond. "I'll—I'll see you at home."

Without thinking, I yank her into my chest and plant my lips on hers, the move so natural that it takes us both by surprise. At first, it's a show—a message to Nathan. But when I hear a breathy little moan escape her throat, I tighten my hold on her hips and glide my tongue gently against hers, teasing, savoring—until I remember where the hell we are.

I pull back slowly, and when we part, she stares up at me, eyes wide.

"Actually, I'm coming back with lunch for you, remember?" I say, hoping she goes along with it. The last thing I want is for this asshole to think I'm leaving her alone.

"Oh yeah," Hazel says, voice breathy as she still recovers from that kiss. She risks a quick glance down at my hard cock pressing against my jeans that I know she felt against her body.

"I'll see you around, Hazel," Nathan calls out to her as he heads for the door, giving me one last side glance before he leaves.

With my fists clenched at my sides, I watch him walk down the boardwalk and climb into a ridiculously expensive car before I get on my bike and gun it toward Catch & Release for the lunch I hadn't planned on bringing Hazel—that now I want to more than anything.

***

"Shit," I mutter as I pull on the door handle at Catch & Release, only to find it locked. Turning back toward the parking lot, I try to think of what else Hazel might want for lunch. Not that I'd know. Since I haven't exactly been the husband of the year, we've only eaten together a few times...

"Hey, Gage!"

I turn back and see Dallas standing in the doorway.

"Hey, Dallas. Sorry, I thought you were open for lunch."

"Only on the weekends. But on Thursdays, I have lunch with the boys." He opens the door wider. "Come join us."

I hesitate, wary of walking into another interrogation. But since I'm hungry and still vibrating with adrenaline, I take him up on his offer. "Yeah, okay. Thanks."

Walking into this restaurant with no people in it is a stark difference to how it felt the other night, vibrating with energy from the throngs of people. Penn and Parker are already seated at the counter, along with Grady Reynolds, a guy I know from his days on the pitching mound. They nod their heads in greeting.

"I found a plus one for our lunch date, boys," Dallas announces as I take a seat on one of the empty stools at the counter.

"I thought we agreed no strays off the street," Penn says. He tips his chin in my direction.

"I'm housebroken, I promise."

Parker chuckles beside me, sliding a basket of french fries in my direction. "Didn't expect to see you here today. How's it going?"

I pop a fry into my mouth. "Fucking great."

All four of them laugh.

"Uh oh, I know that tone," Penn says. "Is our precious little sister driving you crazy?"

"Ha. Yeah, she's definitely part of it. But it's not her that's got my mind spinning right now."

Dallas hands me a glass of water. "What's up?"

I peer up at him. "Do you know Nathan Smith?"

Penn, Parker, and Dallas all immediately go tense, their expressions darkening.

Grady, however, just blinks and asks, "Who's that?"

Ignoring him, Dallas asks, "Why are you asking about him?"

"He showed up at Hazel's studio today, and I instinctively got the urge to deck the asshole in the face."

Penn crumples his napkin and tosses it onto his plate. "All right boys, which power tool should I grab?"

Dallas turns to his brother and arches a brow. "Are you suggesting we deal with him using power tools?"

"Do you not remember what that dick did to her, Dallas?"

Dallas blows out a breath and pushes a hand through his hair. "I do."

I sit up taller on my stool, noting the concerned looks on her brothers' faces. "What the fuck did he do?"

Parker speaks first. "Hazel used to date that twat waffle. Why, I'll never understand."

"But when she called him out for cheating on her, he slapped her," Penn adds, his fist clenching on the bar.

My grip tightens on my glass as something inside me snaps.

That son of a bitch.

Penn shakes his head as he continues, "Hazel insists it was an accident. Says it happened when he was flailing his hands around trying to defend himself, but he's lucky he left town before I could get to him."

Dallas clears his throat. "I was still in the service when this happened, but if I had been here, let's just say the guy wouldn't have been *able* to lay a hand on another woman ever again."

I shake my head. "Motherfucker. Now I regret not going with the urge to deck him."

"Did he say anything to her?" Penn asks.

"Nothing threatening, but he was a dick about her studio."

Parker scoffs. "Yeah, sounds about right. He always thought her photography was a joke. Meanwhile, everything he has came from mommy and daddy."

"Why the fuck did she date this guy?" I ask, growing more furious by the second. The woman I've gotten to know doesn't seem like someone that would put up with that type of shit.

Penn shrugs. "Who the hell knows? I mean, most people have exes they look back on and wonder what the hell they were thinking, but our sister has always been a hopeless romantic. She always tries to see the best in people."

Guilt twists in my gut for robbing Hazel of a life with a man that she deserves because that man sure as hell can't be me.

I force myself to meet Dallas's eyes. "Do you mind starting two burgers for me to go?"

He nods, calling out to the cook. "Is one of these for Hazel?"

"Yeah. I was going to grab her lunch anyway, but I want to head back now to make sure that dickwad doesn't show back up."

Dallas glances at his brothers before turning back to me. "Good idea."

"I honestly don't think Nathan will return," Parker says. "When he comes to town, it's usually just to visit his folks and then he takes off."

"I don't care. I could tell he made her uncomfortable, and I don't want to risk it."

Dallas nods, pulling out his phone. "Let us know if you need back-up." He taps at the screen. "What's your number?"

I didn't really want to exchange numbers with Hazel's family—another tie to Carrington Cove I don't need—but with her safety in question, I won't take any fucking chances.

I rattle off my number to Dallas, then glance up as Grady extends his hand toward me.

"I'm Grady, by the way."

"I know who you are." I shake his hand and reach for the basket of fries again. "I was a big fan growing up."

"Fuck, you're making me feel old," Grady says with a laugh.

"You were one of the best, man. A legend." I cast a glance at Dallas before I say, "But apparently, you suck at cornhole."

Penn, Parker, and Dallas lose their shit, tossing their heads back in laughter.

"Seriously?" Grady darts his eyes between his friends. "You guys have been talking shit?"

Dallas leans over the bar, staring at his friend. "All I know is that when Gage was my partner, I actually won a game for once in my life."

Grady flips him off. "Fuck you. I'll remember that when you want me to play on your team for the Carrington Cove Games this year."

I nearly choke on my fry. "They still do that?" I remember watching a few games as a kid, and my aunt always looked forward to it each year.

"Hell yeah. It's tradition," Parker says. "And Dallas is the reigning champ. But not this year."

"Keep dreaming, little brother."

I turn to look at Parker. "Why not this year?"

"Because everyone is tired of him winning, especially our little sister."

"Hazel thinks if she gets Penn, Parker, and Grady on her photography studio's team, they can claim the title." Dallas rolls his eyes. "But it's fine. I'll let them keep being delusional long enough for me to recruit the most tactical team and clench the title for the third year in a row."

The shit-talking continues, and as I wait for my burgers, I have to admit that this is a good group of men—a group of men that Hazel is pretty fucking lucky to have in her life, even if she wants to beat them at some cheesy-ass small-town game.

***

"I've got your lunch."

Hazel holds open the front door she just unlocked, stepping aside as I walk in the studio.

"Thank you," she says, locking the door behind me.

"Are your clients gone?"

"Yeah. They left about thirty minutes ago."

I set the bags of food on the reception counter and study her for a beat. Her expression is unreadable but neutral, maybe a little guarded. "Are you okay?"

She nods, but it's shaky. "Uh-huh."

"You sure?"

This time her uneasiness sharpens into irritation. "I'm fine, Gage." She grabs a Styrofoam container from the bag and takes it over to her desk. "Honestly, you didn't need to do this. I thought you were just joking when you said you were bringing me lunch."

"I didn't want Nathan to think you would be alone after I left."

She pops a fry into her mouth, not looking at me. "Why do you care?"

My stomach tightens. "Why would I not?" For a moment, I debate bringing up the fact that Nathan slapped her, but think twice when Hazel finally lifts her gaze, her blue eyes stormy.

"I'm a big girl, Gage. I can handle myself. I have been long before you came into the picture."

"I know you can, but the way you reacted to that guy..."

She brushes her hair from her face. "I was just caught off guard." She flashes me a fake smile. "Seriously, I'm good."

I don't believe her. Not for a fucking second.

But I also know Hazel could argue circles around me for days. And if she doesn't want to talk, no amount of pushing will make her. So instead, I choose to let it go for now and head to work before I have to explain to Axel why I'm late. "Fine. Call if you need me. I'm just up the street."

She nods. "Okay."

"See you at home," I say, casting one more glance at her before I head for the door. "Make sure to lock up after I leave."

She stands from her chair and follows me to the door. "I know, Gage."

"Just looking out for you, Spitfire." And then I leave, not enjoying the way my stomach is in knots knowing that this need to protect her is overwhelming me, and I don't know what to fucking do about it.

***

"It's all yours, man." I hand the key for Aunt Diane's house to Penn, feeling like a weight is being lifted as I do. Penn had cash to pay for the house, so we opted for a quicker than normal escrow.

"Thanks, Gage. I know this is hard, but I promise I'm going to fix this place up and make it somewhere people can make some amazing memories."

Staring at the house, I think of all the memories I have inside those walls. "I think my aunt would like that. She was always looking out for people. It's why she wanted the money from the sale to go to the Veteran's Center." I almost mention that it's in honor of his and Hazel's dad, but that's something I want Hazel to hear from me first.

"Damn. Well, that was very generous of her."

"She loved this town," I say.

And I think I'm finally starting to get why.

There's something about the slow pace of life in Carrington Cove that's been surprisingly refreshing. Back in Orlando it always felt like

I was in a hurry to go places, work and go out with my buddies, or keep up with the next new thing. Since I've been here, my life just feels *simpler*. Except for my new wife and the fact that I'm insanely attracted to her but can't touch her the way that I want, of course.

"This place is home," Penn says, pulling me back to our conversation. "There's a reason that a lot of people who grow up here never leave."

"Yeah, Hazel mentioned never wanting to live anywhere else."

Penn nods. "That's part of the reason things didn't work out with Nathan."

Just the mention of that asshole's name has my shoulders tensing.

"Speaking of which, any sign of him?" Penn asks.

I shake my head. "Nope. I followed Hazel to work and hung out around the studio when I could over the past week just to make sure he didn't stop by again. When I mentioned the name to Axel, he said the guy was a doofus and that I shouldn't be concerned, but I know what I saw on Hazel's face when he was there."

Penn clasps a hand on my shoulder. "Well, I'm glad she has you to look out for her, at least for the next few months, anyway."

I clear my throat, trying not to show how the thought of our diminishing timeline affects me, especially after the incident with her ex. "As long as I'm here, she's safe. But just to make sure, are there any other asshole exes I should know about?"

Penn scoffs. "Well, my sister was a bit of a serial dater, so there are plenty of men she's given a chance, but not many she let in as much as Nathan."

My stomach twists. "A serial dater, huh?"

Is that...jealousy?

He laughs. "Hazel has what we like to refer to as hopeless romantic syndrome. She's always dreamed of falling in love, chased the happily ever after and all that, only to be left disappointed."

The guilt that's been hovering like a shadow since the day we got married? It presses in tighter.

Penn pushes a hand through his hair. "Actually, that's a big reason we were so shocked she agreed to this marriage."

I force a casual shrug. "We're adults. We knew what we were doing, and we're keeping things platonic. The last thing I want to do is disappoint your sister."

Penn eyes me curiously from the side. "Well, I know from experience that sometimes we make choices because we think it will keep us safe, when in reality, it just keeps us from getting what we really want." Before I can reply, one of Penn's employees pulls into the driveway.

Penn claps his hands together, calling to the man as he climbs out of his truck. "Come on, Vince! We've got a house to demo." Then he turns back to me. "You wanna stay and see the mess I'm about to make in here?"

"Nah, I've got to get going."

"Suit yourself. See you at dinner next weekend," he says before walking up to the house with Vince trailing him.

Right. The Sheppard family dinner is next week, which means more time with the people closest to Hazel. People who are welcoming me into their family like I might actually be good for her.

I should be figuring out how to walk away. Instead, I just keep getting pulled in deeper.

Chapter Twelve

Hazel

I stare at the recliner that just got delivered, wondering what the hell I was thinking.

"Hello?" Laney answers after the second ring.

"I bought a chair."

"Okay, that's one way to start a conversation."

I kick the dark gray recliner like it personally offended me and scowl as it rocks back and forth mockingly. "I bought a recliner for my husband and now I'm really regretting that choice."

"I feel like you need to bring me up to speed before launching into discussions about random furniture purchases."

Sighing, I sit down in the recliner and instantly feel relaxed. "Some things have happened, Laney, and I don't know what to think."

"Did his dick fall into your vagina already?"

"What? No!" Her laughter fills the line. "This isn't funny."

"It kind of is, but I can tell by your tone that you're not interested in my comedic genius right now, so I'll reel it in."

"Yes, please."

"Fine. What's going on?"

I exhale, rocking gently. "My husband and I went on a date two weeks ago. It was...confusing."

"Confusing how?"

Blueberry jumps onto my lap as I continue to rock. "Well, we started getting letters."

I relay the story, explaining the letters from Diane, the stipulations and the unexpected push toward something neither of us saw coming.

Laney whistles. "Damn. This woman was hell-bent on setting the two of you up, wasn't she?"

"Apparently so. And our date was..."

"Where did you go?"

"Well, first, he insisted we ride on his motorcycle."

"Is that code for his dick?"

"No, Laney! He actually drives a motorcycle. Now focus, please."

"Noted. Continue."

I let out a sigh. "The ride was exhilarating, and then he held my hand—because the letter said to—we shared a meal, and we went to the thrift store to complete the photo shoot. But while we were there, he got a phone call."

"Okay..."

"From someone named Miranda."

"Sounds like a woman's name."

"Right?"

"You said he hasn't made a move on you yet, right?"

"Well, not exactly..." I think back to our kiss last week, contemplating if I would classify that as something Gage wanted to do, or something he felt compelled to.

"Then he either has a girl back in Florida, or he's gay."

"I know he's not gay."

"How?"

"Because I felt his dick get hard when he kissed me in front of my ex."

Laney whistles again. "Whoa! Okay, now we're getting somewhere. Give me a play-by-play."

I spend the next several minutes telling her about Nathan showing up at the studio, Gage acting all territorial, and the explosive kiss.

"And how did you feel about the kiss, about him calling himself your husband?"

"Disgusted," I say, not believing the words myself as they slip out of my mouth.

Laney snorts. "Yeah, okay. Try selling that lie to someone else."

Groaning, I lie back in the chair and pop up the footrest as Blueberry curls up in a ball between my legs. "I honestly don't know what to think, especially because the only reason he was at my studio to begin with was because he brought me apology socks."

"Okay. Now that's actually adorable."

I smile, remembering how embarrassed he seemed when he gave them to me. "It kind of was, but it was confusing too—things got intense after our date."

"So was that what he was apologizing for?"

"Yes. I finally confronted him about the day we met. All of the details of our date, the way we fought and laughed, and then that mysterious Miranda...it just all kind of came to a head and I broke."

Confronting Gage about the day we first met was only a matter of time, but I certainly didn't anticipate his reaction. For a moment, I swear I saw remorse in his eyes, regret mixed with guilt—and that only made me feel guilty for falling apart on him.

He never could have known what that day meant to me, but after the thrift store and him finding the wind chime, I couldn't stop thinking about the circumstances that brought us together.

It felt too strong to ignore anymore—just like my growing attraction to him.

"Well, that's to be expected. You guys are navigating a tricky situation."

"I know. But then I went and bought him a chair."

"Yes, the chair that started this phone call. Why did you buy it again?" I recall the conversation we had about something that would make Gage feel more comfortable in my place.

"I see. So, what's the problem? He did something nice for you, and you did something nice for him."

"I know, but he gets so touchy—always sure to remind me this is temporary. He's so closed off. I want to know him better, but every time I think he's actually going to open up, he shuts down. Like the other day when kids came up."

"What did he say?"

"He said he used to want kids, but now it's not in the cards."

"Okay, that's cryptic."

"Right? And he didn't elaborate. Add in the mysterious phone call and I'm not sure what to think or feel right now."

Laney exhales, like she's turning it over in her head. "Damn, Hazel. I'm confused too. Why would he be so quick to claim you in front of your ex but push you away every time you start to get closer?"

"I know. It makes me think he's hiding something."

"I hate to say it, but I think you may be right. Another possibility here is that he's developing feelings for you and it's scaring him."

"You think?"

"I mean, you said yourself you've seen his reaction to you. And kissing you? He didn't *need* to do that."

I think back to our kiss last week, how unexpected it was, how good it felt to feel his lips on mine again.

How right it felt too.

I've kissed a lot of guys, but I've never felt the electricity that I have with Gage.

And it's not just the physical. It's the way he stands up for me, challenges me, makes me laugh, and anticipate our evenings together after a long day that turns my stomach in knots.

And that's the number one problem—he said no feelings and I'm already developing them.

"No, I can't go there, no matter how badly I wonder what he would be like in bed."

Laney laughs. "If you *hadn't* been wondering that, I would be more concerned."

I groan. "This is going to be the longest six months of my life."

"Hey, you're already a month and a half in. Just keep doing what you're doing. If he's going to be closed off, let him. If he pushes you, push back."

"Oh, believe me. I have been."

"And if he wants to go full caveman and protect you from a shitty ex, then let him. Maybe a little danger will make him realize how incredible you are, and then..."

I don't hear the rest of what she says because Gage walks through the front door, and his eyes immediately lock onto me like I've committed a crime.

"Hazel?" His voice comes out tight, edged with suspicion.

"Hey, Laney... I gotta go."

"Okay, but call me when you two have sex!" she yells through the phone as I scramble to hang up.

I scoop Blueberry from my lap and set him on the ground, standing as Gage steps further inside.

"What the hell is that?" he asks, pointing to the recliner.

I blink dramatically. "This? This is what most people call a *chair*, Gage. It's a place to sit after a long, hard day."

His expression remains flat, his tone dripping with disbelief. "Did you get this for me?" He takes a tentative step closer to the recliner, like he's afraid it might come to life and swallow him whole.

"I did."

He turns to face me, his green eyes full of something I can't quite place. "Why?"

"Well, as you know, the thrift store didn't have any ottomans...so I ordered this instead."

"That doesn't answer my question." He takes another step, closing the space between us. "*Why* did you buy this?"

I lift my chin, refusing to break eye contact. "Because I want you to be comfortable here."

His jaw flexes, and his eyes bounce back and forth between mine for so long, I wonder if we're going to stand here all night. Finally, he clears his throat, blinking himself back to reality. "You didn't have to do this."

I shrug. "I know I didn't."

His lips press into a thin line. "You *shouldn't* have done this."

Crossing my arms, I reply, "When are you going to learn that telling me what to do isn't going to work out well for you?"

He scoffs and pushes a hand through his hair. "Listen, I've told you—I'm leaving as soon as our time is up. You shouldn't be making decisions based on me."

"Oh my God, Gage. It's just a chair."

My chest is heaving, my pulse hammering, and my eyes burn with angry tears. This isn't the reaction I thought I'd get over a damn recliner. But then again, I shouldn't be surprised—this man is so hot and cold, I never know which version of him I'm going to get.

One day, he's closed off and distant. The next, he's kissing me breathless in my studio.

I reach down and pick Blueberry up, turning toward my bedroom. "If it offends you so much, you don't have to use it."

I wait for him to say something. Anything.

But he doesn't.

And I remind myself that it's for the best.

The more we avoid each other, the less likely I am to fall for a man who's already got one foot out the door.

***

The sound of the doorbell ringing pulls me from my coloring book. I should be editing, but my focus has been shit for the past few days, especially after Gage's reaction to the recliner.

He could have at least said "thank you," but since then, I've barely gotten two full sentences out of him.

Marriage. What a dream.

Standing from the couch, I walk over and open the front door. Once again, there's no one there, and my eyes drop to the doormat, where a crisp pink envelope rests on top of a brown cardboard box.

"Just great."

I take the box into the kitchen and remove the envelope from the top, setting it to the side before opening the package and pulling out a small box labeled, *Truth or Dare for Couples.*

Seriously, Diane?

Staring at the box, I can already picture Gage's reaction when he gets home.

Blueberry barks at me from the floor. "Did you know your mom was up to all of this stuff?" His head tilts to the side. "I wish you could speak so you could tell me what's going through your mind." I scoff. "Then again, even my husband can't seem to do that, so…"

"Are you talking to yourself in here?"

I jump at the sound of Gage's voice. He comes around the corner holding a six-pack of beer, looking delectable in his signature all-black outfit, his hair a mess from his bike helmet.

Fuck. He's like every teenage girl's fantasy and exactly the type of guy their dad would threaten with a shotgun.

"*Actually*, I was talking to Blueberry."

Gage looks down at the dog and then back to me. "Not sure that's any better."

I sigh. "Why do you care?"

"I don't, I was just …" But his words trail off as his gaze lands on the counter, where the pink envelope and box sit like a ticking bomb.

His shoulders fall. "Is that…"

"The next letter?" I finish for him. "Yep. This one came with a box and I'm sure you're going to be just as thrilled about its contents as I am."

Gage peers inside the cardboard box at the game and scowls. "What the fuck?"

"Yeah." I reach for the envelope and slide my finger under the seal. "Shall we see what your aunt has in store for us this time?"

Gage heads to the fridge to deposit his six-pack, taking one bottle out and popping the top. "Why the hell not? The sooner we read it, the sooner we can get it over with."

"God, I'm so lucky to have married someone with such a positive outlook on life," I say mockingly, pulling the paper from the envelope and unfolding it.

Gage and Hazel,

It's time for your next task! If I know you both like I think I do, I imagine not much has transpired between you since your last date. So, instead of waiting for your two-month anniversary, I thought you two should get to know each other a bit better, sooner rather than later.

Truth or Dare is the perfect way to get you to open up to each other—or at least have a few laughs at the other's expense.

Life is unpredictable, messy, and sometimes unfair, but if you can laugh together, you'll always have something worth holding onto.

Have fun and good luck. I'll be rooting for you.

Love,

Diane

I set the letter back down on the counter. "Well, do we do this tonight or put it off?"

Gage chugs half of his beer. "Let's just get it done. At least I have alcohol for the occasion."

I study his beer bottle and then an idea pops into my head. "How about we play Truth or Drink?"

"What do you mean?"

"Well, I don't know about you, but I'm not about to go streaking down the street in my underwear for a dare." Gage's eyebrows lift in surprise, but I press on. "You know what I mean. Lord knows the kind of shit we would have to do for a dare. So, we throw those cards out, and if you don't want to answer a truth card, you have to drink." Since Gage isn't a big drinker, but he brought beer home with him, I assume he's in the mood to put a few drinks away.

Gage dips his eyes to the glass bottle in his hands and then back up to me. "Deal."

I fill a wine glass and we reconvene in the living room after Gage has changed into a pair of athletic shorts that do absolutely nothing to hide the bulge between his legs.

It's ridiculous how my mouth waters from seeing just the outline of his cock.

God, it's been far too long since I've had sex. That's it. That's why I feel feral every time I look at him. I'm just horny. Looks like a date with my vibrator is in store.

"Okay." I set my wine glass on the table, take the truth cards out of the box, and shuffle them before placing them in a stack on the coffee table. "Do you want to go first?"

"I don't fucking care," Gage grumbles.

"Yeah, I'm beginning to understand that." Rolling my eyes, I reach for my phone. "Let's take a picture really quick to document this for Timothy."

He doesn't protest, so I take that as permission to approach.

Sliding next to him on the couch, I lean in close and flip the camera to selfie mode. What I see on the screen takes me by surprise.

Gage's eyes are closed and his nose is buried in my hair. When I hear him inhale, something tightens in my chest.

I close my eyes and snap the picture, wanting to capture this moment as a reminder that he's not always the grumpy man I've become so used to.

He opens his eyes, finds the camera poised above us, and says, "Are you gonna take the picture or what?"

"Um, yeah."

I smile while Gage keeps his lips in a flat line, and I take a few more pictures before settling back in my original spot on the couch, willing my heart rate to come back down.

What the hell is going on with this man?

I pick up the first card, clear my throat, and read the question out loud. "What's the grossest thing you have ever eaten?"

Gage narrows his eyes. "I'm supposed to answer that?"

"Yes, Gage. That is how the game works. It's not that shocking of a question, but if you don't want to answer it, you can always take a drink."

He shakes his head, staring down at his beer bottle between his spread knees. "Fine. Probably my belly button lint." I scrunch my nose. "Ew, that's disgusting."

"Yeah, well, some kids ate boogers. I ate my belly button lint."

I stare at the man sitting across from me, not sure if I like where this game is headed. "Okay then, I feel like I'm starting to understand you better already."

Gage smirks as he reaches for a card. "Describe your most embarrassing moment."

"Oh, that's an easy one. I was photographing a wedding and my leggings split right down my ass crack. I was bending over, talking to everyone all night long with my bare ass sticking out since I was wearing a thong."

"You didn't feel a breeze or anything?"

"It was an outdoor wedding, and it was already chilly outside, so I didn't think anything of it. Luckily, I have a nice ass, but still. I'm sure I was the talk of that wedding for years afterward."

His gaze drops down my body, slow and appraising, before he clears his throat. "That's pretty embarrassing, Spitfire."

I shrug, reaching for a new card. "Nothing I can do about it now. Okay, next question. When was the last time you cried?"

Gage's face instantly grows serious. "The day I walked into my aunt's house to clean it out." He takes a swig from his beer and picks up the next card.

I reach out to place my hand on his. "Gage..."

"Don't, Hazel. I answered the question, now let's move on."

Sighing, I return to my spot on the couch. "Fine." But for just a split second, I learned something about Gage—he does have a heart under that tough exterior, and maybe he hasn't dealt with his aunt's death as well as I thought.

Gage clears his throat. "What's the worst date you have ever been on?"

I roll my eyes. "Oh, this is easy too. It was about a year ago and it's actually the reason I swore off men—including you, since Diane was determined to set us up."

"What happened?"

I spend the next few minutes recounting my date with Derek, the thunder guy.

"Are you fucking kidding me?" Gage finally says, shock written all over his face.

I take a sip from my wine glass because I deserve a drink after getting through that story again. "I wish I were."

His fingers drum against his knee, nostrils flaring. "I've never wanted to throat punch someone so hard that I've never met. The way he treated you..." He clenches his jaw. "You deserve someone better than that, Hazel."

"I know, but I'm done looking for him because that night I finally admitted that he may not be out there." Gage's eyes remain locked on mine. I can hear my pulse in my ears, and that's when I know that I need to keep moving this game along, or I might start daydreaming about him potentially being my person.

Sitting here with him, having a drink and talking—albeit forced—is exactly the type of relationship I've always wanted. I want to be with my best friend, someone I can be honest with. And part of me wants to let Gage see who I really am. It's not like I have anything to lose—this marriage has an end date, so who cares what he thinks of me at the end of this?

Gage breaks our stare first, so I reach for the next card. "What is your biggest fear when it comes to love?"

He doesn't even hesitate before taking a drink from his beer, choosing to avoid the question.

I put my hands on my hips. "Seriously?"

"Hey, you gave me the option of drinking if I don't want to answer, so that's what I chose."

"Fine, then I'll tell you mine." I sit up straighter on the couch. "I'm afraid of ending up alone, but part of me thinks it would be better than settling for someone who doesn't see me."

"What do you mean?"

I stare down into my wine. "When I find my person, I want to know that when he looks at me, there are no doubts." I lift my gaze to his. "I want the kind of romance that feels effortless because there were no other people in the world for us but each other. I want the kind of love my parents had."

"And what kind is that?"

Looking him straight in the eyes, I say, "I want someone who will fight *with* me and fight *for* me." I shrug. "It's really that simple."

Before Gage can reply, his phone rings. When he fishes it out of his pocket and sees the screen, he launches from the couch. "Hey, sorry. I've got to take this."

"Yeah, okay."

I can feel our moment break, but I don't regret anything I've said. Gage looked as if I had spoken his worst fears out loud. I wish he'd had the chance to respond, to let me see him a little too.

He heads down the hall to his room and I hear him say, "Hey, Miranda."

Fucking Miranda.

Biting my bottom lip, I look at Blueberry sleeping peacefully in the recliner, and then I glance down the hall to Gage's room. I can faintly hear his voice through the walls, but if I went to his door, I could probably hear more.

Do I want to know who this Miranda person is? Will it make me feel better, or will it just expose something I'm not prepared for?

Why do I care about him talking to some woman on the phone anyway? For all I know, she could be his cousin.

But Gage said he doesn't have any family left.

As soon as I start to stand, intent on eavesdropping, he comes out of his room and back toward the living room. "Sorry about that."

"No worries," I say, heading to the kitchen as if that was my plan all along. I pour more wine in my glass, even though I haven't actually had much since we started the game. When I return, I find Gage staring off across the room.

His jaw is tight, his shoulders stiff. But when he sees me coming back, he smooths his expression, forcing something neutral.

"Whose turn is it?" he asks as we both settle back into the couch.

"It's my turn to answer a question."

"That's right." He reaches for the top card from the stack. "What is your favorite part of my body?"

Both of our heads snap up at the same time, our eyes locking.

"That is not what it says!" I challenge as my pulse climbs.

He twists the card around to show me, and when I verify he's telling the truth, I bring my wine glass to my lips and make a show of taking a long drink.

The corner of Gage's lips lifts. "Interesting."

I smack my lips in appreciation of the wine, buying myself some time. "I'm just drinking so I don't have to lie to you."

"And what exactly would you be lying about?"

"That I find any part of you attractive."

"You're a shitty liar, Spitfire." His eyes dart down to my nipples that are suddenly standing at full attention.

"Ugh." I take down half of my wine before wiping the back of my mouth with my hand. "Fine. You're a decent-looking guy, okay?"

Gage's smile spreads wider. "Just decent, huh?"

"Yes. And that's all you're getting." I lean forward and pull the next card from the stack, eager to move on from that question. "What is one thing you wish I would stop doing?"

"Hmm, where to start..." He taps his chin as if deep in thought.

I playfully whack him with a throw pillow. "Watch it!"

Still smiling, he looks over at the recliner. "I wish you would stop being so thoughtful."

"What?"

He brings the beer bottle to his lips, keeping his eyes locked on mine. "You heard me."

"And why would I do that?"

"Because."

I scoff. "Wow. Hard to argue with that logic."

He shrugs and then picks up the next card. "Have you ever had a dream about me?"

God, really? What is with these cards?

"Yes," I answer honestly, remembering several that have infiltrated my sleep recently.

Gage's eyes darken, but he remains perfectly still in his seat across from me. "That makes two of us then."

The temperature in the room seems to skyrocket as heat blossoms all over my body, a current traveling right between my legs.

Is he trying to get me even more *riled up? And if he is, what's the point when he's not going to do anything about it?*

"Next card." I pick up the one on top. "Have you ever wanted someone you knew you couldn't have?"

"Yes," he says without hesitation before lifting the beer bottle to his lips.

I freeze.

Is he talking about me?

He picks up the next card. "Do you think we met for a reason?"

Holding his gaze, I say, "I think we already know the answer to that question."

"Have you changed your mind about it though?"

"What do you mean?"

He leans his head on the back of the couch, staring up at the ceiling. "I don't know. I mean, I know that my aunt arranged this, but lately…" Blueberry starts barking in his sleep, pulling our attention over to him, and when I turn back to Gage, he's taking a drink from his beer bottle and avoiding my gaze. "Never mind. Next card."

I pick up the next card from the stack. "Have you ever lied to me?"

The silence is so thick I can hear my heart hammering as I wait for Gage to answer.

But he doesn't.

Instead, he abruptly stands from the couch and says, "I'm done with this game." He drains the rest of his beer and heads to the kitchen, tossing the empty bottle in the recycling.

I practically launch off the couch, pissed. "Seriously, Gage?"

"Goodnight, Spitfire."

Without a backwards glance, he walks down the hall to his room and shuts the door behind him, shutting me out even more in the process.

But what keeps me up that night is the question he refused to answer.

What is Gage lying to me about? And does it have anything to do with Miranda?

Chapter Thirteen

"There you two are!" My mother swings the front door open before Gage and I can even knock.

"Here we are," I say sarcastically, bracing myself for dinner with my family while this time pretending that everything is fine between Gage and me.

And technically, I guess it is. We don't really speak unless necessary, we're both very busy with work, and when we do talk, it's very surface level, especially after our game of Truth or Drink the other night.

This back and forth with him just gets more intense, especially when the letters come, and I'm not sure how much longer I can put up with his bullshit.

He sure as hell isn't trying to make things more comfortable for me, so why should I bother?

"Nice to see you, Catherine," Gage says, shoving his hands in his pockets.

"I feel like it's been ages. We all live in the same town, and I barely see my children anymore."

Parker comes out of the kitchen, eating a cracker. "Hey, it's the newlyweds!"

"Watch it," I say, sidestepping him and heading toward the kitchen where I know there is wine.

"Oh, do I sense some trouble in paradise?" he taunts.

Cashlynn appears at his side and pokes him in the ribs. "Leave them alone, Parker." She pulls me into a quick hug. "You looked like you could use one of those."

I chuckle. "Thanks, but I'm fine."

She arches a brow. "You sure?"

I glance over at my husband, who's now engrossed in a conversation with Parker. "We can talk later."

Cashlynn nods. "Yes, please. I'm sorry I haven't been a good friend lately, but the gallery has been insane, and planning a wedding is taking it out of me."

I hold my hand up to stop her. "No need to apologize. Work has been crazy for me too, but tonight we can catch up."

She looks over at Gage and Parker. "How are things going?"

"I honestly don't even know how to answer that."

Astrid and Willow walk into the kitchen from the back deck.

"Hey, Hazel! We were just talking about you," Astrid says.

They come closer and Astrid lowers her voice. "Did you know they opened a sex store in Castle?"

"What? No."

"Yep, finally! Willow, Cashlynn, and I are planning on checking it out soon."

The other two nod eagerly.

"Well, I'm sure you'll have fun."

"You don't want to go with us?" Cashlynn asks.

My eyes find Gage across the room. "Nah, I'm good."

The girls exchange worried looks.

"Oh, does that mean—" Willow starts, but I cut her off before she can finish that thought.

"Nope. Don't even go there."

Willow tilts her head toward the deck. "Let's go outside so we can talk more openly."

I fill a wine glass and follow them out back.

"Okay, now spill," Willow says once we're all settled on the back deck. "What's going on with you two?"

Sighing, I look out at my parents' backyard, taking note of how big the trees have grown since my father planted them when I was a kid, how beautiful the roses look, and how gorgeous the sun looks as it begins to descend in the distance. "Nothing. Absolutely *nothing* is going on."

Astrid snorts. "Okay. That's a lie."

"No, you know what? There is something going on," I say. "My husband has two personalities, and I never know which one I'm going to get. One moment he's apologizing to me with socks and I'm buying him a freaking recliner, and then the next we're playing Truth or Drink, and he's telling me to stop being so thoughtful—but also that he's had dreams about me."

The girls just stare at me, blinking.

Willow recovers first. "Okay...that is a lot to unpack."

"Tell me about it! And don't even get me started on the strange phone calls he gets from mysterious *Miranda*." Tipping my glass back, I take a big sip of wine.

Astrid holds a finger up. "Who the hell is Miranda?"

"That's what I'd like to know!" I shout, my pulse racing.

Cashlynn places her hand on my shoulder. "Just breathe, Hazel."

I set my wine glass on the railing and bury my face in my hands. "I'm just so frustrated and confused."

Astrid rubs my back. "Forgive me if I'm wrong, but could that be because you're developing feelings for him?"

I lift my head. "But we agreed...no feelings."

Willow chuckles. "Yeah, well, I think the three of us can safely say that the biggest issues we've had in our relationships were usually the result of not being honest about our *feelings*."

I glance back to the house. "He's getting under my skin. The more we talk—*when* we talk, that is—the more I want to know him. And he has these moments when I see something in his eyes, like he's holding himself back, but then he immediately shuts down...so I do the same."

Astrid claps her hands together. "Oh my God! What if Diane was right? What if you two are meant to be together?"

I give her a look. "Right. Because nothing says *destiny* like a man who refuses to open up and a woman who should know better than to get her hopes up."

"Maybe you need to push him a little," Cashlynn suggests. "I mean, as I recall, last year you were the one telling me to push your brother into admitting *his* feelings. Now it's your turn to give Gage the same treatment."

Willow bounces with excitement. "Yes, I support this idea one thousand percent!"

Astrid claps again. "Me too!"

I shake my head. "No. I am not *pushing* him to admit his feelings. He either wants me or he doesn't."

"Goose, Michael's calling for you." Dallas appears in the doorway, holding my nephew. As soon as Michael sees Willow, he lights up and reaches for her, stretching his little arms as far as they will go.

"Hey, baby boy!" She beams as she takes him in her arms. "Of course you were calling for momma—because you're momma's boy, aren't you?" She peppers his cheeks with kisses and he squeals excitedly.

"Momma!" My nephew smashes Willow's face in his hands and presses a kiss to her lips.

My heart aches at the sight of them—because the further I get into this marriage, the more I realize I may never have that life.

Even if things worked out with Gage, he said kids aren't in the cards for him anymore, so would I even have the option of being a mom?

And what does that mean, not in the cards? Did he have a vasectomy? Can he not physically have kids at all?

Oh God. What if Miranda is his secret wife and they have like 15 kids together? Maybe that's why kids aren't an option anymore! He's closed up shop!

"Time to eat, by the way," Dallas says, snapping me out of my spiral.

Astrid and Cashlynn follow Willow inside, but my brother waits back for me. "You look like you're trying to solve world hunger over here," he says. "Everything all right?"

I let out a heavy sigh. "I'm fine."

"I don't believe you, but we can talk later." He pats his stomach. "I'm starving and can't offer sage big brother wisdom on an empty stomach."

***

"Well, it's still early, but we just wanted to let everyone know…" Willow glances at Dallas, fighting to contain her smile. "We're having another baby!"

The dining room erupts as my siblings and mother all shout their congratulations. I glance at Gage beside me, curious to see his reaction.

His smile is sincere, but it doesn't fully reach his eyes, like there's a limit to how much he's willing to show.

"Congratulations, you two." I lean across the table and place my hand on top of Willow's.

"Thank you. We actually found out the day you announced you were getting married, but…"

"She didn't want to steal your thunder," Astrid finishes for her.

"No thunder has been stolen," I assure her.

"This means I'm not going to be able to drink at the bachelorette party," Willow says across the table to Cashlynn. "But that just means I can be the designated driver."

Cashlynn smiles. "As long as you're feeling up to it."

I raise a hand in the air. "Please do, because I, for one, really need a night out."

Gage raises his eyebrows. "Oh yeah? When exactly is this night out happening?"

"Next weekend," Parker answers. "And the weekend after that, the boys are going to Blossom Peak for a fishing trip. That includes you, Gage."

Gage glances at me. "Uh…"

"I'm not taking no for an answer," Parker cuts in. "Besides, we deserve to let loose too."

I can tell that Gage feels uncomfortable, so I reach under the table and squeeze his thigh. "You're part of the family now, remember?"

Gage sighs. "Well, I'm putting it out there now—I may be a pro at cornhole, but I can't catch a fish for shit."

Parker laughs. "Not a problem. We bring real food so we don't starve."

"Then count me in."

Astrid looks at me and raises her eyebrows. "Does that mean Gage is going to help build Michael's jungle gym next weekend while we girls have our day?"

I look at Dallas. "You guys are building him a playset?"

He nods. "Yeah. He's climbing everything in sight, and we have the space. I'd rather him climb a jungle gym than the walls. But we could use another set of hands." He peers around me to Gage. "You busy next weekend?" "I have an appointment with a client in the afternoon, but my morning is free. I could definitely stop by for a few hours."

Dallas nods. "Any help is appreciated."

I turn to Gage. "Thank you."

He leans in and presses a kiss to my cheek, catching me off guard. "That's what husbands are for, right?"

I'm so stunned, I freeze for a moment.

When I turn back to my plate, I can feel everyone's eyes on us, but I don't look up. How the hell am I supposed to explain that when I don't even understand it myself?

Dallas, ever the instigator, seizes the moment. "Well, if you want to help some more, you could play on my team for the Carrington Cove Games in September," he says.

I snap my head in his direction so fast I nearly give myself whiplash. "No way! You can't recruit *my* husband!"

He shrugs. "Why not? I mean, it's not like y'all are actually together."

Gage clears his throat. "No offense, Dallas, but if I'm going to play in those ridiculous games, it's going to be with my wife."

The girls' eyes go wide at that. Meanwhile, my heart is thrashing so wildly in my chest that I feel like I'm about to pass out.

My wife.

Every time he says that, my vagina levels up in her pursuit of luring him inside. She's feral, and containing her is starting to become challenging.

Dallas raises an eyebrow, casting me a curious glance. To my relief, he just shrugs and turns back to his food. "That's fine. I don't need family to win."

Willow chuckles. "Your confidence is getting a little out of hand, babe."

"Come on, Goose. As long as I have you, I'm good."

"Uh, are you forgetting that I'll be nice and round by then?"

He kisses her temple. "It's your mind that I love most about you anyway. I've got the guys from the restaurant for the physical stuff."

Astrid leans forward in her chair, a wicked grin on her face. "I hope Hazel's team wipes the floor with you, Dallas."

"Is someone still bitter about losing to me two years ago?"

Penn chimes in. "Just keep talking shit, Dallas. We'll see who gets the last laugh when we beat you by a landslide."

Gage clears his throat and turns to my mother. "Not gonna lie, Catherine—I'm a little concerned what state your family will be in when this is all said and done."

She looks at my husband. "I'm not. They all know that if they ever want to eat my cooking again, they'll squash their pettiness before they walk through the front door."

And just like that, the matriarch has spoken.

***

"So what's going on with you and Gage?" Dallas walks up to me as I step out of the bathroom.

I lower my voice. "Nothing."

"Yeah, I'm not buying that. He called you his wife."

"Technically, that's what I am."

He shakes his head. "No, that wasn't just a label. That was something else."

I try not to think about what he's insinuating. "We're just trying to get through the next four months."

He arches a brow. "I thought you agreed no feelings."

"We did."

He glances toward the living room and then motions for me to follow him further down the hall. He leads me into my old bedroom, shutting the door behind us. "I'm sorry, but the way that man is acting, I'm *telling* you—there are feelings involved."

My pulse starts to climb. "Why do you say that?" I debate how much I should divulge to my older brother, but at this point, maybe I need a man's opinion.

"I have eyes, Hazel. I know that look on his face."

"Things are...complicated."

"Would that have anything to do with Nathan?"

I whirl around so fast I nearly topple over. "How do you know about Nathan?"

"Gage came to my restaurant for lunch that day, remember?"

It hadn't even occurred to me that Gage might talk to my brothers about Nathan's visit.

"What did he say?"

"He was asking about him, wanted to know if he should be worried because—"

"Are you two plotting world domination in here, or just talking shit about me?"

I whirl around, finding Penn leaning against the doorframe, arms crossed, smirking like the pain in the ass that he is.

Dallas sighs. "Don't you knock?"

"It's my parents' house. What am I knocking for?" He steps inside, shutting the door behind him before dropping onto the bed. "So, what's this about?"

I pinch the bridge of my nose. "Dallas was just telling me that my brothers have been gossiping about my exes with my husband, apparently."

"You talking about lunch the other day?" Penn asks, and I nod, growing more irritated. "Yeah, well, he wanted to know if Nathan was a threat."

"And what did you all tell him?"

Dallas exchanges a glance with Penn before answering. "We told him the truth."

Fury starts to boil in my veins as I point at my two oldest brothers. "You had no right."

Penn stands and takes a step forward. "That's where you're wrong. We have every right to protect you."

"But *he* doesn't," I say, jabbing a finger toward the living room where everyone else is.

Penn's eyebrows draw together. "Last I checked, you're married and he's living with you, so yeah, he has a right to know if there's a potential threat to your safety. And frankly, if he didn't care, I'd be more concerned."

I shake my head, vibrating with anger. "I'm not some defenseless little girl! I have been surviving just fine on my own for years, and he is just counting the days until he can sign the divorce papers and leave Carrington Cove."

Dallas takes a step closer to me and lowers his voice. "Hazel, listen to me. Any man who is that concerned about your safety? Who stands up for you in front of your entire family? Who declares that he's on your team over anyone else's? That's not just a boy playing house. That's a man who has real feelings for you."

I stand there, blinking, because I don't have any words left.

Is Dallas right? Has all this back and forth really been because Gage is struggling with his feelings as much as I am? That's what the girls suggested too, but this is coming from my brothers, two of the men that I respect the most. Sure, my brothers annoy the hell out of me, and their protectiveness is borderline barbaric sometimes, but I don't know what I would do without them in my life.

It still doesn't change the fact that I don't have answers to their questions or that I care to admit that they could be right. My annoyance is skyrocketing and all I want to do is leave—now.

"I appreciate your concern, but I'd appreciate it even more if you two would mind your own business for once." I march to the door, but as I move to open it, Penn's voice stops me.

"You and Gage don't have all the time in the world, Hazel. If you want to know if there's real potential for you two, put yourself out there and figure it out. At least then you'll know where you stand."

His words strike me square in the chest—because I know he's speaking from experience. He almost lost Astrid before he finally pulled his head out of his ass.

I know my brothers are just trying to look out for me, but I need time to process everything they just threw at me. So, without another word, I leave the room.

When I step into the living room, my irritation is simmering just under the surface, ready to boil over. But then I see Gage sitting on the couch, talking with my mom, grinning from ear to ear.

He looks happy. He looks comfortable. He looks like he belongs here, with us.

And that just pisses me off even more—because I know he'll never admit he wants to stay.

***

I didn't say a word to Gage during the ride home from my parents' house. My mind was spinning, trying to decide whether I should even bring up his conversation with my brothers, or just let it go.

But when we got home, I found something on my bed that I wasn't expecting.

With the stack of drawings in hand, I march into the living room and finally let the anger that's been simmering all night boil over.

I find Gage on the couch, scrolling on his phone.

"What the hell is this?"

Gage looks up from his phone. "I'm sorry?"

I wave the drawings in front of his face. "What is this?"

Setting his phone on the coffee table, he stands and takes a few steps toward me, a smirk playing on his lips. "Looks like paper to me."

"I know it's paper, dickhead. These drawings...did you make them?"

"I did."

I toss them onto the coffee table, watching them scatter. "Why did you leave them on my bed?"

He shrugs, still smirking. "I figured you could use some new coloring material."

I flick my eyes back and forth between his, trying to understand his motives, how he can be so cold and guarded then do something thoughtful.

He sketched my name, a hummingbird, and 'Spitfire,' all in hollow letters with intricate designs, something very similar to what I would find in one of my coloring books.

And they're beautiful, an expression of Gage's talent as an artist.

But why did he do that for *me*?

"Why did you go to my brothers about Nathan?"

Gage's head rears back. "Where the hell did that come from?"

Crossing my arms, I straighten my spine and decide enough is enough. "You don't get to ask my family about my ex when you won't even talk to me about anything real."

He watches me for a beat, his jaw flexing, something unreadable flickering in his eyes—like he's debating his next move.

Then he takes a step closer, his chest nearly brushing mine. "You want to talk?" His voice is low, rough. "Then tell me the truth right now. Tell me why you moved closer to me the second that asshole walked into your studio."

I lift my chin, refusing to break eye contact. "No. You don't get to see all my scars when you've shown me none of yours."

His nostrils flare. "And there's your answer. I went to your brothers because your reaction told me something was fucking off with that guy, and you sure as hell weren't going to tell me."

I huff out a laugh. "That's rich, coming from the guy who's taking secret phone calls and pushing me away anytime I get too close...because you're clearly hiding something from me."

His jaw ticks. "You don't need to know everything about my life, Spitfire."

"Right back at you, asshole."

A slow smirk tugs at the corner of his mouth. "Is that my new nickname?"

"It's not new. I've been calling you that in my head since the moment I met you...the second time."

He clenches his fists at his sides, and his eyes drop to my lips, darkening. Then his voice drops to something lethal. "God, I'd love nothing more than to turn your ass red right now."

A wave of heat rushes through me at those words, pooling low in my stomach, setting every nerve on fire—because I *want* that. I *want* him to spank me, to show me how much I get under his skin—I want him to admit that he wants me too.

God, this is so messed up.

But hell, I want to see how far I can push him.

So I spin around, bend over the arm of the couch, and push my ass out.

"Fine," I say, my voice breathy. "Do it. Do whatever you want with me."

Silence.

The kind that coils tight, charged, humming with restraint about to snap.

I can hear Gage's breathing—sharp, uneven.

But then he takes a step toward me. Then another.

Finally, I feel his heat right behind me. His hand grazes over my ass—slow, testing, fingers pressing lightly into the curve.

A soft moan of anticipation slips past my lips.

"Fucking hell, Hazel."

"Touch me, Gage."

I turn my head slightly, peeking at him over my shoulder, waiting for the sting, the sharp bite of his palm.

But it never comes.

Instead, he backs away from me, brushing a hand through his hair like he's trying to physically rip himself out of this moment.

"Go to bed, Hazel," he rasps, turning for the hall.

I whirl around, my pulse hammering. "You're a coward, Gage Kingston!"

He huffs as he walks away. "Yeah, I am. If you only knew just how much..."

The sound of his bedroom door closing makes me sigh in defeat.

But if there's one thing I learned tonight, it's that Gage is holding himself back in more ways than one, and I have a feeling it's just a matter of time before he snaps.

At this point though, it might just be me that snaps first.

Chapter Fourteen

"That's it. Hold it right there." I steady the beam so Penn can drill in the bolt that will hold the structure together. "Perfect."

Reaching up, I wipe the sweat from my brow with the back of my hand. "Fuck. It's hot out here."

It's a sweltering Saturday in July and I'm helping the Sheppard men build the jungle gym for Hazel's nephew, as promised. The girls started their bachelorette day for Cashlynn early this morning at a spa a few towns over, and later they're going out drinking at a pub.

When Hazel left this morning, she barely said two words to me, which has been our norm since last weekend—when she went off on me and then asked me to spank her.

The number of times I've jacked off to that mental image is probably unhealthy, but fuck if I didn't want to color her ass red for calling me on my shit.

I shouldn't have left those drawings on her bed. But I worked on them in my spare time at the tattoo parlor last week—when all I could seem to think about was her. So I guess I wanted to give her something that would make her think of me.

And that's the fucking problem. I told myself I wouldn't let my feelings get involved, but here we are. And I think it's safe to say that Hazel is developing feelings too—the most prominent of which is lust.

God, I want nothing more than to fuck her and finally release all this pent-up energy between us. Giving in would solve a lot of my immediate issues—sexual frustration being the main one. But the aftermath would be messy, and Hazel doesn't deserve that.

She doesn't deserve the lack of a real future she'd have with me. Because she deserves everything.

"You sure you don't want a beer?" Dallas holds out an ice-cold Coors Light.

"Nah, I'm good." I pat my stomach. "Trying to watch my figure."

Part of me wants to say the hell with it and give in, but I've already had more alcohol than I'm supposed to since I moved to Carrington Cove. If Miranda found out, she'd give me the lecture I'd deserve.

"You have to have a few beers with us next weekend while we're in Blossom Peak." Parker comes up behind me, slapping me on the back.

"I'm not a big drinker, but I'll probably have a couple." The Sheppard brothers stand side-by-side, studying me now. "What?"

"Shall I go first?" Penn asks his brothers.

Parker shrugs. "Sure. I'll follow your lead."

Dallas doesn't say anything, so Penn continues. "What are your intentions with our sister?"

My pulse spikes. "Excuse me?"

Penn takes a step closer to me. "Look, I'm going to be the first one to admit that I wasn't pleased with the circumstances of this marriage. But after seeing you two together and getting to know you these past few months... You fit in well with our family and you've proven that you have Hazel's back, so continuing to have you as a brother-in-law wouldn't be so bad."

Parker nods. "Yeah. What he said."

Dallas clears his throat. "But you two have obviously not talked about what's going on between you."

"And what's going on between us?" I ask, crossing my arms and hating how transparent our issues are that even her brothers are picking up on them.

Parker smirks. "At dinner last weekend, she looked like she either wanted to murder you or jump your bones."

Penn smacks Parker on the back of the head. "Don't say shit like that about our sister."

Parker scoffs. "Are you seriously naïve enough to think that those two haven't already fucked?"

I decide that's my moment to chime in. "Don't fucking talk about our sex life, all right? Mainly because we don't have one...not that it's any of your business."

Dallas takes a few steps toward me. "Look, I'm not a moron. I see the way you look at our sister, man. All I'm saying is don't fuck with her feelings. If this is just platonic for you, keep it that way. Hazel feels shit hard, and the last thing I want is to watch her try to pick herself up after you tear her down." He pauses for a second before making sure I hear his threat fully. "Because if you do? I'll make damn sure you feel every ounce of that pain."

"I see."

"As intimidating as my older brothers are trying to be, take it from the three of us," Parker tosses his thumb at his brothers. "We all had moments with our women that required us to make some fucking decisions. I recognize that same look on your face, man. Just make sure whatever you decide that our sister knows where you're at mentally. She's going to get hurt in this no matter what, but the level of that hurt can be diminished if you figure out what *you* want."

I nod, not sure what else I'm supposed to do.

Parker claps his hands. "Good. Now, before we can accept you fully into our family, we have devised a way for you to prove your loyalty."

Penn shakes his head. "I wasn't in favor of this, but apparently I'm being dragged into it anyway."

I turn my attention to Dallas. "What the hell is going on?"

He rolls his eyes as Parker speaks again. "What's going on is that we need your assistance for a little…payback." He rubs his palms together, a mischievous grin on his face.

"Payback?" My eyes dart between the brothers. "For what?"

Parker wraps his arm around my shoulder. "Don't worry. I'll explain everything."

Penn rolls his eyes and hikes up his tool belt on his waist. "Now that that's settled, let's finish up this jungle gym so I can actually put my feet up for a bit today."

We get back to work, and I try to keep my heart rate under control for a multitude of reasons.

***

I'm in my room, grabbing some clothes on my way to take a shower, when I hear the front door open and shut.

"Blueberry! Oh my God, I missed you!"

Fuck. My wife is home.

I make my way down the hall, coming to a dead stop when I find Hazel sprawled on the floor, letting Blueberry cover her face in slobbery kisses. As my gaze tracks lower, I realize she's wearing the most pathetic excuse for a dress I've ever seen—strapless, barely grazing her mid-thigh, and so sheer it hides very little of what's underneath.

Fuck me.

"Oh look, it's my husband!" she exclaims. She pushes up off the floor, straightening her dress and batting her hair from her face while trying to maintain her balance. In other words, drunk as a skunk.

I fold my arms and lean against the wall. "Well, you look like you had fun."

Hazel snorts. "Um, yeah. You could say that." Winking, she kicks off her heels and stumbles toward the fridge. "I need some pizza."

I follow her, watching her dig through the fridge like she might manifest a Domino's order from thin air. "We don't have any pizza, Hazel."

Her frown is instant. "Ugh. That's dumb!"

I watch her open and close cabinets until she finds a bag of Doritos. "Jackpot!"

I bite back a laugh. It's been a long time since I've tamed an intoxicated woman, but seeing Hazel like this makes me more than a little curious as to how bold she might be with a little alcohol in her system.

"Let me get you some water," I say, rounding the counter.

Hazel groans as I reach into the cabinet for a glass. "God, why do you have to be so hot?"

Twisting to face her, I try to contain my smirk. "You think I'm hot, huh?"

She rolls her eyes, a reaction I've come to expect from her by now. "Oh, come on, Gage. You have eyes. Surely you've seen me checking you out."

I flex my bicep mockingly. "It's the tattoos, isn't it?"

Hazel sighs. "The tattoos, the pierced tongue..." She falls into my chest, gripping my shirt. And fuck, she feels amazing pressed up against me like this, her soft to my hard, her smell directly under my nose so that I have no choice but to soak it in.

"Do you have any other piercings?" she asks breathlessly, her eyes darting to my mouth and then back to my eyes.

"Wouldn't you like to know?" I tease, but my dick is swelling in my pants, eager to show her the other jewelry on my body.

No, Gage. This is dangerous and she's fucking drunk.

Eyes wide, Hazel licks her lips. "I would. I *really* would." She runs her hand down my chest, slowly working her way lower.

My brain finally kicks in, and I grab her hand. "You're drunk, Hazel."

"Duh." Stumbling back, she brushes her hair from her eyes. "Did you just realize that?"

Walking around her to the fridge, I fill up a glass of water and grab a few ibuprofen from the medicine cabinet. "Here. Take these."

Reluctantly, she takes the pills and water from me, downing them in a few seconds before placing the glass on the counter. "There. Happy, Dad?"

"I don't have a Daddy kink, but good to know that you do."

She groans, pushing her hair behind her shoulders. "Ugh, you're infuriating."

"So you've told me."

I take her by the shoulders and steer her toward her room. When we step inside, she turns around and runs her palms over my chest. The heat of her touch makes me burn for her even more.

"Come on, Gage..." Her hands keep climbing and she runs her fingernails up the back of my neck. "You know it would feel good to take out some of this frustration on each other."

"Fuck, Spitfire." Closing my eyes, I fight to control my pulse—because she's not wrong. "You know that's not a good idea."

"I think it's an amazing idea. No one would have to know. We can scratch this itch and..."

I exhale hard and catch her wrists, pulling her hands from my neck as I take a step back. "You should go to sleep."

I can see the hurt in her eyes, the sting of rejection lingering there before anger takes over. "You're an ass."

"You've said that before too."

"God, I guess I've been reading this all wrong." Spinning away from me, she heads toward her bathroom.

I can't let this woman think I don't want her. Because I do—even though I shouldn't.

I stalk behind her, pressing my rock-hard cock into her back and pinning her against the wall, trapping her wrists above her head. Her breath hitches, the warmth of her skin feels like fire under my hands, and the thin line I'm teetering on feels like it's about to break.

"Does this feel like you've been reading this all wrong?"

The gasp she lets out makes my dick twitch. "Gage..."

"You have no idea how close I am to snapping, Hazel."

"Then do it." She pushes her ass back into me, rubbing it against my cock for good measure. "Show me what happens when you do."

I drag my nose up the column of her neck, watching her skin pebble under my touch. "I want to," I murmur against her pulse, "but it's only going to make things more difficult."

"That's not true," she mewls, arching into me. "It's going to feel *so* good, Gage. *So* fucking good."

I bite her shoulder softly, and her moan sends a lightning bolt straight to my cock. "God, woman, you're maddening."

She wiggles her ass against me again, making me groan. "I learned from the best."

I grip her hips, pulling her ass tighter against me. "The only reason I'm telling you this right now is because you're drunk, and the likelihood that you'll remember it is slim."

She exhales sharply. "Telling me what?"

I drag my lips along the shell of her ear before telling her all the thoughts I shouldn't say out loud, but at this point, I don't fucking care.

"The number of times I've dreamed about burying my face in your cunt, Hazel, is fucking obscene. I fantasize about how you'd taste, how you'd scream..." I trail my hand down her stomach, slipping between her thighs to cup her there.

Hazel moans, sharp and needy, her head falling back against my shoulder.

"I think about how pretty you'd be on your knees. Sucking my cock, licking each barbell on my shaft as I slide down your throat until you gag. But most of all?" I press my fingers against the damp fabric of her thong, curling them slightly, feeling just how soaked she is. "I think about how this pussy would feel wrapped around my cock, sucking in every inch of me."

"Oh my God..."

I move my hand from her pussy to her ass, palming the soft flesh before delivering a sharp smack.

She gasps, jolting in my arms, pressing back into me instinctively.

"I've dreamed of fucking this ass too, Spitfire."

Hazel stills. "I've—I've never done that."

"Fuck," I growl, grinding my cock against her ass and sliding my hand back between her legs. "That would make it even more of a dream."

She whimpers. "Gage, I can't take it anymore."

Tilting her hips, she presses her pussy into my hand. "*Please* touch me."

Snatching my hand away, I take a step back and fight to get my breathing under control.

"That isn't going to happen, Spitfire."

She spins to face me, chest heaving, her eyes full of fury. "You want me just as much as I want you."

"I do."

More than you know.

"Then what's holding you back?"

The words are on the tip of my tongue—the truth.

But Hazel was right. I *am* a coward.

"Go to bed, Hazel."

"Fuck. You." She tugs her dress down in one swift motion, letting it pool at her feet, leaving her in nothing but that black silk thong.

Yeah. Fuck. Me.

I scrub my hand down my face as she spins on her heel and stalks toward her bathroom, hips swaying. My dick aches behind the zipper of my jeans, hating me for having a goddamn conscience right now.

But there's no way I would touch Hazel in the state she's in. And before I self-destruct, I go back to my room, grab my clothes, and head straight for the shower to unleash the demons inside me.

Chapter Fifteen

Hazel

I stare down at my shaking hands as I stand in my bathroom, the sting of rejection burning through the alcohol haze.

All I could think about all night was Gage. Listening to the girls all talk about their men and how they planned to go home and jump their bones made my need build to an ungodly level.

I've never been this horny in my entire life. Probably because I've never lived with a bona fide bad boy who won't let me take my aggression out on his dick.

So, on the ride home, I decided I was going to offer myself to him, give him permission to take what we both know he wants.

But his stupid conscience got in the way.

He probably thought I'd regret it, which is bullshit. I knew exactly what I was doing. And the second he admitted he's pierced below the belt, my curiosity spiked into full-blown obsession.

After stewing in my bathroom for a while, still burning with frustration, I decide I need water. I swing the door open and head toward the kitchen. But when I hear sounds coming from Gage's bathroom, I stop dead in my tracks.

"Fuck," I hear him mumble from behind the closed door, and because I'm a curious creature, I lean against the wood, seeing what else I can hear.

At first, there's not much besides the sound of water against the tile—but then a grunt echoes from inside.

My pulse spikes.

Oh my God. Is Gage...jacking off?

The thought of him stroking himself hits me like a live wire. And before I know what I'm doing, I'm turning the doorknob.

I step inside and am welcomed by the sight of Gage's backside through the glass doors, his ass cheeks clenched, the muscles in his back rippling, one hand braced on the wall, the other slowly stroking his length.

Water slides down his inked skin, tracing every ridge, every groove. His grip tightens and he groans.

I can't stop the whimper that escapes.

He immediately twists his head over his shoulder. "Hazel..."

"Gage," I practically moan, but try to keep my libido in check.

He clenches his jaw. "You should leave."

He keeps stroking himself, and I feel wetness pool between my legs.

"Really? Because it looks like you want me to stay." I step further into the room, my entire body vibrating with need.

His eyes close as he turns to face me, giving me a full frontal view of his gloriously naked body. Every sculpted muscle flexes—his abs tightening, his forearms straining—as he fists his cock, stroking over the barbells along his length.

Fuck, I want to lick those piercings. I want to drop to my knees, take him down my throat, and watch him crumble above me.

But it's his eyes that are captivating me, full of anguish, remorse, and yearning.

"This is what you fucking do to me, Hazel," he finally says, still running his hand up and down his cock, groaning every time he squeezes the tip before sliding back down.

And his cock is glorious—long, thick, and teasing me with each stroke of his hand.

I bite back a whimper. "Then let me touch you."

He shakes his head. "I...can't. I don't deserve you yet." His jaw clenches, his free hand pressing against the glass door as his strokes pick up. "But I'm about to finish what I started, Hazel. So you can either leave or you can stay and watch...while you get yourself off."

The idea of touching myself in front of him has my breath hitching and my body yearning for more than he's willing to give me. But if this is the only way I get to have him tonight, then I'm giving myself over to him without hesitation.

I want to trust this man with my body. And my heart is slowly catching up to the idea too.

Without another word, I push down my thong, stepping out of it and kicking it aside.

Gage's nostrils flare as his eyes rake over me, devouring me, memorizing every inch as he takes in my fully bare body for the first time.

"Fuck. You're exquisite."

"So are you," I breathe, sliding my hand down my stomach, sliding my fingers through my pussy that is drenched with need for him. I shudder as I press against my clit, rubbing slow circles around that magical button.

"Sit on the counter," he commands. And I do as he says—because that tone, the one he gets when he's about to lose control? I'd do just about anything he asked.

"Now spread your legs. Let me see that pussy, Hazel."

I brace my hands behind me and plant both feet flat on the countertop, spreading my legs wide and baring myself to him completely.

"Show me how you like to be touched."

A needy whimper escapes as I slip two fingers inside myself. "I want you to be the one touching me, Gage."

"Touching you would break every rule we agreed to."

I know what we agreed to, but that was before I knew him, before I knew how he would make me feel. But clearly, I'm not getting my way tonight.

Stubborn, frustrating, infuriating man.

"Then tell me what you want me to do to myself."

"*Fuck*, Hazel." He fists his cock tighter, pumping faster as his gaze stays locked between my thighs. "Keep fingering yourself, baby. Rub that clit. Spread your arousal around and let me watch you."

I bite my lip as I obey, dragging my fingers deep before circling my clit with slow, deliberate strokes.

Gage groans. "Jesus Christ."

"I wish this was your cock, not my fingers."

"Fuck, Hazel. You're testing my fucking restraint yet again."

"You're testing mine. I just want to be with you, Gage," I say as my spine tingles with awareness that my orgasm is about to light up my entire body. My eyes fixate on Gage's cock, his fingers moving expertly over his pierced length, the part of him that I've yet to get to know and now it's all I can think about.

"Show me how you touch yourself when you're alone. Show me how your pussy drips and pulses when you're thinking of me."

I move my other hand between my legs, one working over my clit, the other moving in and out of me. Gage's eyes dilate at the sight. He presses his forehead to the glass, like he wants to break through it, shatter all over the floor on his way to me. His veins pop from under his skin, his tongue dances over his bottom lip, and the way his green eyes darken makes my orgasm build in record time.

"Holy fuck. I'm there, baby," he groans, his palm slapping the glass, his gaze locked on me—my body, my pussy, my pleasure unraveling before him.

"Me too," I pant.

"Come with me, Hazel," he growls.

We both cry out at the same time, my orgasm tearing through me just as his cum hits the glass in thick, hot ropes.

His face tenses, his body shuddering, his chest rising and falling with ragged breaths, like he's just been fucking ruined.

When the final wave of my orgasm subsides, I pull my fingers from my pussy as Gage's gaze follows the movement.

"Suck on those fingers, Spitfire," he growls.

I hesitate for only a second before I put the same fingers that were just inside me into my mouth, swirling my tongue over them and tasting myself, moaning softly as I draw out the moment just for him.

"Jesus fucking Christ. You are trouble, woman."

I remove my fingers with a pop, watching his reaction with a self-satisfied smirk. "And you're confusing as hell."

He shuts off the water and slides the glass door open, reaching for a towel to wrap around his waist, his cock still hard. Then he moves across the room and stands right in front of me. "I'm not trying to be, but..." He reaches up to touch my face, and I flinch on instinct—not because I don't want him to touch me. God, I do. But after everything we just did, after everything we can't admit, I can't take that touch right now.

He pulls his hand back before he makes contact. "You scared of me now, Hazel?"

Biting my bottom lip, I say, "Fucking terrified."

He scowls. "Why?"

Tilting my head, I fire back with, "Why are *you* scared of *me*?"

Silence stretches between us before he reaches for my hand and places it right over his wildly beating heart, his eyes so captivating, they're holding me hostage. His throat bobs up and down before he says, "This is why, Hazel." His pulse is firing rapidly beneath my palm, his heart trying to break free from his rib cage.

I'm so confused. "Wh—what do you mean?"

Before he can answer, there's a scratch at the door.

Closing his eyes, Gage sighs. "Blueberry."

With a laugh, I hop down from the counter and grab a clean towel from the rack, wrapping it around myself. "He probably needs to go outside."

Wobbling on my feet, I head for the door, but Gage stops me.

"I'll take him out so you can get ready for bed."

I blink up at him. "Okay."

With a nod, he leaves.

As I turn and look at myself in the bathroom mirror, the room begins to spin. God, waking up tomorrow is going to suck. Not just because I'll have to face the consequences of the alcohol, but because I have no idea how Gage is going to act after tonight.

After I put on a pair of silk pajamas and brush my teeth, I stumble to my bed, burrowing under my blanket.

At some point, I swear I feel the weight in the bed shift and a hand stroking my back.

But when I wake up in the morning, I'm alone.

***

"Wow. Mutual masturbation is really fucking hot," Laney says through the phone. "Perhaps one day I can fulfill that fantasy as well."

"It was one of the most erotic moments of my life."

"Well, that's saying something—considering you hold sex toy parties for fun."

I giggle—then groan as soon as a fresh wave of throbbing hits my temples. "Oh God, don't make me laugh."

"Had a little too much to drink last night, did ya?"

"Let's just say that the liquid courage was in full force, and the second I woke up, I brushed my teeth because I swear, it tasted like a cat shit in my mouth while I was sleeping."

Laney laughs. "The joys of drinking. But I think it's a good sign that he denied you… Repeatedly."

I frown. "Are you kidding? I mean, I did still get an orgasm out of it, but…"

"Well, it shows he's not a creep who takes advantage of drunk women, and he's not just into you for sex. I mean it sounds like you *threw* yourself at him. Multiple times. Like, low-key kinda desperate—"

"Hey, I was not desperate! I was drunk and horny—there's a difference."

"Uh-huh. And he wouldn't touch you, or let you touch him, even though he clearly wanted you. He must care about you."

"Or he's just terrified of my brothers…"

We both laugh.

I think about our conversation afterward…when I asked him why he was afraid of me and he responded by placing my hand over his heart. I have no idea what that meant, but the only logical explanation is that he's feeling something for me too.

"Well, I'd love to ask him about it, but I have no idea where he is. Probably back to avoiding me and pretending nothing happened, as usual."

"God, I seriously just want to strangle the two of you."

Groaning, I open the medicine cabinet and grab the bottle of ibuprofen. "I know...Enough is enough. When he gets home, I'm going to *make* him talk to me. I can't do this anymore."

As if I summoned him, Gage walks through the front door, holding a box from Astrid's bakery, two coffees, and a bottle of Pedialyte. Our eyes meet and the corner of his mouth lifts. "Hey, Spitfire."

"Uh, Laney, I gotta go."

"If you don't text me after you two talk, we are no longer friends."

"Noted." I end the call and set my phone on the counter. "Hey."

Gage's eyes dip down to my nipples peeking through the silk of my pajamas for just a second before he shakes his head and makes his way into the kitchen. "I brought breakfast."

"I see that. Thank you."

He sets everything down on the counter and just stands there, his fists clenched at his sides.

Taking a deep breath, I decide to lay it all out there. "Look, Gage—"

Before I can form a sentence, Gage closes the distance between us in one stride, gripping my face in his hands and slamming his mouth to mine.

God, yes.

His tongue swirls against mine, the piercing immediately elevating the experience to erotic as I wrap my hands around his neck and pull him closer.

"Are you feeling okay?" he asks between kisses.

"Better now."

"Fuck, Hazel."

Gage lifts me onto the counter, pressing himself between my legs, letting me feel how hard he already is. The sounds of our labored breathing fills the space.

Chest heaving, he says, "I know we need to talk, but I really need to fuck you first."

"Yes. Now. Please." Apparently, my vagina is running the show—because any intention of talking just flew right out the window.

Gage leans back, his hands still gripping my waist, eyes dilated. "Are you sure?"

"Yes."

He leans his forehead against mine, breathing heavily. "We can't go back after this."

I shake my head against his. "I don't want to go back."

When he lifts his head from mine, I can see the moment he's made his decision, when he finally allows himself to give in to what he wants.

He reaches behind his neck and pulls his shirt up, tossing it on the floor behind him. I run my hands up his bare chest, admiring his tattoos before he takes my hands and moves them back to his neck. "I hope you know what you're asking for."

"I do. Now, fuck me please."

Gage smashes his lips to mine again and the dizziness returns, but not from the hangover. No. This dizziness is overwhelming as all of my senses go haywire, feeling every electric jolt of his touch as he pulls me closer to him, pressing his cock against the heat between my legs.

"I want you so fucking bad," he murmurs.

"I can tell," I tease, tracing my fingers over his inked chest.

"This isn't going to be gentle, Hazel."

"Good. I don't want gentle. I want you to show me how much you want me."

He lifts my silk tank from my body, tossing it aside before dipping his mouth to my pierced nipple, licking it and pulling it gently between his teeth.

"This is so fucking sexy," he rasps between licks.

I gasp, my head falling back, my body arching into him. "Oh God, don't stop."

His tongue dances on my skin, licking, sucking, and nibbling before moving to my other breast, giving it the same attention. Gage pinches my pierced nipple as he licks the other, and I can already feel how soaked my panties are from this alone.

Suddenly, he grabs my thighs and lifts me off the counter, my legs wrapping around his waist on instinct. He carries me into the living room, setting me down in front of the couch, kneeling in front of me.

Our eyes stay locked as he hooks his fingers in the waistband of my silk shorts and pulls them down my legs slowly, holding me steady as I step out of them. Leaning forward, he buries his nose in my slit and inhales deeply. "Fuck, I need to taste you."

He hooks his thumbs under the strings on my hips and pulls my thong down, barely allowing me to step out of it before pushing my legs apart and guiding me onto the arm of the couch. He dives between my legs, licking through my entire slit before finding my clit and flicking it softly.

"You taste so fucking good, Spitfire," he mumbles against me, tightening his grip on my hips, anchoring me. With one hand gripping his hair, I brace myself with the other on the back of the couch, and it's a good thing because my entire body is trembling each time his tongue passes over me, every instance when his tongue piercing hits my clit.

Part of me can't believe this is happening, and the other part is fixated on the sight of this beautiful man between my legs doing wicked things with his mouth because I don't want to ever forget this moment—how I feel, how it sounds, how all-consuming this pleasure is.

"Holy shit, Gage," I gasp, tightening my grip on the back of the couch.

He licks two of his fingers and slides them inside me, curling them softly upward, stroking a spot that has my back arching, nearly bowing off the couch. Gage digs his fingers into my hips, keeping me in place as his tongue returns to laving at my clit, swirling the ball of his piercing around, over and over again. Every muscle in my body tightens and my breathing grows shallow as I feel an explosive orgasm quickly building.

Then it hits—and I'm screaming and coming harder than I ever have in my life as pleasure crashes over me, rolling through me, wave after dizzying wave. Gage keeps licking, stroking, letting me ride it until I can't take anymore.

When my body finally relaxes, Gage rises from the floor, looking down at me as he unbuttons his jeans. "I'm not even close to being done with you, but that was the perfect appetizer."

"I can't feel my legs," I say, breathlessly.

His lethal grin spreads across his lips. "Well, in a moment, you won't be able to feel your ass either."

Chapter Sixteen

Gage

"Bend over, Hazel."

My body is buzzing with need, and it feels fucking amazing to finally let go. The woman before me has invaded every corner of my mind for nearly three months now, and it's time for me to show her how she makes me feel.

And then I will *tell* her as well.

My wife—*my sinfully gorgeous wife*—does as I ask, turning and bending over the same couch she did not so long ago, asking me to spank her. And I'm finally going to give in.

I leave her there for now, letting the intensity build, and walk to the kitchen. My fingers close around the box of condoms I bought this morning, knowing there would be no more hesitation when it comes to this woman. After last night and feeling the electricity between us as we watched each other get off, I knew I was done fighting this.

When I return to the living room, Hazel is peering over her shoulder, her breath shallow as I set a condom on the back cushion of the couch. Her eyes blaze with hunger.

"Gage, please hurry."

I smack her ass, making her jump. "If you think I'm rushing through fucking you, you've got another thing coming."

I take a step back, admiring the way her creamy skin turns pink under my touch, before I push my jeans and briefs down my legs, kicking them aside. The sight of her bare and waiting has me gripping my cock, already aching for her.

Closing the distance, I smooth my hand over the skin I just spanked and lay my cock between her soft, smooth ass cheeks.

"I think you need to be spanked a few more times before I give you my cock."

Hazel moans, arching her back. "Yes, spank me."

I cover her back with my chest, my lips brushing her ear. "You sure you can handle it?"

She turns her face and kisses me softly, retracting far enough that I can see the trust in her eyes. "Yes."

"If it's too much or if you want me to stop, say the word and I will."

"Okay, but I don't think that will be a problem."

Needing this woman more with each passing second, I straighten and drag my palm over the swell of her ass before delivering another sharp smack. Hazel releases a shriek, then stills for a moment, as if adjusting to the sting.

When she finally exhales, it's a shaky, desperate sound. "Oh my God..." she gasps, her hands fisting against the couch.

"That was for making me want you."

She shudders, a whimper catching in her throat.

"This is for making me feel shit." *Smack.*

Her body jerks forward before she arches her back, silently begging for more.

"This is for thawing the ice around my fucking heart." *Smack.*

She gasps, pressing her forehead to the couch.

I keep her on edge, slowly reaching for the condom and covering myself before delivering the final handprint on her skin that's blooming with heat.

"And this is for making me break my rules." *Smack*.

The sharp crack fills the room and Hazel shudders, her body quaking. She moans as I lean over her again and whisper in her ear, "But you are so fucking worth it."

Then I line myself up to her entrance and thrust forward.

"Fuck," she mewls, bracing herself against the back of the couch as I push deeper inside, feeling her stretch around me for the first time, knowing I'll never be the same again. "Oh my God, Gage! It's too much."

I grip her hips harder as I stand up to gain better leverage. "You." A sharp thrust. "Can." Another, harder, making her gasp. "Take." She glares at me over her shoulder as I slam into her again. "It." Her lips part with a mixture of shock and pleasure as I bottom out inside her.

I tip my head back and groan. "Fuck. Me." And then I start to move, pulling and pushing back in slowly so we can both feel every inch of each other.

"That's it, baby." I smack her ass again. "Take it. Take every fucking inch and count those fucking barbells as I slide in and out of you. Don't lose that tenacity on me now."

Hazel moans with each stroke, the sound of our bodies slapping together echoing in the room.

Blueberry is snoring on his bed in the corner, completely unbothered, but even if he weren't, there's no way in hell I would stop fucking my wife.

Hazel continues to curse and moan as I fuck her hard, relentless, desperate—letting the past three months of need pour into each thrust, unleashing a part of me that's been dormant, waiting to be freed.

And this woman is the one who beckoned him.

"Oh God, I'm gonna come," Hazel announces, reaching between her legs to rub her clit just as I slow my pace, wanting to keep her on edge just a little while longer.

I stick my thumb in my mouth to wet it before I press it against her tight, untouched hole, teasing her as she shudders, her orgasm just out of reach.

"Let me feel that pussy quiver for me," I rasp, pressing my thumb inside of her as I thrust a few more times before she explodes, shaking uncontrollably as her orgasm pulses through her body.

I pull out and lift her into my arms before she can go completely limp, her body trembling against me as I carry her down the hall to her bedroom. Kicking the door shut, I lay her on the bed and slide right back inside her.

Hazel gasps as we connect again. "Jesus..."

"You are so fucking sexy when you come," I growl in her ear, fucking her hard and deep, loving how her body feels under my hands—her soft skin, her curves, her warmth.

I wasn't lying when I said she's thawed my frozen heart.

I feel like I've been hiking Mount Everest for years, and suddenly I'm in the tropics, sun kissing my skin for the first time in forever.

Hazel leans up and kisses my neck, dragging her tongue along my skin. "This feels so good..."

"I know..."

"Your piercings..." Hazel's nails dig into my back, dragging across my skin. "Don't stop, Gage."

"Oh, Spitfire, I'm not going to stop. I'm going to pound this pussy until neither of us can see straight. I'm not going to let you leave this bed for a long fucking time."

She turns her head to the side, closing her eyes as the pleasure races through our bodies. "Oh, God, I'm going to come again."

I lean down and latch onto the piercing in her nipple and pull her knees up higher and over my shoulders. "Come all over me, Spitfire. Take me there with you."

She clenches around me, growing tighter and hotter, and with a few more thrusts, I feel the first drop of cum leave my body. "Fuck..."

"Gage!" she cries, coming apart beneath me.

Tremors of pleasure race through my body as Hazel clings to me, both of us fighting for air as our orgasms crash over us.

As the final wave crashes over us, I lift my head, meeting her heavy-lidded gaze.

"That was..." she whispers.

But she doesn't have to finish, because we both know.

Everything just changed.

Chapter Seventeen

Hazel

Exiting the bathroom, I find Gage sitting against the headboard, still shirtless with only the sheet draped over his bottom half, covering his glorious dick.

It's official. Those piercings have ruined me.

His chest is still damp from the exertion of fucking me within an inch of my life, but it's not his muscles or tattoos that I'm mesmerized by—it's his smile. It's the first real one I think I've seen from him.

"Get that beautiful ass over here," he commands.

As I step closer, still bare from head to toe, he grabs my wrist and pulls me toward him, flipping me effortlessly so I'm flat on my back, staring up at him.

"Who are you and what have you done with my grumpy husband?"

He trails a finger down my cheek, making my skin break out in goosebumps. "Turns out sex was all I needed to put me in a better mood."

I roll my eyes and try to escape from his hold, but he pins me down with a little more pressure. "Hazel..."

"If this was just about getting your dick wet—"

He cuts me off with his lips, swirling his tongue deep against mine, stealing my words and my breath.

God, I'm in trouble.

When he lets me come up for air, he says, "This is more than sex, Spitfire. Please tell me you know that."

My eyes bounce back and forth between his. "I do."

"Good." With one more kiss, he lets me sit up and then guides me to straddle his lap, his cock already hard beneath me.

I think about how I can still feel him between my legs, yet I could already go for round two. But I need to know where his head is at first. "What changed, Gage?"

He leans his head back against the headboard and sighs. "You are a hard woman to resist, Hazel."

"I know." Smirking, I reach up to cup his jaw. "But..."

"Would you believe me if I told you that your brothers helped change my mind?"

My eyebrows draw together. "My brothers?"

"Yeah." He clears his throat before continuing. "They said they could tell I was struggling with how I feel about you and that I needed to make a fucking decision—or at least tell you where I stand."

I swallow past the lump in my throat, nervous for what he'll say next. "What did you decide?"

He buries his hand in my hair, pulling my forehead to his. "I want you, Hazel, even though I shouldn't."

"Why shouldn't you?" I ask breathlessly, my heart in my throat.

"It's complicated."

"So then un-complicate it."

He shakes his head and releases me. "All I know is that not giving into my desire for you—for both your body and mind—was causing me more pain than I stand to feel later. So, I'm waving my white flag. I think my aunt may have been right."

I snort. "Oh my God."

That smirk of his returns to his lips. "It's insane."

I lean forward and press my lips to his once more. "I think she might have been right too." As the words leave my lips, a weight lifts from my chest, like all the resistance between us was preventing us from admitting what's been there all along—a connection, and it's not just physical.

"You drive me crazy, Spitfire, but getting to know you, fighting with you, has made this the best three months of my life. You amaze me," he says, cupping my jaw. "The way you speak your mind, the way you see the world through your camera, the way you continued to care for me even when I was trying to push you away." A pinch forms between his brows. "God, I hated every minute of it."

"Then why did you do it?" I place a hand on the center of my chest. "I've been going out of my mind trying to understand you, Gage. Because everything that you just said? I feel that too."

"Because I was scared, Hazel. Scared of falling for you and hurting you, or losing you, or doing anything to fuck things up. I don't know what the future holds and—"

I hold up a hand to stop him. "No one does, Gage. So why don't we forget about the timelines and deadlines, just take it one day at a time?"

He's quiet while he considers it, and I'm glad he doesn't reply right away—because although I am truly starting to see a future with this man, I know that admitting his feelings was a huge hurdle for him. My romantic heart wants to believe this was all kismet, but the little sliver of a realist in me is bracing for the eventual crash that every other relationship has ended in.

"Okay."

One word. That's all I needed to hear.

My heart is pounding as I stare at the man I married for 5.1 million dollars but eventually found myself wanting in every way imaginable.

I move to straddle his lap and admire his ink, my hand gliding across his shoulders and down his arms, memorizing the array of roses and skulls, with the occasional random object like a boat and a compass-looking thing.

I have so many questions about him that I've been afraid to ask for months. "Do your tattoos mean anything, or do you just throw a dart at the wall and go with whatever it lands on?"

Gage chuckles, shaking his head. "Honestly, I just thought they looked badass." He points to the compass. "But this is the Viking Compass. I included that to pay homage to my heritage."

"What does it represent?"

"Traditionally, it symbolizes a safe passage through wind and rough water."

I drag my finger over the black ink. "It's beautiful."

"Do you have any tattoos?"

I gape at him, dumbfounded. "You've seen me naked."

He cups both of my breasts in his hands. "Sorry. I was more focused on these and your pussy."

Fighting the urge to forgo the conversation and ride his cock that's hardening beneath me, I reply, "No tattoos. I want one, though."

He leans forward and latches onto my nipple piercing, sending a bolt of need straight between my legs. "Why haven't you gone through with it?"

"I don't know. I just haven't felt compelled to do it yet and I'm not set on what I want. I guess I'm waiting for when it feels like the right time."

He lifts his head up, locking his eyes with mine. "What about a hummingbird?"

As soon as he says it, my pulse picks up. It would make the most logical sense, but at the same time, hummingbirds are a tie to him now too, and I don't know if I could handle having that reminder on my body everyday if this marriage is only temporary.

"Yeah, that's a good idea," I say instead, not wanting to feed into the doubts that I know won't go away until he opens up to me more, until I allow myself to fully give in to what I feel.

He grins and flips me onto my back. "I know. I'm full of them." Thrusting his cock against my pussy, he drags his piercings up and down my slit, hitting my clit with each pass. "Now, the question is, do you want to be full of me too?"

"Yes," I whisper desperately, but before Gage can grab another condom, he furrows his brow and rolls onto his back. "Gage?"

His hand is in the center of his chest as he closes his eyes and starts taking deep breaths. "Shit."

"Are you okay?" I sit up next to him, not sure what I should do.

"Yeah, I'm fine. I just got dizzy."

"Does that happen often?"

Yes. "It's not a big deal."

"Can I do anything?"

He shakes his head, keeping his eyes closed. "No. I just gotta wait for the dizziness to subside." Popping one eye open, he says, "You made me overexert myself earlier, Spitfire."

I smack his chest playfully. "That was your own choice. You didn't have to fuck me like an animal."

He places his hand over mine. "Yeah, I did. I've been waiting too long not to."

I lie back down next to him, staring into his eyes as he turns to face me. "Well, I'm really glad you finally gave in."

"Me too, baby. Me too."

***

"God, yes. Right there, Gage." With my arms braced behind me, I watch where Gage and I are joined, his cock glistening with my arousal as he pulses in and out of me.

"Fuck, the sight of your pussy sucking me in is so fucking perfect, baby."

I toss my head back and groan. "Keep going."

Gage spreads my legs wider as he snaps his hips forward, hitting a spot inside of me that has me detonating in seconds. As I scream through my release, I'm grateful the walls between the shops on the boardwalk are pretty thick.

Gage finds his release moments after me, stilling inside of me as he comes down from the high, resting his forehead on mine. "Fuck, Hazel."

"So good," I murmur in his ear before leaning back and kissing him softly.

Before either of us can move, though, he begins to wobble on his feet.

"Whoa..." Gage grabs onto my arms, steadying himself.

"Are you okay?"

He closes his eyes. "Yeah, your pussy just makes me dizzy."

I want to laugh, but I'm more worried than amused. This is the second time this has happened now, and even though we're being more open with each other, I don't want to pester him if it's nothing. I mean, if it weren't, he would tell me...right?

"This isn't funny."

Gage chuckles, opening his eyes back up and loosening his grip on me. "It's a little funny." He pulls out of me and walks over to the bathroom to deal with the condom while I slide off my desk and straighten my dress.

I glance in the mirror, fixing my lipstick and taming my tousled hair, just as Gage comes up behind me, wrapping his arms around my waist and kissing my neck. "Fuck, I needed that."

"Are you sure you're okay?"

"More than okay because I got to be inside you again."

I laugh. "You act like we didn't have sex in the shower before I left for work."

His lips travel over my skin to my ear. "I know, but I'm going to get home late tonight and then I have to leave early Friday morning for your brother's bachelor party trip. I need to have you as much as I can before then."

I close my eyes as his mouth continues to move over my neck. "Just don't go with them then. Stay home with me."

He groans in my ear. "I want to, but Parker insisted, and I don't want to piss them off any more than I have."

"I hate to break it to you, but when they find out we're having sex, they're going to be pissed whether you go on that trip or not."

"Who says they're going to find out?" he asks.

Looking at him in the mirror, I reply, "The grin on your face says it all. You haven't smiled like that since you moved to Carrington Cove."

"The reason I'm smiling is because I'm fucking happy for the first time in a long time, and that's because of you."

My heart climbs into my throat. "You really mean that?"

"Yes." He presses his lips to mine. "You're making me reevaluate some things, which is fucking terrifying, but I promise you, this is more than just sex for me, Hazel. Okay?"

I nod. "Okay."

With one more kiss, he releases me and brushes a hand through his hair. "I have to go. Axel has me doing a bunch of shit before my appointments today."

"Okay. I hope you have a good day."

"You too, baby. Don't forget I want to take you somewhere tonight, all right?"

"I can't wait."

He winks at me and then heads out, leaving me alone for another hour until my next client comes in.

I stare at my desk where Gage just fucked me and sigh, reaching for my phone because I need someone to talk me through everything that has happened this past week.

"Hello?"

"Hey, Laney. Are you busy?"

"I have twenty minutes before my next client, so I'm shoving food in my mouth. But I can listen. What's up? Has Gage been fucking you all week with his magical, bejeweled dick?"

I roll my eyes as I begin to pace my studio. "It's not bejeweled. There are no jewels on it, okay? It's a Jacob's ladder with barbells."

"God, I'm so jealous. That's so fucking hot. I always heard there were men out there who would endure the pain for penis jewelry, but I thought it was just a myth."

"Not a myth. And I am definitely enjoying every inch of his."

Laney giggles. "I'm glad."

"But..."

"Oh no." Laney groans. "Buts are never good."

"Well, it's not a bad but, more like a concerned but."

"Okay..."

I sink into the chair behind my desk. "Well, for starters, I'm terrified to ask him what happens in three months when the six-month arrangement is up."

Laney hums. "Yeah, that's valid. But it's only been a week since you two finally admitted your feelings, right?"

"Yes."

"Then don't freak out yet. Just keep enjoying the sex for the time being."

"Oh, I am. But that's the other problem."

"Jesus, I knew this man was too good to be true. He's a fast shooter, huh?"

"What? No!"

Laney laughs. "Okay, then what's the issue?"

I look across my studio, wondering if I'm making a bigger deal out of this than I should be. "Twice now, right after we've had sex, Gage got dizzy."

"Your pussy must be magical."

I roll my eyes, even though she can't see me. "I'm serious, Laney. I feel like something is off."

"How many times has it happened?"

"Twice."

"And how many times have you two had sex now?"

I try to count in my head, but it's useless. "I've lost count, girl."

She laughs. "Well, did you ask him about it?"

"I mean, I asked if he's okay, and he just jokes that the sex was so good..."

"Getting dizzy after sex doesn't sound too serious. I mean, they do exert themselves quite a bit, if I remember correctly. Although, it's been a while since I've enjoyed a dick that wasn't made of silicone and battery-operated, and Seth lasted about five minutes each time, so I'm no expert."

I cackle. "So I take it that you still have no plans to get drunk and come on to Fletcher again the next time you see him? I would almost bet money that he can fuck you better than Seth ever did."

Laney snorts. ""I'm sure any man, not just Fletcher, would make that happen. But finding out would require me to talk to Fletcher, and the last thing I want to do is open up that wound again. This thing happening between you and Gage is different though…"

She doesn't even have to finish her thought. "I know, Laney. You're right. I'm sorry for the bad joke."

"It's okay. Just know that the chances of me ever coming on to him again are slim to none. Honestly, I hope he forgot about it and it's not even a blip in his memory. Unlike for me, where I relive it late at night when I'm trying to fall asleep." We share a laugh. "But hey, I need to get ready for my next client."

Sighing, I lean back in my chair. "Okay, but do you really think I'm making too big of a deal with Gage's dizzy spells?"

"If he's not worried, I wouldn't stress about it. Just enjoy the pierced dick for every other woman out there who has the fantasy but hasn't found her unicorn yet."

Laughing, I let out a heavy sigh. "Okay. Thanks for talking me off a ledge."

We end the call and I turn in my chair, waking up my computer so I can do some work before my client arrives, trying like hell to stop overthinking everything that's happened with Gage in the past week—because if I don't, I have a feeling this might end up like every other relationship I've ever had—a disappointment.

***

"This is where your aunt told you to take me?" My gaze moves around the store, where I'm feeling very out of place, even though I throw parties for this kind of stuff regularly.

"I think we can both agree that my aunt was not afraid to think outside the box. I'm more impressed that she knew we'd be having sex by now and planned the delivery of this letter perfectly." Gage places his hand on the small of my back and guides me toward the bondage wall.

"She knew you'd only be able to resist me for so long," I tease.

When Gage told me the latest letter from his aunt was addressed only to him, I found it odd, but everything about this arrangement is odd, so I didn't think much of it. But when the letter led us to Cum and Get Sum, the new sex shop the girls told me about, I couldn't help but wonder if Diane was just fucking with us at this point.

"I'm surprised I lasted as long as I did." He wraps his arms around me from behind and presses his lips to my neck.

We walk past a display of lube before we come to an assortment of whips, chains, and nipple clamps, where he tugs me to a stop.

He leans in and his lips graze my ear as he whispers, "What do you fantasize about, Spitfire? Tell me what you want."

So many ideas form in my mind at once that I don't know which one to voice first. "I've always wanted to be tied up," I say under my breath.

His grip on my waist tightens. "Hmmm, we could make that happen." Another brush of his lips makes my skin break out in goosebumps. "What else?"

"For some reason, the idea of you fucking my boobs is really hot," I admit, turning to meet his eyes. "Especially with those piercings."

He pushes his cock into my back. "Fuck, baby. That sounds perfect."

"And then you mentioned anal…"

"I did…"

I reach for one of the silicone anal plug sets, plucking it from the wall. "Well, that's something I'd love to try with you."

A throat clearing behind us makes me freeze. I twist slowly and come face to face with two of the last people I'd want to run into here, even though I knew Willow wanted to visit this place.

I just didn't think she'd do it on the same night as us—and with my brother.

"Dallas? Willow?"

Willow's cheeks turn bright pink, and my brother looks like he's about to vomit.

"Uh, hey, Hazel. Fancy seeing you here," Willow says, breaking the awkward silence.

"Um, yeah." I turn in Gage's arms, concealing his raging hard-on behind me. "What are the chances?" I flick my eyes over to my brother.

He grunts, but Willow keeps rubbing his arm. That's when my eyes drop to what he's holding and I almost lose my shit.

"What the fuck?"

A voice pulls my gaze to the left where I find Penn holding the biggest dildo I've ever seen while Astrid casually inspects a lace teddy like we're at a damn farmers' market.

What the fuck is going on?

"Penn? Astrid?"

Astrid waves like this is completely normal. "Hey, Hazel! Isn't this place great?"

My eyes dip back down to the two-foot-long dildo my second oldest brother is holding. "Uh…"

"Hey, guys," Gage says, reaching out to shake my brothers' hands.

I look over at him and mouth, 'What the fuck?'

"Let's pretend this never happened," Dallas says, taking a step back and avoiding my eyes. But when he shifts, something slips from his grip, clattering to the floor.

"Shit," Dallas mutters.

I gape. The image of my oldest brother scrambling to retrieve a bondage kit, a strap-on, and another dildo is burned into my brain forever.

"Uh..." I manage, still stuck in horror paralysis.

"You guys have a nice night," Gage finally chimes in, steering me away from my brothers and the evidence that they do, in fact, have sex lives. Apparently, very kinky sex lives.

I shudder, burying my head in my hands. "Oh God, oh God..."

Gage is trying not to laugh as he continues to guide me away. "I'm sorry, baby. But fuck...that was hilarious."

"I'm never going to be able to look my brothers in the eye again."

"Oh, come on, Spitfire. Everyone has sex."

"Not my brothers."

Gage scoffs. "I thought you were the one who encouraged Cashlynn to sleep with Parker to get him to snap? And didn't you hit Penn in the head with a dildo at one of your passion parties?"

"That was different. There were no personal details or insights into their kin—" I can't even say it without gagging. "How do you know about that anyway?"

"Oh, I learned all kinds of shit about your brothers while I was helping build Michael's jungle gym... Like how siblings will go to some weird lengths just to get payback."

The moment he says the words, I freeze. "What did you just say?"

Gage's grin is growing wider by the second.

I take a step toward him, but my phone dings in my pocket before I can speak. When I take it out and see a text from Parker, I curse. "Fuck."

Parker: *Your face was priceless *laughing face emoji**

I lift my head to find Gage practically vibrating with glee, just as Dallas and Willow come around the corner, fighting to keep their composure. Penn and Astrid slide out from behind the display of condoms just as Penn whacks me on the back with the two-foot-long dildo he was holding earlier.

"I almost lobbed this at your face by the way, but I'm not as mean as you." He tosses it to the side.

The chime above the door rings as Parker and Cashlynn come running in, laughing hysterically. "Oh, fuck! That was great!" Parker holds his stomach as he fights to control his laughter.

That's when I spin around to find Gage shaking hands with Dallas and Penn, and then Parker. "You were in on this?"

"Payback is a bitch, little sis!" Parker exclaims, pulling Cashlynn into his side.

Gage shrugs. "I'm sorry, Hazel, but I only agreed to let him do this to you if we were all in on it, that way I wasn't the bad guy."

Astrid and Willow shrug, but they're laughing too. "You have to admit that this was pretty funny," Willow says.

"Funny? This was traumatizing!" I shriek just as an employee comes over to us.

She lowers her voice. "You're making other people in the store feel uncomfortable. So, unless you plan on making a purchase, please put your items back and exit the building."

Everyone mutters their apologies, replaces the items, and makes their way to the sidewalk outside.

"Ah, fuck. I feel like a changed man now," Parker declares, amusement radiating off of him.

"How? How did this change *you*?" I fire back.

He leans forward and bops me on the nose. "The amount of therapy you'll probably need after this should be equal to the amount of torture you put me through with Cashlynn."

I point to his fiancée. "Yeah, but you got something good out of my meddling," I argue.

He smiles at Cashlynn. "I did."

"And in return you're giving me *trauma*?" I turn to Gage. "And a husband I can't trust, apparently."

Gage laughs and pulls me into his chest. "I was being tested, Spitfire. They had to make sure I could hang with the family when push came to shove."

"But you're supposed to be on my side."

"I will always be on your side from now on," Gage says, nodding toward Parker. "That was the deal."

Parker nods. "Yes. I promise not to recruit Gage against you ever again, and that is what makes us even." He holds out a hand for me to shake.

I stare at him long and hard. "You are deranged! Do you know what I saw our older brothers holding in there?"

Parker shudders. "No, and I don't want to know."

I take a step toward him. "How about I tell you what Gage and I were going to buy instead?"

The girls laugh as Parker covers his ears and closes his eyes. "For the love of God, Hazel...please!"

"You know what? Fine. Consider us even then because I could keep this going if I wanted to, Parker, just remember that." I point a finger at his chest as his eyes pop open. "I could build this into a prank war of epic proportions..."

He holds his hands up in surrender. "Okay. It's done. I'm not going to do anything else, I swear!"

"Good." I turn to the rest of my family. "Now, if you'll excuse us, I have to go home and fuck my husband." And with the last word, I smile, knowing that, although I may be scarred for life, I can't deny that Gage being in on it actually makes me happy.

***

"Squeeze those tits together for me, baby." Gage lets the lube slowly drop from the bottle and fall over my chest. I stare up at him, watching him stroke his cock as he straddles my chest.

"You sure you want this?"

"I do."

Slowly, he pushes his length between my breasts, the barbells hitting my flesh as he pulls out and pushes back in. "Jesus, you look fucking perfect right now."

I stick my tongue out, teasing him every time he thrusts forward, catching his tip with quick flicks.

"You want my cock in your mouth, too?"

"Yes," I moan, rubbing my thighs together to help dull the ache building between my legs.

Even though the start of our evening was ruined by my brothers, Gage is making it up to me by fulfilling a few of my fantasies.

My hands are holding my breasts together, creating as much friction as I can as he continues to slide between them. "Let me taste you."

This time when he reaches my mouth, he doesn't stop, sliding his perfect dick between my lips, allowing me to swirl my tongue around the head, tasting the strawberry-flavored lube, before he pulls back out.

"Fuck." He reaches behind him and finds my clit with his thumb, stroking me. "You're fucking soaked. You love this, don't you?"

I nod. "Yes."

"You want more?"

"Uh-huh."

He pulls my hands from my breasts and reaches behind him for two silk ribbons. Just the sight of them makes my pulse spike.

"Grab onto the headboard."

I do as I'm told, watching my husband tie one wrist to the steel bar, and then the other, leaving me helpless from the waist up.

"God, you're so fucking sexy like this, Hazel. Trusting me, offering yourself over to me like this."

My next words slip out before I can even think. "I do trust you."

Gage's eyes lock with mine, but he doesn't say anything. And he almost doesn't have to—because the look of reverence in his green orbs tells me that this isn't just some fantasy-fulfilling night for him either.

He's in this moment with me.

We're crossing another line.

And as he makes me come as many times as I can take, every line I thought we drew vanishes. I have no idea where we began—or where we might end.

Chapter Eighteen

"Do you remember that time that Dad made us read the newspaper because we told him we were bored?" Parker asks as we cruise along the highway.

Dallas and Penn are in the front seats of the truck, while Parker, Grady, and I are packed like sardines in the backseat. We're on our way to Blossom Peak and have already been on the road for four hours. Only three more to go.

The conversation has shifted from work to sports to kids, and then Penn brought up Mr. Sheppard, leading the brothers to reminisce about their dad and feeling his absence as Parker embarks on his marriage.

Dallas starts to laugh. "Yeah, and then it backfired because we found the sports section and started asking him a bunch of questions about hockey and football."

Penn sighs. "I still can't see a newspaper without thinking about him."

Parker chuckles. "Same." Then he grows quiet. "I can't believe it's been over three years."

Dallas sighs this time. "I know."

"Your father was a good man," Grady interjects. "He'd be proud of the three of you. You've continued to give back to the town he loved so much. You're all good men and good friends."

Parker nods at Grady. "Thanks, man. I guess it just feels weird that I'm getting married and he's not here." He turns to me. "Was it weird getting married without your dad there?"

My throat grows tight. Honestly, I didn't even think about my father when I agreed to marry Hazel, but that's probably because I have a lot of resentment toward the man.

"My dad's gone too, so..."

Dallas clears his throat. "Sorry to hear that, man."

"It is what it is." I have to shrug it off because I can't tell them the truth. His death changed everything for me—just not in the way they think.

"How did he die, if you don't mind me asking?" Parker asks, looking at me from his seat to my right.

"Heart attack." And right on cue, my heart starts beating wildly.

All I want is to get through this weekend without reminders of what's at stake, given how the dynamics of my relationship with Hazel have changed. But we're not even at our destination yet and I'm already uneasy.

I packed my meds, I plan to stay away from alcohol as much as possible, and if these guys want to go on a hike, I'm going to stay back so I don't risk passing out in the middle of the damn forest. Of course, I can't tell them any of that without opening a floodgate of questions I'm not ready to answer, especially since Hazel deserves those answers first.

I just have no idea how she's going to react.

Somehow, in the past few weeks, my wife morphed from someone I was trying to avoid to the person I want to spend the most time with. And it's not just about the sex, even though that's fucking mind-blowing.

It's her—every word that comes out of her mouth, every smile I can pull from her lips, and every time she touches me and makes me yearn for things I swore off years ago.

Yet, that's the problem. I know I shouldn't have crossed the line that I drew in the sand upon agreeing to this marriage, especially since my reasons for doing so haven't changed. In fact, they've been reminding me what's at stake every time I fight the dizzy spells after Hazel and I have sex.

But I can't stop. The pull to her is too fucking strong.

I just have to keep hoping and praying that Miranda knows what she's doing and can help me get my condition under control before it's too late.

"Fuck. That sucks," Parker says. "Were you two close?"

"Nah. My dad loved his job more than anything, hence why I was so close to my aunt. I spent a lot of time up here during the summers with her."

"What about your mom?"

I turn to look out the window. "My mom took off when I was two."

"Damn," Penn chimes in. "I'm sorry, Gage. That's tough."

"I've made my peace with it." I turn to face him and offer a placating smile, one I've perfected over the years, because the last thing I want is fucking pity. "Your dad had cancer, right?" I ask, trying to get the focus off me.

Parker nods. "Yeah. It hit fast too. Hazel took it the hardest."

"Yeah, I kind of gathered that."

"She talked to you about it?" Dallas asks as he continues to drive.

"A little in the beginning, but she hasn't mentioned it much since then." My mind goes back to that conversation when she told me the meaning of the hummingbird to her, making my chest ache like it always does from the memory.

"Doesn't surprise me. She tries to be the strong one, but she and Dad had a bond like no other. Maybe it was because she was the youngest or because she was the only girl, but I remember every time I'd come home from deployment, if they weren't home, they were at that damn lighthouse on the coast, staring out at the ocean or playing poker together."

Interesting. Hazel never mentioned that. Looks like I still have a lot to learn about my wife.

Fuck, I wish I was lying in bed with her right now so I could pick her brain some more—a thought I've been fighting for so long that it feels good to finally give in to it and ignore the fear lurking in the background.

"And if Dad wasn't there, he was at the Veteran's Center in town," Parker adds. "He was a Marine for ten years. Honorably discharged."

"Didn't you serve as well, Dallas?" I find his eyes again in the rearview mirror.

He nods. "Yup, against Dad's wishes."

"Why was he against it?"

He scoffs. "It's a long story that definitely requires a beer or two."

"Well, there's plenty of beer to go around this weekend, right?" Parker interjects, trying to change the melancholy mood as he slaps his brothers on the shoulders. "'Cause I'm getting married, you guys!"

Penn looks over his shoulder, annoyance written on his face. "Yeah, we know, Parker."

He slaps Penn on the shoulder again. "Hey, it's taken me a long time to get to this point, where I feel like I can actually be fucking happy. And that's all because of Cashlynn, all right?"

Penn smiles at his younger brother. "I am happy for you, asshole. You deserve this, and I'm proud of you for working through your shit to get there."

And in that moment, I wonder—do I even get to be happy? Because my secrets will come out at some point, and I'm worried they'll destroy everything I'm finally letting myself hope for.

"God, last night was epic, though," Parker declares, the ever-present smile on his face returning. "Granted, I know my little sister played a role in me getting to this point, but she deserved being given a taste of her own medicine."

"Yeah, but don't ever ask me to do anything like that ever again," Dallas says from the driver's seat.

"Me too. The only reason I agreed is because Astrid did," Penn adds.

I turn to Parker. "You already know I only got one pass, so count me out of all future ploys to get back at your sister."

Grady chuckles from his seat in the truck. "God, this family is a trip."

"Do you want to see the picture of Hazel's face?" Parker asks Grady, reaching for his phone from his pocket.

Grady holds his hand up. "Nope. I'm good. I trust that you enjoyed yourself, though."

He smiles again. "I did. Worth every ounce of shit I'll get from her for the rest of my life."

***

"I don't think you brought enough wood." Parker stares down at the pile of scraps that Penn is continuing to unload from the truck.

Penn tosses one more piece on the top of the pile, the sound echoing into the forest around us. "Better to have too much than not enough."

"It's summer though. It's not like we're going to freeze to death." Parker kicks one of the logs that fell from the stack.

Penn stands tall in the bed of his truck, placing his hands on his hips. "Let me educate you for a minute, little brother, since I know your precious hands don't see much dirt or the outside." Parker scoffs as I get comfortable, crossing my arms over my chest, waiting for Penn to teach the youngest Sheppard a thing or two.

And if there's one thing I've learned since meeting these guys, it's that Penn and Dallas grew up a bit differently than their younger brother did.

"Yes, it is summer, but that means that the bugs are in full force and once the sun goes down, it will get a lot cooler up here than you're used to. So, the point of the fire is twofold—keep you from being a snack for the bugs *and* prevent you from complaining about being cold later."

"If Cashlynn were here, I wouldn't have to worry about being cold."

Penn laughs. "Yeah, well you wanted a good old-fashioned guys trip for your send off into married bliss, so no girls are allowed."

Just the mention of their women has me venturing back to thinking about Hazel for the hundredth time since we left for this trip this morning. After a seven-hour drive, you'd think I would feel more at ease about being away from her, but the opposite has happened. Right now, I want to be near her even more.

"Isn't that right, Gage?" Penn's voice pulls me from my thoughts as he hands me a beer.

My eyes drop down to the silver can, taking it with the intention of sneaking it back into the cooler at some point. "Sorry, I spaced out."

Parker slaps me on the shoulder. "Yeah, I could tell. What's going on, man? Are you afraid we're gonna bash you on the head with a shovel and bury you out here so our sister gets the full 10 million, or what?"

Dallas smacks Parker on the back of the head. "What the hell is wrong with you?"

"Ow." Parker rubs the spot Dallas just hit. "Come on. You don't think Gage has wondered that same thing?"

"Honestly, it never crossed my mind until you just said it," I say, much to his dismay.

"Well, shit." His eyes grow wider. "Uh, just so you know, that wasn't the plan."

I chuckle. "I sure hope not, especially since your sister is growing on me."

Grady walks up to the four of us standing in a half circle. "I was wondering how long it was going to take before she made you snap."

Rubbing the back of my neck, I stare down at the ground, but none of them miss the smile on my lips. "Well, let's just say that things have definitely progressed..."

Dallas holds a hand up, cutting me off. "Look, I'm glad that you finally figured out your shit, but that's still our little sister. And judging by the look on your face, I'm gonna say you're probably thinking about shit I don't want to know anything about. So, for the sake of the weekend and so I'm not tempted to make Parker's wild idea come true, let's refrain from mentioning how entranced you are with Hazel, yeah?"

Grady laughs as I nod. "Sounds good."

Dallas, Penn, and Parker head back toward our camp to finish setting up the tents, leaving Grady and me alone.

"Since Hazel's not my sister, if you need someone to talk to, I'm here."

I blow out a breath. "Thanks. I just hope I'm not making a mistake—for Hazel's sake."

Grady's brows draw together. "Care to explain?"

I push a hand through my hair. "It's complicated."

"Ha. It always is. But let me tell you from experience, when you find the right woman, she's worth the fight, man. My wife made me work for her—I mean, *really* work for her. We had a long history, and she *still* didn't want to let me in, even after I knocked her up." I have to rein in my shock at that admission. "All I could do was prove to her that I wasn't going anywhere, and eventually, she knew she could trust me."

"Yeah, but that's the problem. I might *have* to go somewhere."

"Like back to Florida?"

Without divulging too much information, I reply, "Something like that."

"Well, whatever you have to deal with, just ask yourself if Hazel is worth the bullshit that comes with it—*all of it*." He slaps me on the shoulder. "And if the answer is yes, then embrace your marriage and be grateful that your aunt knew what the hell she was talking about, even though you were too stupid to believe it."

***

"So, I was thinking a family of geese." Dallas points to his left pec.

Parker claps loudly. "That's fucking genius."

"Then I need a bag of frosting." Penn points to his rib cage.

"Frosting?" I ask.

Penn waggles his eyebrows. "There's a reason, but y'all don't need to know."

"Oh!" Parker nearly launches from his chair, but Dallas steadies him before he face plants into the fire. "Then I need rock, paper, and scissors."

Grady stares at him. "That's random."

"More random than a bag of frosting?" I say.

The brothers keep talking about their tattoo ideas as I reach for another soda, trying to conceal the can as I pop it into my koozie.

"Hey, no need to hide that you're not drinking," Grady murmurs to me from his seat beside me.

"Tell that to the drunk triplets over there."

Grady laughs. "Touché. But seriously, if you don't want to drink, don't let them guilt you into it."

I conceal my drink and then sit back in my chair correctly. "Alcohol just makes me feel like shit, you know?"

"Oh, I get it. I avoided it like the plague back when I was playing professionally."

"Sucks about your shoulder, Reynolds. Like I said before, I was a big fan."

Grady shrugs as he stares at the fire. "It took me a long time to get over it, the anger mostly. I felt robbed, but at the same time, it was my fault. I knew something was off and I didn't listen to my body."

My heart starts pounding as he speaks because I know exactly where he's coming from. I saw the signs too and didn't want to believe it.

"But now? I look back on it with gratitude. I mean, hell, it wasn't like I was going to be able to keep playing until I was seventy, right?

And then when Scottie came back into my life, everything fell into place. If I hadn't lost baseball, I never would have found her again."

"Are you still upset about it?"

"Not really. I get to coach now and watch Chase play, which just reminds me of how much I love the game."

The embers of the fire glow as they drift up toward the sky, extinguishing as the breeze hits them.

"Well, I'm still fucking angry." I admit.

"About what?"

"Fuck, now I want to go home," Parker whines before I can answer him. "I miss Cashlynn, man."

"You'll see her in a few days," Dallas says and then sighs. "But fuck, I miss Willow too. And Michael."

Penn takes his phone from his pocket, holding it up toward the sky. "I wish there was better reception so we could at least call the girls."

Grady and I share a laugh, but my chest aches with the thought of wanting to talk to Hazel right now too. I wonder what she's doing... Is she editing on the couch? What socks does she have on? Is Blueberry on her lap or in his bed?

And that's when it hits me.

I'm starting to get used to this life.

Fuck. That means that I now have something to lose.

"No, I'm going first!" Parker launches from his chair, stumbling over to where I'm sitting, lifting up his shirt. "Gage, you gotta tattoo me first, man!"

"No, me!" Dallas shoves Parker aside, lifting his shirt up now. "I need my Goose and goslings right over my heart, Gage! Right now!"

Penn comes up behind them. "Where do you think I should put the bag of frosting, Gage? I was thinking my ribs, but what about my butt cheek?" He starts to unzip his jeans, but Grady stands up to stop him.

"I think you all need some water and food," he says, leading Parker over to the picnic table that's covered with snacks. We brought enough food for a small army, but none of us are small men, so I'm sure the majority of it will get eaten by the end of the weekend.

"Um, I think that's a good idea. Besides, doing tattoos in the middle of a forest is not exactly sanitary, not to mention I don't have any supplies with me," I say, actually enjoying being the sober one as I watch my brothers-in-law act like children.

Fuck. I have brothers-in-law.

"Damn it, Gage. You should have brought your stuff." Penn follows Grady and Parker pouting, but Dallas stays behind, staring down at me before I can stew on that realization for too long.

"Uh...you okay, Dallas?"

He arches a brow at me. "Are you in love with my sister?" he says, followed by a hiccup.

Trying not to laugh at him, I rise from my spot so I can look at him eye to eye. "I think that's between me and her."

He nods. "I respect that, but I want to make sure that *you* respect *her*." He takes a step closer to me. "I'm so proud of that girl—how honest she is, how hardworking she is, how talented she is, and how hard she loves."

"I agree with everything you just said."

"Then care to explain these?" He holds up my pills, and my stomach instantly drops.

I pause before responding so I don't overreact. "Where the hell did you get those?"

"They fell out of your bag when we were unloading."

I reach for the bottle, but he holds it further away. "Give me back my fucking medicine, Dallas."

We stare at each other, our jaws clenched tight, until he finally shoves the bottle into my chest. "I'm no doctor, but I know that if you're taking those, there's something going on that I'm guessing you're not being transparent about."

"Why don't you mind your own business?"

He lowers his voice. "The second you married my sister, your business became my business. Does Hazel know about this?"

I don't back down, looking him straight in the eye. "Not yet."

"Are you planning on telling her?"

"When the time is right."

"Which is? Before or after she falls in love with you?" I don't say anything as the truth dawns on him. "Fuck, she already is, isn't she?"

"I don't know, but I know how I fucking feel."

Dallas pushes a hand through his hair, stumbling a bit. "You'd better fucking tell her soon, or I will. Up until a few hours ago, I was rooting for this to work out. But this isn't something you can hide forever, Gage. Hazel deserves to know what she's signing on for if you two stay together."

"I know, and I plan on telling her. I just need more time to figure some shit out."

He nods. "You have until the wedding."

"Dallas! Come eat!" Grady yells across the campsite.

Dallas glares at me a beat longer before he stumbles over to the others. "Don't get your panties in a bunch, Reynolds! It's going to make you suck at cornhole even more!"

"Good thing I'm not on your team for the games then, huh?"

"I don't need your sorry ass to win!" Dallas fires back. "I'm the champion for a reason!"

"Stop fucking yelling or you're going to attract bears," Grady grates out, looking over at me while crossing his eyes in frustration.

I try to laugh off his annoyance, but my worst nightmare just came true. Time's running out to come clean to Hazel about my health, and if I don't figure out how to tell her soon, Dallas will do it for me—ruining any chance I have of a future with Hazel, even though I know I shouldn't want one in the first place.

***

The line keeps ringing, making my anxiety build.

"You've reached Hazel Sheppard. I'm sorry I missed your call, but leave me a message and I'll get back to you as soon as I can."

I end the call again as I pace around our empty apartment.

The guys dropped me off about an hour ago and I was fully prepared to ambush Hazel and make up for lost time the second I walked through the door. But the only person—or should I say animal—that was here to greet me was Blueberry.

And it's not that I wasn't happy to see him but I've called Hazel three times without an answer, and I'm getting worried because I have no idea where my wife is and it's getting dark.

Not to mention that the conversation with Dallas from the other night is still on repeat in my mind, and another letter was delivered and she wasn't here to receive it. But it doesn't matter since this one is only addressed to me anyway.

In a last-ditch effort to find her, I call someone I swore I wouldn't lean on unless I absolutely had to.

"Gage?"

"Hey, Catherine." I run my hand through my freshly washed hair as I continue to pace.

"Is everything okay?"

"Well, I hope so. I, uh...I don't know where Hazel is and she's not answering her phone."

I can practically hear the smile in her voice. "Oh."

"Do you have any idea where she might be?"

Catherine grows silent for a moment. "You're worried, huh?"

"Yes. She's not here and I just got home from Parker's bachelor trip, and I..." I blow out a breath. "I need to fucking see her."

Catherine chuckles. "The only place I can think of would be the lighthouse, then."

Fuck. Why didn't I think of that?

"Thanks, Catherine."

"Anytime, Gage. Glad to know you missed her."

And even though it pains me to admit it, I say, "Yeah, I did."

Chapter Nineteen

Hazel

I let out a sigh as I snap another picture, enjoying the sound of the waves crashing on the rocks below me.

Watching the sunset from this view will never grow old.

"Oh good. You're alive."

"Jesus Christ!" I spin around, placing a hand over my chest, willing my heart to calm down, but staring into the piercing green eyes of my husband is not helping. "What the hell, Gage? You scared the shit out of me."

"You're one to talk." He crosses his arms. "I came home to an empty apartment and tried calling you three times with no answer."

I glance over at my phone on the desk my dad put up here for me all those years ago. "I must have had my phone on silent."

"Nice. Well, thankfully your mom suggested checking here. Hell, I wouldn't have even known about this spot if your brothers hadn't mentioned it this weekend."

"You called my mom?" I ask, setting down my camera and giving him a once-over. And damn, he looks good wearing his signature black on black outfit, the crinkles at his eyes hinting at the sliver of amusement he's finding in our reunion.

"I did. And I know I shouldn't have."

Taking a few steps toward him, I inhale his scent, immediately comforted. The past three days have been so long and lonely without him in our apartment. I missed sleeping next to him, I missed arguing with him, and I can't deny that I missed his mouth and cock as well.

He's fucking ruined me.

"Then why did you?" I ask, standing just a few inches away from him now.

He reaches to cup my face. "Because I needed to talk to you, to see you." Leaning down, he presses his lips to mine softly. "I realized something out there in the mountains this weekend."

Smiling, I say, "What was that?"

He pauses before continuing, his eyes bouncing all over my face as the corner of his mouth curls up. "I really fucking missed you."

I stifle the snort that wants to escape my mouth, but inside, my heart melts. "You sound pained to say that."

He huffs out a laugh and rests his forehead on mine. "Don't make this harder than it already is for me, Spitfire."

My heart rate climbs again. "So what are you saying, Gage?"

"I'm saying that I'm falling for you and I'm tired of not letting myself." He leans in and kisses me again, this time deeper, swirling his tongue against mine and making me soften in his arms, letting his entire body and presence overwhelm me.

When he releases me, I'm breathless. "It's about time you finally admit it."

"What can I say? I'm a little slow to come to grips with my feelings."

I laugh. "Yeah, you can say that again."

He lifts me into his arms, and I wrap my legs around his waist as he carries me back over to the window, setting me on the cushioned seat, kneeling between my legs. "You've fucking marked me, Hazel." His fingers trace the line of my jaw. "Like ink."

I swallow hard because hearing those words is the validation that I needed, especially after this weekend. I was so afraid that while he was gone, he'd realize what we'd done, how we'd broken the rules we set out three months ago when we agreed to this. I was afraid that I'd be back up here, in this lighthouse, crying yet again over lost love and feeling alone for the thousandth time.

But he's not saying those things. He's saying the opposite. And as I study the pure and honest look in his eyes, I finally know in my heart what my head has been resisting for so long—*I'm in love with this man*.

"Well, if it makes you feel any better..." I pause for dramatic effect. "I really fucking missed you too."

The smile on his face makes my knees weak, so it's a good thing I'm already sitting. But when he launches himself at me, smashing his lips to mine and burying his hands in my hair, I pray that the risk I'm taking with my heart this time is worth it.

That this was all meant to be and Diane was right.

"Fuck, I need you," Gage mumbles against my mouth between kisses.

"There's no bed here."

"I don't need a fucking bed." He yanks my head back by my hair, kissing a path up my neck. "But let me at least taste you before I take you home and fuck you properly."

"If you insist."

Gage pushes my dress up around my waist, releasing his hold on my hair to pull my underwear down. He props my legs up on the ledge, guides me to lean back against the window, and then drags his tongue all the way through my slit as I let out an embarrassing moan.

"Fuck, I missed this pussy," he mumbles against me, circling my clit with his tongue, using his piercing with precision, and running his fingers through my wetness before pushing two inside of me.

I bury one hand in his hair, bracing the other behind me for support. "God, don't stop, Gage."

He continues to slide his fingers in and out of me, curling them expertly to hit that spot that will make me come undone. No other man has touched me like he has, no other man has made me feel so out of control, and no other man has forced me to admit how wrong I've been about everything I thought I knew.

Gage makes me want to trust, to stop guarding my heart, and to give in to everything I feel for him.

"You're fucking dripping, Hazel," he mumbles against me, bringing me back to the present. His touch escalates and then subsides, building me higher before bringing me back down, teasing me relentlessly until my body is primed to release.

"I'm close."

"I can tell. Your pussy keeps tightening around my fingers. I can't wait to feel you around my cock again, baby."

His tongue keeps moving over my clit with just the right amount of pressure and his fingers rubbing me deep inside where I need him to as the first flash of white heat sparks behind my eyes. "God, yes! I'm coming!"

And then I break, screaming and gasping through my release, holding his face to my pussy as he draws every last tremor of pleasure from my body.

When I come down, he's there to catch me, holding me to his chest. "I need to get you home, now."

"Gage..." I press a kiss to his neck and then one to his lips, tasting myself on his mouth. "I really missed you," I murmur, spent as my body relaxes.

"Me too, Spitfire. I fucking missed you too."

***

"Feels like this pussy missed me too." Gage stares down into my eyes, his hand wrapped gently around my neck, my knees up by my ears as he fucks me deep and hard, picking up where we left off at the lighthouse, making up for lost time. "So hot, so wet, dripping all over my balls."

"You're so deep," I cry out as he picks up his pace, relentlessly pounding into me.

"Doesn't feel deep enough." Our eyes remain locked as Gage's breathing grows shallower. "Come with me, baby."

"I'm there," I gasp, clenching around him just as he groans, burying himself deep as we both come undone.

Gage rolls off me, pulling me onto his chest. He kisses the top of my head, his chest still heaving beneath me. "You okay? I wasn't too rough with you, was I?"

"Not at all."

He grows quiet for a few moments before surprising me. "It sounds like your dad was an amazing man."

I lift my head to find his eyes. "Weird time to bring up my dad, but okay..."

Laughing, he urges me to lie back down. "Your brothers were talking about him a lot on the way out to Blossom Peak. That's when they told me he used to take you up to the lighthouse."

Smiling at the memory, I sigh. "Yeah. That was our place."

"You must really miss him."

I swallow past the lump in my throat. "Every day."

Gage kisses the top of my head. "I'm sorry."

"Thank you."

"But there's something that I need to tell you."

"Okay..."

He grows quiet again, the sound of crickets outside providing background noise. "My aunt wanted the proceeds from her house to be donated to the Veteran's Center."

I launch up from the bed. "What?"

He nods. "In honor of your dad."

"Really? Why would she do that?" My heart is hammering in my chest.

"Because she knew how much your dad meant to you, and you meant a lot to her."

"Wow..."

He cuts me off. "Either way, I'm taking the money to the Veteran's Center this week, and I want you to come with me." He lifts my hand, kissing it softly.

My eyes well with tears. "Gage..."

He leans up, presses his lips to mine, and pulls me back down to the bed with him, situating me across his chest. "This whole thing is crazy, Hazel. But at this point, what choice do we have but to embrace it?"

Sighing, I close my eyes and try not to overanalyze the bomb he just dropped, focusing instead on the progress we are making in our relationship.

"It *is* crazy, but it feels right."

He hums in agreement before stretching and releasing an exaggerated yawn. "God, you wear me out."

I giggle. "Well, get ready for round two. You've been gone for three days and it's hardly fair not to make up for lost time."

He pulls me into him, dusting his lips across mine. "Nothing about this is fair, Spitfire, but I'm beginning to understand why."

Chapter Twenty

Hazel

"Hey, you okay?" Gage squeezes my hand as I stare at the Veteran's Center, preparing myself to go in. This building holds so many emotions for me—pride, sadness, honor, grief. And that last one is why I haven't been here in years.

"Yeah, it's just hard to walk in here."

"When's the last time you were here?"

"When they honored Dad the year he died."

Gage pulls me into his chest, holding me tight and reminding me I don't have to face this alone, that I can handle whatever emotions come when we walk through those doors.

"This money is going to help so many people, baby."

"I know." I sniffle against his shirt before leaning back to look at him. "I still can't believe Diane did this, but I'm also so grateful."

He lifts my hand to his mouth, pressing a kiss to the top of it. "My aunt knew it would be put to good use. And she obviously cared about you."

Steadying myself, I take a deep breath and head inside, only to find my mom and brothers standing next to the front desk. "What are you guys doing here?"

Mom takes a step toward me, pulling me in for a hug. "Gage asked us to be here, sweetie."

I look back at my husband, standing there with his hands shoved in his pockets, like he didn't just make me fall even more in love with him.

He wanted my family to be here for this, to share in the legacy that Diane is leaving behind in our dad's name.

I choke back a sob as my mother pulls me into her again. "It's okay," she whispers so only I can hear.

"I wish he were here, Mom." The heartache that's always lurking under the surface bubbles over and overwhelms me.

"I know, sweetheart. Me too."

When she releases me, Gage steps forward, smirking at me knowingly. "You didn't think I was going to do this without your family present, did you?"

I rise on my toes and press a kiss to his lips. "Thank you."

Gage's smile is soft as he looks up at my waiting family. "Mr. Sheppard obviously had an impact on my aunt, and Hazel did too, so I wanted you all to be a part of this moment. The money being donated today comes from the sale of her house, just as she wanted, and I think it's safe to say she was honoring Mr. Sheppard in her own way." He clears his throat, peering around the space as my family and I share looks of surprise. "Now, I think we're just waiting on..."

"Ah, the Sheppard family!" First Sergeant Hank Lyle walks over to greet us, offering a warm smile. "And you must be Gage Kingston." He steps up to my husband, shaking his hand.

"It's a pleasure to meet you, sir."

"The pleasure is mine, Mr. Kingston. On behalf of the entire center, we can't thank you enough for this incredible donation. This will go a long way in supporting our veterans, helping with housing, medical assistance, and transition programs."

"This was my aunt Diane Kingston's wish, and I'm honored to carry it out on her behalf," Gage says, his voice steady but thick with emotion.

Hank nods solemnly. "She must have been an incredible woman. And Mr. Sheppard—he left an unforgettable mark on this place. It's a privilege to honor his memory in this way. We're incredibly grateful."

Gage squeezes me tighter, and I can only imagine the emotions coursing through him.

Hank clears his throat, glancing around at my family. "Alright, we've got everything set up. If you'll follow me, we'll get a few photos and make this official." He waves for us to follow him down the hall toward the main room.

But Dallas grabs my hand and pulls me to the side.

"I just wanted to check on you." He wipes his thumb under my eyes where my mascara is undoubtedly running. "This is a huge, unexpected gesture, and it's...overwhelming."

"I know."

"For some reason, I feel like Diane and Dad were friends."

"Gage asked me if they were the other night," I say. "I honestly don't know, though."

"Do you think Mom knew about this?"

I shrug. "I could ask her later."

Dallas nods. "Yeah... I just feel like we're missing something here."

Nodding, I begin to walk away, but he pulls me back. "Wait."

"What's up, Dallas? They're waiting on us."

His brows knit together. "Are you happy?"

His question throws me off. "What do you mean?"

"Gage...does he make you happy?"

I can't deny that the timing of this question is irritating me, but I see genuine concern in my brother's eyes.

"I am happy...but I'm also terrified." I sigh and finally admit the thing that's been weighing on me, aching to get out. "I'm falling for him, Dallas. And he'd been adamant about no feelings, but he has them too. I'm just worried something will happen to make him change his mind."

Dallas cuts me off. "If he can change how he feels at the drop of a hat, then he's not the right man for you."

"I know."

"Have you talked about the tough stuff yet, though?"

"Like what?"

"Like if you want kids, where you'll live, his family history, or—"

My pulse picks up. "Whoa, slow down, Dallas. Where is this coming from?"

He shrugs, shoving his hands in his pockets. "It's just... Sometimes people aren't honest about everything, you know? I just think you should really get to know him more before you commit to this one hundred percent."

"I thought you liked him?"

"I do. But I *love* you, Hazelnut. And I just don't want to see you get hurt..." He stares right into my eyes when he says, "Again."

"I hear you, big brother, I do. There's still a lot we need to figure out, but it feels like too many things lined up for this to just be coincidence. Diane saw something in us we couldn't even see ourselves. That has to count for something, right?"

"You two coming?" Penn calls from the end of the hallway.

"Yeah, be right there!" I respond before turning back to Dallas. "I know what I'm getting myself into, okay?"

He sighs, but nods. "Okay. Just know that I'm here for you no matter what, all right?"

"I know."

Dallas wraps his arm around my shoulders and leads me to the room where everyone is gathered.

"Hazel, why don't you and your mom stand in the middle, and your brothers and Gage can spread out on the sides?" Hank suggests as we get into place.

But when my eyes land on the check, I nearly drop it. "Holy shit! Is that number right?"

Penn grins. "Yeah, sis. Why do you think I got into real estate investment? I can't believe she did this. Dad would be honored."

And as we smile and pose for the pictures, I get the feeling he is.

***

"Hazel?"

Gage steps out from the back of the tattoo shop, smiling when he sees me. He steps around the counter and pulls me into his chest, pressing a quick kiss to my lips. "What are you doing here?"

Honestly, I didn't have a reason for stopping by other than just wanting to see him. "I was in the neighborhood, so..."

His brows draw together, but he's still grinning. "You're always in the neighborhood. Your studio is just down the boardwalk."

"If you're busy, I can leave. I just..."

He presses a finger to my lips, silencing me. "You just caught me by surprise, Spitfire." He removes his finger and then kisses me again. "Wanna come back to my station? I'm finishing up a piece."

"Sure."

Gage grabs me by the hand and leads me down a hallway to his room, where his client is lying face down on the tattoo table—shirtless. His very *female* client.

She lifts her head and smiles at me. "Hey there."

Shit. She's gorgeous, and her boobs are pressed into the leather bench, doing nothing to conceal their size.

Jealousy flares in my chest.

My husband is touching this beautiful woman.

Oh God. How many women has he tattooed? How many intimate places has he seen?

"Hazel?" Gage's voice pulls me from my mental spiral.

"Huh?"

"I said you can sit over there." He points to a chair in the corner as he puts on a fresh pair of latex gloves. "I've got about twenty minutes left with Shyanne, and then maybe we can get some lunch?"

I nod, trying not to let words fly that I can't take back—because jealousy isn't an emotion I'm very familiar with.

With other men I've dated, I either didn't worry about other women, or I didn't care enough to worry.

The realization slams into me like a freight train.

I never worried about losing those other guys.

But I am worried about losing Gage.

"Shyanne, this is Hazel, by the way."

She lifts her head again, grinning. "Ah, the wife."

Gage has talked about me? Well, that makes me feel a little better.

"Yeah, the old ball and chain." Gage winks at me over his shoulder before returning his attention to his work.

"How long have you two been married?" Shyanne asks, putting her head back down.

"A little over three months now," I say, though the words feel heavier than they should. Because the closer we get to the end of our six-month agreement, the more unsettled I feel. "Newlyweds! Well, I was married for ten years and let me tell you—if you don't talk about the hard stuff early on, you'll regret it. Take it from me."

"I'm sorry it didn't work out," I say, but take note that this *tough stuff* seems to be a theme with married people giving advice.

"Don't be. My husband lied to me about all kinds of things. It started small, but before I knew it, I was married to a stranger. I found out he was racking up credit card debt in both our names—had no clue until it was too late."

Her words strike a chord with me, reminding me that there are things I still don't know about Gage, and details that I want to ask him about—like who the hell Miranda is and if he actually wants a future with me beyond our six-month arrangement.

But this weekend is Parker and Cashlynn's wedding, and I just want to make it through that without any drama. After that, I'm done tiptoeing around my feelings and my questions. I plan on making Gage talk to me because I can't keep living in this state of in-between, not knowing what our future holds. Three months is too damn long to be in the dark about where we stand.

"Is that Hazel Sheppard?" A deep voice booms behind me, making me jump.

"Axel?"

He walks further into Gage's room. "What's up, girl? Long time no see."

"I've been around. You haven't."

He laughs. "Fair enough. If I'm not here, I'm at home, counting the days till I can retire."

"I thought Suzie would have forced your hand by now."

"She's trying, but I don't want to abandon the shop." He juts his chin toward Gage. "Maybe if you could talk your husband into taking over for me, that might help me win some points with the wife."

My eyes slide over to Gage, who doesn't bother to look up. But by the clench in his jaw, I can tell he's listening.

"He's always wanted his own shop," I say carefully, watching for his reaction, but his eyes remain locked on Shyanne.

"Really? How come you never said anything when I brought this up before, Gage?"

"I told you, I'm not interested."

Axel darts his eyes over to me. "Well, that's a shame."

I keep my gaze on my husband, trying to fight my disappointment, but do a piss-poor job of it. "Yeah, it is."

Finally, Gage's eyes lift to mine. "Hazel..."

Axel clasps a hand on my shoulder. "Say, while you're here, I wanted to book a photo shoot for our fortieth wedding anniversary."

"Oh my gosh, yes! Let's do it." Grateful for the distraction, I take my phone out of my back pocket. "Suzie will love that."

"Such a good husband," Shyanne interjects from the table. "Gage, you should be taking notes."

My husband grunts, but he looks over at me and winks again. That tiny gesture helps ease some of the anxiety building in my chest. Because when Axel brought up Gage taking over CC Ink, for a second, I thought maybe—just maybe—there was one less thing standing between me and Gage choosing each other for real.

But Gage's response shut that down real fast.

"I'll be sure to take more notes once I'm done with this shading," Gage mutters as he continues to fill in the Harry Potter piece on Shyanne's back. The detail of Hogwarts castle and the characters surrounding it is astounding.

God, the man is so talented—and not just with a tattoo gun. Watching him hunched over and deep in concentration reminds me of all the other talents he possesses, and suddenly, I wish we were alone so he could spread me out on that table.

Axel and I settle on a date for his photo shoot just as Gage finishes up the final touches.

Before Shyanne jumps off the table, Gage hands her a towel. "You can cover up with this."

She looks at me over her shoulder. "Such a gentleman." When she sees the final product in the mirror, she gasps. "Fuck, Gage. It's perfect."

"It turned out good," he says, walking over to her, checking out his work in the light. "You didn't bleed too much either—should heal fast."

Axel nods beside me. "You fucking nailed it, Gage."

Gage cracks a smile, but I can tell the praise makes him uncomfortable. "Thanks."

"You sure I can't persuade you to be the next boss of this place? You could mentor so many new artists."

This time when Gage's eyes meet mine, the corner of his mouth lifts. "Maybe it's something we can talk about after the wedding this weekend."

Oh my God. Does that mean...

Axel's eyes light up. "Sounds good. I'll take you out for a proper business dinner."

"Appreciate it, Axel." Gage walks over to me, lifting my chin as he leans down and presses a kiss to my lips.

Shyanne grabs her shirt and bra from the chair in the corner. I watch Gage apply the appropriate cover and lecture Shyanne about the aftercare, to which she rolls her eyes. "This isn't my first time, Gage. I'm not a tattoo virgin."

He laughs and finishes bandaging her. "I'll meet you out front for payment, Shyanne."

"That tattoo turned out beautifully, Gage," I say, watching him as he makes his way toward me.

"Thank you. Does that mean you'll let me draw on you for real one day?"

I reach up and smooth his hair away from his face. "I'm thinking about it."

"I'll take it."

"Will you really consider Axel's offer?" I ask timidly, almost afraid of his answer.

"I think I might." My heart rate climbs. He leans down and presses his lips to mine once more. "But let's save that talk for next week, okay? The only thing I want to focus on this weekend is Parker and Cashlynn's wedding."

I swallow roughly, nodding. But inside, hope is unfurling.

Everything in my body is telling me that this man wants the same future that I do, that we really are on the same page.

But you know what I'm beginning to realize about hope?

My life is just a graveyard full of hopes I've had to bury, and this could be one of the most painful losses yet.

Chapter Twenty-One

Hazel

"Cashlynn, I don't know what I ever did to deserve you, but I'm so grateful I've earned the right to spend the rest of my life with you. You have made me a better man, a better brother, and I promise to be the best husband to you that I can be...as long as you promise to never unplug the appliances in our house ever again."

I fight back my laughter, reaching up to wipe the tear from my cheek with my free hand, the other holding my bouquet. I'm standing beside my new sister-in-law as one of her bridesmaids, so incredibly proud of my brother and everything he has overcome to get to this moment with the woman who is perfect for him. The look on his face can only be described as pure joy, the kind of joy that makes you want to be infected by it as well.

The sun is setting over the ocean in the distance as the ceremony comes to a close on the beach just outside the main cove in our town. Cashlynn insisted they get married by the water, and I can't blame her. Staring at the water on our coast never gets old.

"Parker, you helped make my dreams come true before you ever really knew me." Cashlynn dabs under her eyes with a tissue. "Your generous heart, your strength and intelligence, and your unconditional love are the reasons I can't wait to spend the rest of my life with you...even if you iron your socks."

My brothers shake their heads across the aisle as everyone chuckles yet again. I look out at Gage who's grinning from ear to ear. When his eyes find mine, his smile softens to a look of adoration in his eyes as he stares at me so close, yet so far away.

The pastor says a few more words then Parker and Cashlynn seal their union with a kiss, officially making them husband and wife.

As I walk down the aisle in the procession, I find Gage looking at me yet again, undressing me with his eyes this time. Ever since he saw me earlier in my light blue bridesmaid dress, I could tell where his thoughts were—that he couldn't wait to strip me out of it. Believe me, I'm looking forward to that too.

After the ceremony, everyone drives over to our parents' house for the reception under a white tent, complete with a DJ, catering, and black-tie waitstaff.

"God, he can't take his eyes off you," Astrid says in my ear as we pose for pictures in the backyard. Gage watches from the side, his hands in the pockets of his blacks slacks. In true fashion, my husband is dressed in all black, but those piercing green eyes are the sexiest part of him that I can't look away from.

"I was about to say the same thing," Willow adds. "When Dallas looks at me like that, I swear, I could get pregnant from a glance alone."

My ovaries jump at that thought, but then I remember what Gage said about having kids.

Shit. Add that to the list of things we need to talk about this week.

As the weekend winds down, my anxiety is only building. Next week I'll know where my husband of convenience and I stand—if this marriage that started out as a business arrangement might have transformed into something real.

"Is that why you're already expecting baby number two?" Astrid teases as she bumps her shoulder with Willow's.

Willow rubs her belly where her new baby is growing. "Yup. This was from one of those looks."

"Well, not to burst your bubble, but Gage and I are nowhere near that stage." I smile as the photographer asks us to pose. After this last shot, it's the boys' turn for photos. I'm glad I have the night off from that responsibility for once.

Astrid, Willow, and I head over to the side where a waiter comes by with a tray of champagne. Astrid and I take one, and Willow asks for a glass of water.

The sun bathes the sky in a golden hue, but the heat still lingers—especially the heat in Gage's eyes.

"So, you two have discussed kids?" Astrid asks.

I take a sip from my glass. "No, not really."

"Well, what if you end up pregnant, Hazel? You should probably know how he'd feel about that."

"I'm still trying to figure out how he feels about *me*, Astrid."

She huffs out a laugh. "I can't believe you're questioning it. Anyone with eyes can tell that the man is in love with you."

Willow nods. "It's true."

"Well, he hasn't said as much, and until he does, I'm not getting my hopes up." I take another sip of my drink.

Astrid hums. "Oh no. That means she already has."

I drop my glass by my side and lower my voice. "The truth is, I know what I feel and I'm pretty sure he feels the same, okay? But there are still a lot of things we need to talk about, which we agreed to do after the wedding. So until then, I don't have any answers for you, and trust me, it's killing me too."

Willow reaches out and rubs my arm. "I'm glad you two are planning to talk. I know you're a grown woman and can make your own decisions, but we just want you to be happy, Hazel. That's all."

Astrid nods. "You're our sister. We love you, and I can't believe it, but Diane was right. You two belong together." She taps the center of her chest. "I can feel it, we can see it, and you two just need to allow it."

The last thing I wanted to do was cry tonight, but these two are doing their best to make that happen. Maybe it's the wedding, maybe it's my impending period, or maybe it's the limbo I'm stuck in with Gage—but knowing I have these two women supporting me no matter what? That's something I will never take for granted.

"I appreciate and love you both so much."

"Sorry to interrupt, ladies." Gage comes up behind me, placing his hand on the small of my back. "But I'm stealing my wife for a dance."

Willow and Astrid exchange knowing smiles as I hand Astrid my glass of champagne and let Gage lead me to the dance floor. He guides me past the crowd of people until he finds a more secluded spot he deems perfect, spinning me into his chest. "Fuck. You look stunning, Spitfire. I couldn't just stand by watching anymore."

I breathe him in deeply as he begins to move. "You don't look so bad yourself."

His hand tightens on my waist as he sways us back and forth to the music. "I can't wait to pull this string at your waist later and unveil what's hiding underneath this dress."

"Who says I have anything on underneath this dress?" I tease him, nipping at his earlobe and drawing a growl from his lips.

"Fuck, Hazel. You have no idea what you do to me."

I drag my nails through the hair at the back of his head. "I might have an idea." He lifts his head and locks his eyes with mine. "This wedding turned out beautifully," I say, moving to a safer subject.

Gage hums. "Not as beautiful as you."

I roll my eyes. "Are you trying extra hard to get laid tonight, Mr. Kingston? You already know I'm a sure thing."

He cups the side of my face. "I'll never stop reminding you how badly I want you, Mrs. Kingston."

Mrs. Kingston.

That's the first time he's ever called me by my married name, and the shiver it sends through me feels like recognition—like something clicking into place.

"God, I hate the way you look at me sometimes," I whisper, not wanting to listen to these doubts that keep popping up when my heart is telling me to trust what it feels.

Gage's brow furrows. "How do I look at you?"

Like you could love me if you'd only let yourself.

"Like there's something you want to say, but you're holding yourself back," I say instead.

His mouth falls open. "Fuck, Spitfire." He leans his forehead against mine but says nothing, and I don't know if it's silent confirmation that he does have something to say or that he doesn't feel the way that I do.

Just then, a hummingbird comes flying into the tent, darting through the crowd. A few kids shriek in surprise, but I just stand there, mesmerized.

I watch the bird hover, its iridescent green and pink feathers catching the last rays of sunlight. It's beautiful, weightless—a fleeting moment that somehow feels like a sign.

Gage pulls me closer, kissing my temple. "You okay, baby?"

I can hear my heartbeat in my ears as I close my eyes to fight off the tears. Then I smile, knowing my dad is with us today. "Yeah. I'm good."

The song ends as Gage guides us to stop. "You want another drink?"

"Yes, please."

He kisses me before taking a step toward the bar. "I'll be right back."

I watch him go, placing my hand over my chest trying to calm the emotions swirling inside me. Every time I'm around him, something shifts—something falls into place while something else unravels.

He's the man I'm supposed to be with.

I'm still staring at my husband when Willow and Astrid reappear. "God, you two look good together."

I tilt my head, admiring how hot my husband is. Clearly, Diane knew her nephew was totally my type. "We do, don't we?"

Astrid laughs. "The boys sure do seem to like him."

I turn to her. "You think?"

"Penn has had nothing but great things to say, which you know says a lot coming from him."

When I turn my attention back to Gage, I see Dallas has now joined him at the bar. And even from here I can tell Gage's back just stiffened.

Willow hums, drawing my attention to her. "Dallas has some concerns though, even though I probably shouldn't be telling you this."

I turn to look at the two men talking again, intensity written on Dallas's face, making me grow worried. "Yeah, well, I think it wouldn't matter who I was with, he wouldn't approve."

"I don't think it's that." Willow lowers her voice. "Dallas feels like Gage is hiding something."

My pulse spikes. "He does?"

Astrid chimes in. "Like what?"

I don't want to add to their curiosity, but I feel like he's hiding something too.

Dallas steps in closer to Gage, practically in his face, and then both of their voices start to rise.

Willow grabs my arm. "What the hell is going on?"

The last thing I want is for Dallas to cause a scene at Parker's wedding, so I head in that direction.

But before I can reach them, Dallas shoves Gage's chest, making him stumble backward.

My breath catches, waiting for him to steady himself, to push back, to retaliate.

But that's not what happens.

Because Gage never finds his footing.

No.

His face drains of color. His body sways. And he collapses.

That's when I know something is wrong—terribly, terribly wrong.

***

"Gage?" I shake him again, hovering over him while a crowd of wedding guests gather around us. "Gage? Wake up!" My hands are trembling, my voice is wobbly, and I feel like I'm living in a nightmare I can't wake up from.

But this is as real as it gets.

"What the fuck happened?" Penn asks from behind me.

But I don't look back at my brothers, especially the one that was in a heated argument with Gage before he went down. My eyes are fixed on my husband lying unconscious on the ground, wondering if there is something else I should be doing.

He's breathing, but it's shallow. His skin is pale and clammy, and as I pick up his hand and bring it to my lips, I feel his pulse in his wrists, but it's weak.

Parker and Cashlynn come running over, stopping short at the sight of Gage lying on the ground.

"Oh my God, Hazel. What happened?" Cashlynn asks.

"I—I don't know."

"The ambulance is five minutes away," Willow announces.

"They need to hurry! I don't know what to do." I shake Gage again, desperation clawing at my throat. "Gage...Gage! You have to wake up!"

"Was he feeling off today?" Astrid asks. "Like dizzy, or..."

Realization dawns on me. "No, but he has had dizzy spells before..."

"Fuck," Dallas mutters, raking his hands through his hair.

My head snaps up. "What did you do, Dallas?" My voice shakes with anger.

"I pushed him..."

"Why?" I shove at his legs, making him stumble back. "Why were you trying to start a fight?" Sirens echo in the background, signaling that help is almost here.

Dallas doesn't say anything as he stares at my husband lying unconscious on the ground.

"Gage," I choke out through a sob, tears spilling down my cheeks. "Please, baby, wake up."

And that's the last thing I remember before the paramedics arrive and take my husband to the closest hospital as I hope and pray with everything in me.

***

"Any updates?" Parker asks as he and Cashlynn enter the waiting area, still in their wedding attire.

I feel horrible that their wedding was cut short, but that's an apology I can worry about later. The only thing I care about right now is knowing if my husband is dead or alive.

"No, not yet," Mom says, rubbing my back as she has been since we arrived. She drove right behind the ambulance and has stayed by my side, telling me over and over again that everything is going to be okay.

I want to believe her. Hell, I always want to trust anything that comes out of my mother's mouth. But I'm not a child anymore. I've loved and lost enough to know that life doesn't always play fair, dreams don't always come true, and some goodbyes are forever.

I just hope that isn't the case for Gage.

A nurse approaches us. "Mrs. Kingston?" she asks.

My mother taps my leg. "Hazel, that's you, honey."

Launching myself from the chair, I rush over to her. "Yes, that's me."

"Come this way, please."

I don't bother looking back at my family as I follow the nurse down the hall. "Your husband is stable, but his heart is experiencing irregular rhythms. That's expected, given his condition."

My heart lurches. "What condition?"

She stops outside a room, placing a reassuring hand on my forearm. "You weren't aware of your husband's HCM?"

"No." I shake my head, my entire body trembling. "We haven't been married long, and didn't know each other well before that, and—"

"Mrs. Kingston, breathe."

That's when I realize I'm borderline hyperventilating.

"That's it. Deep breaths."

I blow out another. "I'm sorry, I just—I don't understand what's happening."

"No need to apologize. The doctor will be in shortly to explain everything." She gestures toward the bed. "You can sit with him."

Nodding, I follow her inside the room and freeze.

Gage is lying in the bed, his face pale against the white sheets, wires and tubes attached to him.

I stifle a sob with my hand.

"He's going to be okay. He's resting. He regained consciousness about thirty minutes ago, but he's going to be in and out of it for a bit." The vision of him grows blurry through my tears as the nurse hands me a tissue. "Take a seat. The doctor will be in shortly."

Slowly, I walk to the chair by his bedside and sit, dragging it closer to him as I dab away the tears under my eyes.

"Oh my God, Gage," I whisper, reaching for his hand, relieved to feel his warmth. He's still alive. He's still here. But I have no idea what the nurse was talking about, and suddenly I wonder if this is what he's been keeping from me, just like Dallas suspected.

I sit there staring at him before resting my head on the bed right next to his arm and feeling the adrenaline start to subside from the past hour. Just as I feel myself drift off to sleep, Gage moves and startles me.

My head pops up to find his eyes open, staring at me. "Gage?"

When he sees me, his eyes widen and then close just as fast. "Fuck."

"You're okay. You're in the hospital, but..."

"Fuck, fuck, fuck!" he yells, pressing the button on the remote next to him, paging the nurse.

The same nurse from before comes barreling through the door. "Mr. Kingston? Is everything okay?"

"No. I need to get out of here." Gage starts pulling at wires, but I grab his hand.

"Stop!" I grab his hands. "What are you doing?"

"Ah, Mr. Kingston, you're awake." A doctor enters the room and Gage freezes. "I highly recommend you refrain from pulling any chords, sir, or things could get worse before they get better." Then he turns to me. "You must be his wife?"

"Yes, but forgive me. I honestly have no idea what is going on here."

Gage mutters again through clenched teeth. "Fuck."

I turn back between him and the doctor. "And since there only seems to be one word my husband is capable of speaking, could you please explain it to me?"

The doctor extends his hand. "Well, I'm Dr. Owens, but I've been in contact with Dr. Miranda, who is Gage's heart specialist back in Florida, so I've been brought up to speed on his condition."

"Dr. Miranda?" I ask, looking back at Gage. "*That's* who Miranda is? Your doctor?" But Gage doesn't say anything, so I take a seat on the edge of the bed and grab his hand, even though I can feel him stiffening beside me. "What condition?"

"Your husband has something called Hypertrophic Cardiomyopathy, or HCM."

"What is that?" I ask as I look back at Gage, who's avoiding my eyes now.

"It's a condition where the heart muscle becomes thickened, making it harder for the heart to pump blood. Symptoms include shortness of breath, dizziness, and fainting, which is what led him here today. Some cases are mild. Others, like your husband's, are more severe."

"Fuck," Gage mumbles again.

I glare at him. "Yes, we've established that's your new favorite word, babe. Now, if you would, please let the doctor finish."

"You shouldn't be here, Hazel," Gage says suddenly, taking me by surprise.

"Where else would I be?"

He shakes his head, looking away from me. "You need to go."

The doctor clears his throat. "I'm going to give you two a minute. Nurse Hailey and I will be right outside if you need us."

I watch them leave and then stand from the bed, staring down at the man that has much more explaining to do before I let him off the hook. "I'm not going anywhere until you tell me what the hell is going on."

"You heard the doctor. I have HCM."

"And what does that mean?"

He finally turns to face me. "It means that you shouldn't be here. That I never should have agreed to this marriage. That—"

"No." I cut him off, stabbing a finger in his direction. "You don't get to push me away right now. You need to talk to me. Help me understand."

He pinches the bridge of his nose, inhaling deeply. "This is why I didn't want to get involved with you, Spitfire. My dad died from this condition, and who the fuck knows when my time will come." When he opens his eyes, I see a pain there that I've never seen before—like hopelessness, sadness, and grief all rolled into one.

"I don't know what the future holds for me, Hazel. I don't know how serious this could get, how limited my life might be. The last thing I want to do is put that burden on someone, and that's why I never should have married you. That's why I wanted to keep feelings fucking out of this!"

My heart breaks for him. He's been holding this inside, keeping this life-changing condition to himself for God knows how long.

I swallow hard. "Well, it's a little too late for that, isn't it?"

He shakes his head. "No, it's not. I want you to leave. Fucking go." He turns away from me again, closing his eyes as his voice cracks. "Please."

I reach for his chin and turn his face back to mine as tears fall down my face. "No, Gage. You don't get to make that decision on your own. You made me fall in love with you, and now that's a choice we have to make together!"

His eyes fill with tears as he reaches up and squeezes my hand. "You think I don't love you too, Hazel? You think it doesn't kill me to know that I told myself *not* to fall in love with you and want things that I can't have? Things that you deserve and I can't fucking give you?"

"Then talk to me," I beg, sitting on the bed and cradling his face in my hands as we both cry. "Talk to me so we can figure this out."

He shakes his head again. "There's nothing to figure out. You don't need this in your life."

A sob wracks through my body. "Yes, I do, Gage."

He pushes my hand from his face. "You need to leave."

"But I'm your wife."

His eyes snap open, dark and cold. "Only on paper, Hazel." I flinch at that. "We married for money, not love, remember? I don't give a fuck about the money anymore. I just want to be left alone." He closes his eyes and turns away from me once more.

He might as well have stabbed me right in the chest.

That agreement we made months ago feels like a cruel joke now—because nothing about this, about us, resembles what we were then.

Part of me wants to fight him on this, but how can I when he already decided I'm better off without him? And I can see how exhausted he is from what his body just went through.

And even though I know he's full of shit, part of me needs some space too—to process everything I just learned, to come to grips with the fact that the man I married is still a stranger in ways I never realized.

I stand from the bed, looking down at him. "Fine. I'll go," I say quietly. "But I'm not *leaving*, Gage. I'll give you some space, go home and shower, and check on Blueberry—but I'm. Not. Leaving. You." I say, letting every word land, sharp and deliberate.

He turns back to face me.

"I love you," I say as I place a hand over my heart. "I fell in love with you, Gage. And you don't get to push me away because you're afraid of that." Leaning down, I kiss his lips. "I *will* be back."

I turn for the door, glancing over my shoulder one last time, but he's not looking at me.

He's staring out the window, lost in thoughts I can't reach.

I just hope I can help him find his way back.

***

When I enter the waiting room, my entire family rises to their feet, waiting anxiously for me to tell them what I learned. But hell, I've barely come to grips with it.

Instead, my eyes zero in on my oldest brother and I rush over to where he's standing. "You knew?"

"Hazel—" Dallas starts, but I cut him off, shoving his chest even though he doesn't budge.

"No! You knew there was something wrong with him and you didn't tell me!"

"I was trying to *let* him tell you," Dallas fires back, his voice booming in the small room.

My mother comes over and holds me to her chest. "Lower your voices, both of you. I've had enough drama in this family for one day."

"How could you keep this from me?" My body shakes as I cry.

"What's going on, Hazel? What is wrong with Gage?" Astrid asks, rubbing my back.

"Gage has a heart condition, and I had no idea. But Dallas knew."

Dallas drags a hand through his already disheveled hair, frustration etched across his face. "I just knew something was off because I found his pills when we were on the fishing trip. I didn't know all the details, but I told him he needed to tell you—by today." He exhales sharply. "But when I saw the way you were still looking at him, I knew damn well he hadn't been honest with you."

Penn steps closer. "What kind of pills?"

"Beta blockers," Dallas finishes. "After a quick Google search, I knew there were a few different reasons why he could be taking them, including for the heart." He turns to me. "I swear, I didn't know anything more than that."

A hollow laugh slips from my lips. "Well, thanks to you, he ended up in the hospital and wants nothing to do with me."

Parker takes a step toward me. "He said that?"

"It's not Dallas's fault that Gage is here, honey," my mother says, lowering her voice. And I know she's right, but blaming someone else for this pain feels better than blaming Gage.

God, why did I do this to myself? Why did I let this man in when I knew better?

Because you couldn't fight it, Hazel. And remember, you tried.

"Is he okay though?" Willow asks. "Is he going to be okay?"

I wipe at my nose, taking the tissue Astrid offers. "I honestly don't know. I didn't get much out of him or the doctors before he"—a sob escapes—"told me to leave."

"And you did?" Cashlynn asks, eyes narrowing in disbelief. "That doesn't sound much like you."

I throw my hands in the air. "What was I supposed to do? Maybe he just needs some space."

"He probably hates you seeing him like that," Parker says, looking at his wife. "I know I hated letting Cashlynn see me weak."

"But he's not weak. I mean, he's been dealing with this life-changing diagnosis on his own for who knows how long. That takes insane strength. Or in his case, *stupid* strength."

"What is the condition?" Parker asks.

"Something called HCM." I blow my nose and throw my tissues in the trash as Dallas comes up to me, wrapping his arm around my shoulders.

"I'm sorry, Hazelnut. I wish I'd been wrong. I wish tonight had gone differently. But maybe it's better that you know now."

I exhale sharply, shaking my head. "He would have told me, Dallas," I say. "We had plans to talk about our future this week, and you ruined it." I turn away from him, but he reaches out to stop me.

"I'm sorry you had to find out like this, but I will never apologize for looking out for you, for trying to protect you."

"Well, guess what? I got hurt anyway, and now I have no idea what the future looks like for me and the man I love."

***

"I thought I wouldn't have any more tears left by now, but I guess I was wrong." I blow my nose again and toss the tissue into the growing pile on the couch cushion beside me.

"God, I'm so sorry, Hazel," Laney says through the phone. It's one in the morning, but I can't sleep. Luckily, Laney is going through her own personal crisis, so she was up and called me as soon as she saw my text message. "What do I do?"

"You go back to the hospital in the morning like you told him you would."

"But what if he keeps pushing me away? What if he's dead set on using this as his reason not to be with me?"

"When you have a health condition, it's normal to feel like a burden. Believe me, I know that feeling all too well."

My chest tightens. "I know you do."

Laney has type 1 diabetes, and I've seen firsthand how it's affected her relationships. How it's made her push people away before they could leave first.

"But Gage doesn't have anyone," I whisper.

"Even more of a reason to keep showing up for him."

I let out a sigh. "God, how did I end up here?"

"Diane Kingston bribed you with 5.1 million dollars to marry her nephew."

I nod. "Oh, yeah. That's right."

"And then you went and fell in love with him like she said you would."

"Is this supposed to be helping?"

Laney laughs. "Yes, because even though you thought you were destined to be alone for the rest of your life, somehow she knew better."

Her words hit deeper than I expect. I glance around my quiet apartment, the silence heavier than usual.

I miss him.

"I was wrong. I just hope that Gage realizes he is too."

***

"Um, excuse me? I'm here to see Gage Kingston," I say as the nurse continues to stare at her screen.

"Give me one second, hon." Her eyes bounce all over the screen before her nose scrunches up. "That's weird."

"What is?"

When her eyes lift to mine, I can already tell I'm not going to like what she has to say. "Mr. Kingston checked out about an hour ago."

"I'm sorry. What?"

She nods, looking back at the screen. "He's not a patient in this hospital anymore. I'm sorry. He didn't say anything to you?"

I look down at my phone, expecting to see a text or missed call from him.

But there's nothing—which says a lot without saying anything at all.

Chapter Twenty-Two

Gage

"What are you doing here?"

Dallas Sheppard is the last person I expected to see standing in the doorway of my hospital room. But when I see him holding my helmet and keys, I sense that this isn't a friendly visit, but a sendoff.

"I brought you your bike."

"I can see that. Trying to run me out of town now?"

"No, but I figured you'd want to leave, so I'm just making it easier for you."

I stand from the bed, gaining my footing before walking toward him. My body feels weak, no doubt about that, but the last thing I want to do is continue to lie in this bed when there's a bunch of shit I need to take care of —starting with getting back to Florida as soon as possible.

And Dallas's gesture is sure as hell going to help me get there faster.

"What's the catch?"

He shakes his head as he hands me my helmet and keys. "No catch. But if you're leaving, you'd better be sure that's what you really fucking want." He takes a step closer to me. "I'm sorry that you ended up in the hospital last night. The last thing I wanted was for your health issues to be revealed like that."

"Yeah, right. You probably fucking enjoyed it."

He tilts his head. "You think I enjoyed seeing my sister break apart when you were lying there unconscious? You think I enjoyed watching her cry after you told her to leave? You think that pushing her away is what's best for both of you?"

"She doesn't need me bringing down her life, Dallas."

"That's where you're wrong, Gage. Hazel would never see it that way. You're the one convincing yourself that you're some kind of burden, but that girl? She would never walk away from someone she loves because of a little heart condition."

"It's not that simple," I grate out. "But you know what? Doesn't matter." I move to walk past him toward the door. "Thanks for bringing me my bike."

He reaches behind his back and pulls a pink envelope from his back pocket. "Before you leave, I was told to give you this."

"You were the one delivering these?"

He shakes his head. "No, but I do know who was, and I'm just helping them out."

"Ha. Well thanks."

"Gage?" I pause. "Hazel will wait for you. But if you don't plan on coming back, make sure she knows so she can move on with her life. That's all I ask."

With a tight nod, I walk out.

The second I hit the highway, my engine roaring beneath me, I expect to feel relief.

This is what I wanted.But all I feel is guilt and pain—the type of pain that no doctor can treat.

***

"Well, your episode wasn't the worst one you've had yet, which is good." Dr. Miranda continues to read the chart that the doctors in Carrington Cove sent over after my stay there. When her eyes lift, I can see the concern in them laced with an ounce of hope. "It wasn't as bad as the one you had when your aunt died."

Just the mention of why I wasn't there after my aunt left this earth piles on the guilt I haven't been able to shake for the past two days.

Coming back to Orlando and stepping into my old apartment was surreal because I've called this place home for the past ten years, but it sure as hell doesn't feel like it anymore.

"So what does that mean?" I ask, afraid to know the answer but needing it anyway.

"Well, a few things. That means the medication you're on is helping manage your symptoms, but we could try a different medication to see if we could eliminate the episodes altogether. I'd love to do another scan of your heart while you're here to check to see if the muscle thickness has changed at all."

"And what if it has?"

"Then we discuss your options." Dr. Miranda rests her hands in her lap. "I told you, Gage. This is a process. We take it one step at a time, one symptom at a time, until we get you stable and living a relatively normal life."

"And what if I never get that?" I ask, my voice rough. "What if I end up dying before the age of fifty in my sleep like my father?"

She sighs, leaning back in her chair. "Your father refused surgery that could have saved his life, Gage. We've been over this."

"Surgery has risks."

"So does *not* having surgery, but being open to it is half the battle. My goal is to give you the longest life possible, but you have to stop fighting me."

I stare at the wall, looking at the same damn poster of the human heart I've been staring at for two years. One trip to the ER and then I was here, talking to Dr. Miranda, the same doctor who treated my father.

It was one year after I lost my dad to a heart attack and found out about the heart condition he'd been living with and kept from me.

But that day I'll never forget—that day when Dr. Miranda told me that I inherited HCM from my father was the day my entire life changed.

"But as of right now, surgery isn't an option for you," she says, pulling me back from memory lane. "I'm still optimistic that the right medication and lifestyle changes can drastically improve your life. Sometimes it just takes a while to find the right combination."

"What if I don't have time, Miranda? What if I die tomorrow?"

She leans forward in her chair now. "We all could die tomorrow, Gage. That's no reason to give up."

I stare back at the wall, remembering the look on Hazel's face when I told her that I wanted to be alone, that she needed to leave and remember that this marriage was just for money. She looked like I slapped her, called her the worst names in the book and basically told her that I hated her guts. But that's the complete opposite of how I feel.

I'm in love with that girl, just like I told her that I was, which was my worst fear coming alive.

It's not dying. It's not never seeing another sunrise or sunset.

It's leaving behind someone that I love like my father, mother, and aunt have left me.

I don't ever want to do that to someone else, no matter how shitty or amazing the relationship is.

And the relationship with Hazel is more than I ever imagined it could be.

Fuck, the woman makes me want to *live*—to experience everything life has to offer, to wake up next to her and fall asleep with her in my arms, to open up my own tattoo shop like I said I always wanted to.

She makes me want a future.

I just wish I could get my head and heart to believe in it too.

"Are you planning on going back to Carrington Cove?" Dr. Miranda asks.

"I—I don't know yet."

"Well, how does Hazel feel about all this?"

When I left Florida to move to Carrington Cove, I had to tell my doctor where I was going and why. One thing she's always asked me for is honesty. The woman literally holds my life in her hands, so the last thing I want to do is lie to her.

"Hazel just found out when I had the episode."

She presses a hand to her forehead. "Oh, Gage. Why are you so stubborn?"

I huff out a laugh as I brace my forearms on my knees. "Because I didn't intend to fall for this girl. I didn't think telling her was necessary if I planned on leaving once our six months were up."

"And now? Are you saying that you have fallen for her?"

I sit up tall again and swallow the lump in my throat. "I have."

"And what did she say when she found out?"

My jaw clenches tighter. "She said that we can make decisions together."

Dr. Miranda smiles at me. "She sounds like an amazing woman who's fallen for you too, Gage. So are you going to let her be a part of your life? Or are you going to live alone and hide this like your father did?"

Her words cut deep because I know she's right.

The question is, can I be strong enough to let Hazel see me at my weakest? Because I still haven't gotten used to that version of me—and I don't know if I ever will.

***

I flip the pink envelope over in my hands again for the hundredth time, bracing myself for what's inside.

After everything else my aunt has asked me to do, I'm afraid of what this one will contain. But there's only one way to find out, so I slide my fingers under the seal and pull the paper from inside, unfolding the three pieces of paper and taking a deep breath as I read the words on the page.

My Dearest Gage,

If you're reading this, it means she knows, and I'm glad. It's about time you stop hiding behind your diagnosis and start making the most of your life while you still have one.

And Hazel? She's the type of person that loves with her entire soul, Gage. She accepts people for their flaws and greatness. She has the heart of a saint and the stubbornness of a bull, which means she's the perfect fit for you. She will test you, push you, and love you despite your insistence on not giving or receiving love in return.

I've known it for so long, but time wasn't on my side until now. You've had time together, time to get to know one another, and I can only hope that what you've learned is that fighting with someone for the rest of your life is better than fighting against what life has dealt you.

You needed to realize that your diagnosis isn't a death sentence, and I figured the best way to convince you of that was to give you something, or someone, to fight for. Tomorrow is never guaranteed, Gage, no matter how healthy you are. There are people who eat healthy and exercise every day that die of lung cancer, for crying out loud. But you have the ability to live a normal life. Your children could also. Your diagnosis isn't a death sentence, Gage—it's a reminder that life is short and when you find something worth living for, that's what your focus should be.

And if there is one person who could help you see that, it's Hazel Sheppard. The moment you lost your dad, I knew there were no words of comfort I could offer you. Despite your difficult relationship, he was still your father and the way he left us was going to leave a scar on you no matter what I said.

But Hazel knows what love and loss feel like. She knows how unfair life can be, and when she lost her dad, I saw the same thing in her eyes that I saw in yours—like you lost your person.

So I figured maybe, just maybe, you two could be that person for each other.

Let her in, honey. Let her love you the way you deserve. Let Carrington Cove be the place that makes you feel whole and gives you a chance at a life that you never imagined possible.

I wish there was more that I could have done for you as a child. I still feel guilty about it to this day, but hopefully through my death, I can help you find your future in a way that you never imagined could be yours—with a woman who will love you for all of your triumphs and flaws, heart condition and all.

Love,

Diane

Chapter Twenty-Three

Hazel

"You sure you don't want anything to eat?" my mother asks me from the kitchen.

I'm sitting on her sofa, staring at the TV, but I have no idea what I'm watching. My mind feels like mashed potatoes, which are one of my favorite foods, but even that doesn't sound good right now.

Nothing does—except being wrapped up in Gage's arms.

"I'm not hungry."

My mother sits down beside me. "You need to eat, honey."

Another tear slips down my cheek. Yup, I'm still crying after three days. "I can't. I literally have no desire to eat."

She pulls me into her chest and sighs. "God, I hate to do this to you right now, but there's something I need to tell you, and I don't want you to get upset with me."

Lifting from her embrace, I swipe under my eyes. "What do you mean?"

She stands from the couch and goes over to the mantle where family pictures in frames cover the surface. Grabbing one of the frames from the shelf, she turns it around, unclasps the back, and pulls out a stack of pink envelopes much like the ones Gage and I have been receiving from Diane for the past three and a half months.

I cover my mouth with my hand. "Oh my god."

"I had every intention of telling you once the six months were up, but given how things have changed, I couldn't keep this secret anymore." She hands me one of the envelopes. "I was a bit behind getting this one to you two because of the wedding, but here. Maybe there's a pearl of wisdom in there."

I stare down at the envelope in her hands. "You knew about all of this? You knew Diane's plan?"

She shakes her head. "Actually, no. But I can tell you more about that in a minute." She holds the envelope out to me. "Here, take this one, honey."

I unfold the paper and see Diane's familiar script.

Gage and Hazel,

Happy three-month anniversary! You're halfway through this journey now and one step closer to becoming millionaires.

Yes, I know that you're doing this for the money. But my hope is that you're learning much more about yourselves and each other in this process—so much so that you've forgotten about your impending fortune.

For this task, I want you to do something simple. I want each of you to pick 3 photos from your time together so far, one for each month you've been married.

You're going to share why you picked them, how you felt in that moment, and why it was an important moment for you.

That's it. I just want you to look back on your time together so that maybe you can realize how much time you still have left.

Life is precious, you two. Nothing we ever do is a waste of time. Every moment, every person is a piece of us that we carry through our life.

I only hope that you two will choose to carry each other together through the rest of yours.

Love,

Diane

When I look at my mother, I can see that she's crying as well. "God, the woman had a way with words, didn't she?"

"Yeah." I lean back into the couch cushion and stare at the TV again, letting the tears continue to fall down my cheeks. "Too bad Gage doesn't want to be a part of this anymore."

"Do you honestly think that?"

I turn to her again. "He left, Mom. And I haven't heard from him since."

"I think he's just scared. You scare him."

"Well, running away from me doesn't change any of that. You know, Dad said that I should be with a rule breaker, but I'm beginning to think that men are nothing but heartbreakers."

My mother laughs. "That sounds like something your father would have said."

I sniffle and wipe under my eyes again. "God, I wish he were here."

"Me too, baby." My mother reaches for the stack of envelopes again and hands me another one. "But at least he left you this instead."

I have to blink a few times before her words register. "Wait. This is from..."

My mother nods, tears in her eyes. "Him, sweetie. Your dad wrote you a letter too."

My eyes fall to the pink envelope. "How?"

The sigh my mom lets out is so heavy that I brace myself for what she's about to say. "You know, I thought your father let me in on all of his secrets before he died, but apparently there was one that he kept. I've fought with him in my mind about it since I found out about Diane's will and this marriage. But honestly, knowing your father and myself, I can see why he didn't tell me about the arrangement with Diane."

"What do you mean?"

"Diane got your father's permission for Gage to marry you before she made her will, honey. Your father agreed to let her make the marriage a stipulation of the inheritance."

My mouth drops open. "Oh my God."

"I know." She throws her hands up. "I can barely believe it myself. But after thinking about it, I get why." She cups the side of my face. "Your father knew that your romantic heart would be willing to risk hurt to see the potential on the other side of this. But me? The realist? I would have never agreed to this back then."

"When did they arrange this?"

"Apparently a year before your father was diagnosed with his cancer, right after Diane's COPD diagnosis. Little did we know that he would die before her. He was supposed to deliver the letters, so I was gifted that responsibility. Once you and Gage got married, Timothy called me down to his office and explained the entire thing."

"I can't believe this."

"You and me both, sweetie. But your father never did anything that he didn't believe in, even arguing with Dallas about joining the Marines. He always wanted what was best for his kids. Even if he ended up being wrong, his heart was always in the right place."

"So he honestly thought that an arranged marriage would be good for me?"

"It killed your dad every time that you got hurt in love. He wanted to give you every opportunity to find your person, and when Diane explained Gage's circumstances to him, he knew that even if you two didn't fall in love, that you would be someone he could lean on when Diane died. He knew what it felt like to be alone, to feel like no one understood you. Your father fought demons throughout his life that no human should have to face. So, he wanted you to help Gage not end up like him as well. He knew your heart wouldn't let him."

I can barely see my mother through my tears. "I can't believe this."

My mother holds up a pink envelope that's been handled much more than the others. "Well, I got a letter too."

We share a laugh. "Dad and his damn letters," I say, staring down at the one in my hand.

"Yes, he had a way with words as well. Now, I have no idea what yours says, but just know that I'm here for you if you need to talk about it."

I lunge at my mom, sobbing into her shoulder. "I love you, Mom."

"Oh, I love you too, Hazel. You have no idea how much I love all of my children. You will be okay, no matter what happens with Gage, all right?"

I nod against her. "I know...because I have you."

***

Sitting at the top of the lighthouse, holding a letter from my dad, feels like the past and future coming together at full force.

There was a time when he would be sitting here with me, holding my hand as I navigate yet another heartbreak. And for this one, I wish he were here now more than ever.

At least I have his words, which might as well be the next best thing.

I unfold the stack of papers in front of me and brace myself for what he has to say.

Hazelnut,

Don't panic. I know you must have so many questions, and I hope that I can answer them for you even though I'm not physically there.

First, I love you. My daughter, you are one of the best things I have ever created and nurtured in my life. Your drive, your heart, your capacity for love—I hope you never lose sight of the amazing human that you are and how everyone who knows you is better because you are in their life.

Now, about this marriage. Yeah, I'm sure you are wondering how I, your father who loves romantic movies as much as you, would ever agree to an arranged marriage for my daughter. Well, the simple answer is that even if it blew up in our faces, Diane and I knew you and Gage would be set financially for life.

But the not-so-simple answer is that sometimes your soul knows something that you can't explain.

Diane and I actually became friends when I ventured to the lighthouse for the very first time. It was after Dallas left for his first deployment and I was worried sick about him—how it would change him, how he might not come back alive. Diane was sitting on the beach right below the lighthouse, staring out at the ocean with her own worries and we just started talking. Turns out, she just found out her brother was diagnosed with a heart condition, and she was scared about what it would mean for his son, her nephew, if he died.

From then on, we would cross paths every now and again and as her health got worse, your mom and I would help her when we could.

When she received her COPD diagnosis, she was terrified of what it would mean leaving Gage behind, especially after her brother died unexpectedly. And by that point, you had already formed a bond with her as her photographer.

Well, that's when she approached me with a crazy idea, and said she would only go through with it if I agreed. All I knew was that if she and I could bring two people together that needed one another in ways we couldn't be there for anymore, then it was worth a shot.

And yes, I know that Gage could potentially have a heart condition like his father, but I know that even if he does, that would never stop my girl from loving him if he was the person meant for her.

So, I hope you understand that my intention was never to play God with your life. It was to give you a chance at one you've always wanted. Because even if the marriage didn't work out, you'd have money to do whatever you wanted to.

But I know in my heart that your heart is not meant to travel this life alone, Hazelnut. You are a lover in every sense of the word—because love is showing up for people, even when it's hard.

It's finding humor in pain, and joy in sadness. It's seeing people at their worst and accepting them anyway.

You have given me the kind of love and admiration that a father and man could only dream of, and some day, another man will be lucky enough to receive that from you too.

I love you, my dearest daughter, with all of my heart. And I will always be with you.

Just look for the hummingbirds and know that I am there.

Dad

By the time I'm done reading, I'm sobbing so hard that I can barely breathe, collapsing to the floor and holding the paper to my chest, like I'm hanging on to the only man that has ever loved me as fiercely as I wish another could.

But when I wake up in the morning after crying myself to sleep, I almost wonder if I'm still dreaming.

Because when I open my eyes, I'm in my husband's arms.

Chapter Twenty-Four

Gage

"Gage?" Hazel's voice is groggy and her eyes are swollen from crying. It kills me just looking at her because I know I'm the reason for her pain.

But she's never looked more beautiful to me.

"Shhh...I'm here, baby."

She reaches up to touch my face, dragging her nails through my scruff. "You are?" Blinking, she takes a deep breath. "When did you get here?"

I look at my phone and notice the time. "About four hours ago."

"What time is it?"

"Seven in the morning."

"Does that mean..."

"That I drove all night to get here? Yeah, I did, Spitfire."

She rises, sliding from my arms and putting distance between us. She wraps her arms around her legs and pulling them into her chest. "What are you doing here?"

I reach out to her, wanting her back in my arms. "Come back to me, please."

She shakes her head, her bottom lip trembling. "Why are you here, Gage?"

I crawl across the floor to her instead, pulling her into my chest. I don't blame her for the hesitation, for having her guard up around me right now. I deserve every bit of her disdain and animosity. But if I'm going to have this conversation with her, she's going to be in my arms.

Cupping her face, I lift her chin so she can look straight into my eyes. "I'm here because you're my wife, and I love you, and I'm ready to make decisions together." Her eyes instantly well with tears. "Fuck, Hazel. Don't cry anymore, baby."

But when she launches herself at me, I break apart too, letting every fear of mine go as I hold on to the one person I can't live without. When we both regain our composure, she leans back and holds my face in her hands, straddling my hips. "I love you too."

"I know you do. Why, I don't think I'll ever fucking understand, but I want this." I press my lips to hers. "I want you."

Her grip on me tightens. "Then you can't push me away when you're scared, Gage." Her voice is thick with emotion, but unwavering. "I can be strong for you. I can help you carry the weight, but I can't take you shutting me out. I won't."

"I know, baby. I'm so sorry, I just..."

"Talk to me." She wipes the tears from my face. "Tell me everything. Start from the beginning."

"Before my diagnosis, I felt like I was taking my life for granted, Hazel. When most people get life changing news like mine, they carpe diem. But me, I just got angry." Shaking my head, I run my hands up and down her back. "I withdrew. I decided that I didn't get to have a life like other people, like normal people. And I resented my dad so much for not fucking telling me that I could have this condition as well. He kept it from me, which made that anger even worse."

"Why did he keep it from you?"

"Because we didn't talk about shit like that. Honestly, I never had a great relationship with my dad. I think he thought that by working tirelessly and providing for me, he was doing his part as a good father. But I was alone most of my childhood, especially after my mom took off. She loved drugs more than me, but looking back, I'm glad she left and didn't drag me into that part of her life with her."

"I'm so sorry, Gage."

"When I told you that you have no idea how lucky you are to have your family, Hazel, I meant it. I was jealous of that, but I accepted a long time ago that I didn't get that type of family, so being alone was just how it was supposed to be. And then once I found out about my heart, I felt like that was the nail in the coffin that sealed my fate of solitude."

"Until your aunt left us millions of dollars."

I laugh. "Yeah. And you know...it's not like she didn't try to set us up before, but..."

"We had both sworn off love."

"Exactly."

She sighs, a pinch in her brow. "I wish you would have told me about your heart sooner."

"I wanted to, but it was easier to ignore it, pretend like it wasn't an issue." I rub my thumb along her bottom lip. "You definitely gave me something else to focus on."

"Except when the dizzy spells started happening."

I close my eyes. "Yeah. And it was my fault for not telling Dr. Miranda about them. If I had, she probably could have adjusted my meds before the episode at Parker's wedding."

She shoves at my chest, forcing me to look at her again. "You realize I thought that Miranda was some woman you were talking to back home?"

Chuckling, I say, "Well, you weren't wrong. And I planned on telling you everything when we talked this week. I just didn't get the chance. And then when I woke up and saw the look on your face as I was lying in that hospital bed…it was every fear slamming into me at once."

She licks her lips, pushing her hand through my hair and trailing it down my jaw. "What fears?"

"Even though I wasn't close with my dad, his death affected me. It's like I realized everything I missed out on, everything I could have changed if he hadn't died. And that's when I decided that I never wanted to leave someone else with that feeling, so I was better off just being alone for the rest of my life as well. You looked at me with the fear that I was dying, and the last thing I wanted was anyone to ever feel that way…especially you."

"So you asked me to leave."

"Yes." I swallow past the lump in my throat. "What if I don't wake up next time, Hazel? What if I leave you and a couple of kids?" I shake my head. "This condition is hereditary and I still don't have it under control, and I don't want you burdened by being with me."

"Taking care of you and loving you would never be a burden."

"You say that now…"

She presses a finger to my lips. "No. You listen to me, Gage. Being with you is *my* choice," she says, pointing a finger on her other hand to her chest. "I would rather take that risk than never have another second with you in my life again. Do you understand me?"

I feel tears build again in my eyes. "Are you sure?"

"I've never been more sure of anything in my life." Relief laced with gratitude rushes through me. "Besides, when you love someone, you never really leave them alone, even after you're gone. Look at my dad, look at Diane. They are still showing us they are with us."

I pull her into my chest, closing my eyes as I breathe her in, as the reality that she wants me resonates in my chest. "I'm sorry I asked you to leave. I promise to never do that to you again."

"I won't ever leave, so it's pretty pointless." Her tenacity makes me laugh as tension begins to leave my body. "So what happens now, Gage? What kind of decisions do you want me to make with you?"

"Everything," I say, smiling up at her. "I want you to fight *for* me and *with* me, just like you said."

She brings my lips to hers. "Then that's what you'll get."

Thank fuck.

Chapter Twenty-Five

Hazel

As soon as we get back to the apartment, Gage pins me up against the door. "I need you, Spitfire," he says as he yanks his shirt over his head, revealing that inked chest and lean physique that I can't get enough of.

I toss my shirt to the side and slide my shorts and underwear down my legs. "I need you too."

Not wasting one more second, Gage crashes into me. His hands are everywhere, his lips tease my skin and kiss me so deeply that I can barely breathe when he lets me come up for air. I help him take off his pants and briefs and then he's back on my mouth, claiming me and kissing me like he thought he'd never get the chance to again. When he lifts me up and pins me to the door, I feel his cock pressing against my pussy, ready to slide inside.

"Gage…"

"Can I take you like this, Hazel? Can I take you with nothing between us?"

I nod. "Yes."

He presses himself up and we both gasp as he enters me with very little resistance. "Fuck," he groans. "God damn, Hazel. You have no idea what you do to me."

I hold his face in my hands as he fucks me at a relentless pace. "I do. I feel it too."

"I fucking love you," he says, resting his forehead on mine.

"I love you too."

Gage swivels his hips on his next drive, hitting something inside of me that has me gasping for air. He does it again, over and over until I'm screaming through my orgasm, and moments later he finds his own.

Once we've showered and cleaned up, Gage guides me to lie in bed with him. My body is spent, but my mind is still reeling with so many questions.

"Were you in Florida while you were gone?"

Gage chuckles. "Where else would I have gone?"

"I don't know," I say, drawing circles on his chest with my finger.

"I had to go see Dr. Miranda."

"I want to meet her."

He kisses my forehead. "Then we will make it happen."

"What did she say?"

"She's going to adjust my meds. This episode wasn't as bad as the one I had the week my aunt died, so..."

I lift my head from his chest. "Oh my God. That's why you weren't here, wasn't it?"

He nods. "Yeah, baby. And it killed me."

"I'm sorry for making you feel like shit about that."

He strokes my cheek. "You didn't know."

Sighing, I lay my head back down on his chest. "Does your doctor think a new medication will help?"

"It's the next logical step. But if things get worse..."

"We'll handle them together," I say before he can finish his thought.

His arms squeeze me tighter to him. "Be patient with me, Hazel. Please. This is all new to me, sharing this part of my life with someone."

"Your aunt knew though."

"Yeah, she did."

I sit up again so I can see his eyes. "Did you know that she was friends with my Dad?"

His brows furrow. "No."

I stand from the bed in search of my purse, grabbing the two letters I received yesterday from my mom and bringing them back to the bed. "My dad wrote me a letter."

Gage sits up in the bed, resting against the headboard. "Holy shit."

"Yeah…"

"My aunt wrote me one too."

My eyes widen. "Really?"

It's Gage's turn to leave the bed and come back with a letter. When he settles back in, he hands his to me. "I want you to read it."

I hand him mine from my dad. "I want you to read mine too."

I lean my back against his chest as we both grow silent, taking in the words on the pages that summarize every moment that led to us ending up right where we are. By the time we're done reading, both of us are crying again.

"Fuck." Gage tosses the letters to the side and wraps his arms around me, the wetness of his cheek hitting my shoulder. "Somehow they knew…they knew before we ever did."

"It's so crazy."

"It is, but I'm so fucking grateful, Hazel. I'm grateful that my aunt was looking out for me, and I'm grateful to your dad for raising you, for knowing the person you are and how you could impact my life."

I turn my head so I can see his face. "You've changed my life too, Gage. You made me believe in love again."

"I never believed in it until I met you."

Gage leans forward and kisses me, and my body begins to melt all over again.

"You know, my mom was the one delivering the letters."

Gage huffs out a laugh. "That makes sense. Dallas is the one who gave me mine, though."

"Really?"

"He brought my bike to the hospital."

"What?" I shout.

Gage presses a finger to my lips. "Don't be mad at him. He knew I needed some space, but he told me that if I didn't plan on coming back, to be honest with you because he knew you'd wait for me."

"I would have."

"I know, Spitfire." He kisses me softly. "But I knew the second I got back to Florida that it wasn't home anymore. Home is here with you, in this apartment, in Carrington Cove."

I reach for the other letter. "Then we'd better make sure we finish what your aunt started," I say, handing him the paper. He reads the next task, smiling the entire time. "You only get one life, Gage. You're the one that gets to choose how you live it, but I know what my choice would be." His eyes meet mine. "I don't want to only choose three photos to summarize our relationship, to look back on and remember. I want one thousand photos, Gage. I want every good and bad memory, even if that means our time is cut short. I'd rather have that time with you than none at all."

He reaches for his phone, flips the camera to face us, and holds it up above us. "Then I need more memories to choose from, Hazel. What we had isn't enough and I don't think it ever will be."

***

"Nice to meet you." I reach out to shake Dr. Miranda's hand before taking a seat in one of the chairs opposite her desk. Gage sits down in the chair beside me, reaching for my hand.

"The pleasure is all mine, truly. I'm glad that Gage has someone now in all of this."

I turn to look at him. "Me too." When I twist back to face Dr. Miranda again, I say, "But I have some questions."

"Of course. Ask away."

"Is there anything I can do to help you?"

My question catches her off-guard. "Wow. Well, the best thing you can do is make sure he keeps his appointments with me for regular checkups and scans, and that he's honest with both of us about how he's feeling on a day-to-day basis."

"Done. Next, are there any activities that Gage should avoid so he doesn't risk having another episode?"

Gage rolls his eyes but Dr. Miranda laughs. "As long as Gage listens to his body, he should be all right to participate in most forms of exercise within reason. The medication he's on will help manage his symptoms, but it's not a cure."

"I think Hazel is concerned about my ability to have sex, Doc."

I smack his chest. "Gage!"

The doctor laughs. "She has every right to be concerned, but with the new medication, hopefully we won't have any more dizzy spells."

"And this is the new medication? How long will it take for us to know it's effective?" I ask, focusing my attention back on Gage's doctor, mentally taking note of how I'm going to get back at him for making me look like a pervert in front of her.

Dr. Miranda slides her eyes to Gage. "I like her."

"I knew you would," Gage replies, squeezing my hand. "Hazel, babe—"

"No," I cut him off. "I want to make sure I'm doing everything I can and know as much as possible to keep you healthy, Gage. Okay?" I lift my phone from my pocket. "I've already set an alarm to remind you to take your medication."

He leans forward, cups the side of my face, and rubs his nose against mine. "I love you."

I press a short kiss to his lips and then face Dr. Miranda again. "Continue, please."

She chuckles. "The new medication may take a few months to take full effect. Some things to look out for are dizziness, of course, fainting spells, lack of energy, rapid heart rate. Also, his alcohol intake should be minimal."

"Are you recruiting her to be my babysitter now?" Gage asks.

I whip my head in his direction. "Absolutely."

"You should have known that this was going to happen, Gage," Dr. Miranda says. "When you have someone who cares about you, they take responsibility for your well-being too."

"Don't worry. This man won't be able to so much as breathe without me checking on him from now on," I say, making both of them laugh.

The ironic thing is that sitting here and learning about what our life will look like together is actually making it easier for me to breathe, knowing that together, we can keep Gage healthy.

Chapter Twenty-Six

Gage

"Once I get started, you know there's no backing out."

Hazel rolls her eyes at me in the mirror as she lies on her side on my table. "I'm aware."

"And the ribs? You're sure that's where you want it? Kind of an intense spot for your first tattoo." I stretch the latex gloves over my hands as I stare down at her. My wife is letting me give her the first tattoo she'll ever have, and there's something about this moment that is making me fall in love with her even more.

Maybe it's how much trust she's putting in me. Maybe it's the fact that my art will be on her body for the rest of our lives.

Or maybe it's the fact that the tattoo I'm about to give her is a way to bring this whole story of ours full circle.

"I'm not scared," she says, making me laugh. "I can handle pain, remember?"

Memories of me spanking her among other various activities come to mind. I waggle my eyebrows at her. "Oh, I'm aware."

She shoves me. "Get your mind out of the gutter, Gage Kingston."

I lean forward and press my lips to hers. "My mind will always be in the gutter when I'm around you, Hazel Kingston."

Her smile makes my heart skip a beat, but not in the way that will make me end up in the hospital. No, it makes my heart beat in a way that reminds me I'm alive, and this woman lying here in front of me is the reason why I get to live a life full of gratitude and love.

Today is our four-month wedding anniversary and the letter Hazel's mom gave us from my aunt said to do something you've been afraid to do. Even though Hazel says she's not scared, I know making this decision to finally get a tattoo is one that she's been putting off because of the fear she has about it.

It's not the pain, it's the idea of putting art on her body that will be there forever.

Until last night when she told me that she's not afraid anymore because the art I drew on her is how we first met and that's what she always wants to remember about our time together—where we started compared to where we are now.

I can't deny that her words made me tear up a bit.

But since we are both supposed to do something we've been afraid of, I have my own task to accomplish once I'm finished with her tattoo.

"Just focus on my tattoo, please," she says, pulling me back to reality as I prepare the stencil for her body. Once I have it in place and lift it off, I have her check it in the mirror.

"You like?"

She smiles. "Yes. It's perfect." When she turns to me, I see tears in her eyes. "I want you to leave a mark on me forever, Gage. That's what this represents to me."

I lean forward and kiss her softly. "You left a mark on me the second I saw you, Spitfire. Your strength, your courage, your outlook on life, looking for the glimmers in it all the time..."

She folds in her lips as a tear rolls down her cheek. "That's what my dad used to say about me. That's why he used to call me his hummingbird."

I pull her into me, kiss her softly, and wipe her tears away. Once Hazel gets back in position, I get to work, and honestly, I don't know why I doubted that this girl could handle this. She actually falls asleep on me when I'm about halfway done which makes me laugh because most grown men tear up when they're getting their ribs tattooed.

But while she's out, I complete something extra just for us.

"Hazel?" I gently shake her awake. "Baby...I'm done."

Her eyes flutter open. "What?"

"You fell asleep, baby. I have no idea how," I say through a laugh. "But it's done. You wanna see?" I help her stand and then take her back over to the mirror. She gasps when she sees the finished product.

"It's beautiful, Gage."

"It turned out good."

She swats at me. "It's better than good. It's almost identical to the one you drew on my arm that day. But what is that?" she asks, pointing to the letters that I put in the corner of the wings. "DK and MS?"

"Diane Kingston and Michael Sheppard." Her eyes lock with mine. "I felt like they needed to be a part of it too."

She spins to face me, but as she does, I drop down to one knee. "Gage? Wh—what are you doing?"

"Hazel Marie Kingston..."

"We're already married, Gage!" she exclaims through her laugh.

"I know we are, Spitfire. Will you just let me say what I need to say, damn it?"

She closes her mouth and nods.

"Thank you. Now, as I was about to say before I was so rudely interrupted..." She rolls her eyes, which only seems fitting at this point.

"Hazel Marie Kingston, I never imagined in a million years that the day I was called to draw a hummingbird on you would be the day that changed my entire life. But now, that piece of art is permanently on your body, and there's no better way to signify this day than to make sure you know that being married to you is both everything I never wanted and everything I could ever need."

I reach into my back pocket and take out the ring I bought last week, a princess cut solitaire with two pink diamonds on the sides. "I never bought you a ring when we agreed to this because I didn't think this would be forever. But now I know without a shadow of a doubt that you are the woman that was meant to be my wife, to fight with me and for me, to make my life have meaning. And one day soon, I'd like to have a proper wedding with you, if that's what you want." Hazel's eyes are full of tears, but I continue. "Hazel...will you continue to be married to me for the rest of our lives?"

She kneels down in front of me. "Yes."

I slide the ring on her finger and then pull her face toward mine, kissing her with everything I have.

When we part, she says, "This ring is beautiful."

Peering down at the diamond on her hand, I sigh. "I knew it belonged on your hand."

"But I don't have one for you, Gage."

I lift my left hand and show her the tattoo I had one of the other guys do yesterday, hoping that Hazel wouldn't notice. The solid hummingbird on the base of my left ring finger is still swollen, but it was the perfect way to mark me as hers. "I don't need one. I have you marked on me too."

She covers her mouth. "Oh my God. When did you do that?"

"Axel did it yesterday for me after I told him I want to take over the shop." She gasps, her eyes wide. We haven't talked about me taking over the shop since that day before Parker and Cashlynn's wedding, but making that decision was the thing I'd been afraid to do.

Well, not anymore.

"I'm surprised you didn't notice, but I'm glad so I could surprise you with it."

Hazel launches herself at me as we tumble to the ground. And that's where we stay, laughing and talking until it's time to take her home and celebrate properly.

Chapter Twenty-Seven

Hazel

"Damn, Gage. You did good," Willow says, whistling as she holds my hand in front of her, admiring my ring.

"Thank you." Gage smiles over at me. "Hazel seems to like it."

I can't help but laugh. "I honestly can't stop staring at it."

Astrid grabs my hand from Willow. "With good reason. So are you two going to have a real wedding now?"

"Our last wedding was real," I reply.

"You know what I mean." Astrid turns to Gage, who just shrugs.

"If that's what Hazel wants, then we'll make it happen."

"I honestly don't know. I mean, I love the idea, but I think I'd rather use that money for something else."

Willow rolls her eyes. "In two months, you two are about to have over ten million dollars. I think you can afford it."

I slap my hand to my forehead. "I honestly forget about that."

Astrid laughs. "Damn. What a problem to have."

My mother comes around the corner from the kitchen. "It's almost time to eat, everyone."

"So now that it's official, I guess this means you won't be playing on my team next week," Dallas says, coming up behind us and slapping Gage on the back.

After Gage and I reunited, my brother and I had a long talk, one that Gage joined us for. He apologized for inserting himself into our relationship, and assured us that he would back off now that things were settled. I also asked him if he'd be willing to walk me down the aisle if we decided to have a wedding, which made him practically sob.

I still threatened revenge if he went back on his word because, honestly, I'm not sure he'll be able to keep his nose out of my business—ever. But deep down, I know I'm lucky to have family that cares about my happiness. I wouldn't be here in this moment if they didn't.

My family gathers around the table for dinner, taking their usual seats. Dallas, Willow, and Michael sit together, my nephew growing bigger by the day as well as my niece in Willow's belly that will be here early next year. Astrid, Penn, Bentley, and Lilly are next to them. Parker and Cashlynn are at one end of the table, struggling to keep their hands off of each other. And then right as I take a seat in my chair, my husband sits down next to me, kissing me on the top of my head as he does.

My husband.

I've found my person now.

My mother brings over the casserole dishes and then everyone settles in, dishing out their food and catching up on each other's lives.

It's a usual Sunday afternoon dinner in the Sheppard household, except it feels different too.

The past three years have been full of so much change. Losing my dad was one of the most painful moments of my life, but I also feel that through his death, all of us discovered things about ourselves.

Dallas opened himself up to love thanks to our father and was able to find peace in their tumultuous relationship while he grew up.

Penn finally started to live his life for himself and go after the woman he'd always wanted.

Parker let go of his need for perfection and realized that being alone wasn't the best thing for him.

And I found Gage, but my dad also had his hand in that as well.

"This is really good, Catherine," Gage says from beside me. "I swear, nothing you make disappoints."

My mother smiles proudly. "Glad to hear it."

"Look at this guy trying to be the new favorite son," Parker says, gesturing to Gage with his fork.

Gage flips him the bird. "I'll remember that when you want a discount on your tattoo."

Penn wipes his mouth with his napkin. "Remember, I bought your aunt's house, okay?"

Dallas clears his throat. "I..."

I point my knife at my oldest brother. "You meddled in my relationship, so don't even bother trying to kiss my husband's ass."

All of the women laugh. "So is this what Gage has to look forward to now that he's taken over CC Ink?" Willow asks.

Gage nods. "Apparently so."

"Axel already left you the keys, huh?" Astrid asks, lifting her glass of water to her lips.

"He did. The paperwork for transfer of ownership is being drawn up and Timothy said we can sign in a few weeks. But he was ready."

I reach over and rub Gage's shoulder. "A lot has changed in the past few weeks, but in the best way."

Gage wipes his mouth with his napkin and lifts his glass, holding his gaze on mine. "I know we've already started eating, but I'd like to propose a toast."

Everyone grows silent as they reach for their glasses as well. I stare at my husband, curious with what he's about to say.

He drifts his gaze to my family. "I just want to thank you, all of you, for welcoming me into your family." His throat bobs as he swallows. "As you know, mine is gone. But marrying Hazel has changed so much for me. Not only did I find the most incredible woman who puts up with my shit..." Everyone laughs. "But through her I was given all of you. The Sheppard family—a group of people that love hard and protect each other no matter what. I'm proud to be a part of you now." He raises his glass. "So thank you."

My mother wipes away her tears. "We're honored to have you in our family too, Gage."

"Here, here," Penn says, smiling at Gage and me from the across the table.

"Well, now I feel like I need to say something," Dallas chimes in.

I groan. "Do you really?"

"Come on, Hazelnut. You know it's my duty as the oldest brother."

"No one gave you that job except for you."

Willow laughs, rubbing her growing belly. "Oh, Hazel. Just humor him." She winks at me.

"Fine."

Dallas raises his beer. "You know, I always knew that when Hazel got married I was going to have a hard time with it. I honestly never thought she'd find a man good enough for her." My eyes start to water.

"But somehow, Dad knew what she needed." He turns to Willow. "What I needed too."

My mother sniffles from the end of the table.

"I think I can speak for everyone here when I say that I miss that man, more than I ever thought was possible. But I know he's with us every day—watching over us, keeping us safe, and guiding us to where we're supposed to be. And Gage?"

I turn to look at my husband who looks like he's barely holding it together. His jaw is clenched so tight that he might crack a tooth, but the look in his eyes is one I've been seeing much more from him lately—gratitude.

"Our dad brought you into this family. Your aunt too. You belong here, and I'm proud to call you my brother."

"Absolutely," Parker adds.

"To Gage and Hazel!" Dallas cheers as everyone clinks their glasses together.

I lean into my husband and whisper, "You sure you want to be a part of this?"

"Absolutely, Spitfire. You and your family are my people now."

Gage kisses me and, for a moment, I just take it all in.

My life and journey with love did not pan out the way I thought they would, but I wouldn't change it for anything since it's how I ended up here.And I guess what I've learned in all of this is that *sometimes, somehow, somewhere,* and *someday*, you realize that *someone* you love could know what's best for you before you ever figure it out yourself.

Chapter Twenty-Eight

Hazel

One Month Later

"This is it." Gage whispers in my ear. "You ready?"

Astrid jumps up and down next to us. "We're gonna win! I can feel it."

I smack her arms, pulling her to a stop. "Don't jinx it."

"It's called visualization, Hazel. Manifestation." She points to her temple. "You have to say and believe what you want, then the universe will give it to you."

I roll my eyes. "Fine. Then I want a million dollars and to beat my brother in the Carrington Cove Games."

Gage laughs beside me. "You'll have five million dollars in a month from now, remember, Spitfire?"

I turn to look at him. "Oh yeah."

"How do you keep forgetting about that money?" Cashlynn asks as Timothy MacDonald calls for the teams to line up at the starting line for the final game, a potato sack race that I feel confident we can win.

However, I underestimated Dallas. He recruited people from losing teams over the years that he knew wanted a taste at being on a winning team for a change. They've definitely put up a fight, but I think this last race is ours.

Gage and I have been practicing potato sack racing in our apartment for the past two weeks since I had a feeling it would be one of the games this year. They rotate from year to year and this one hasn't appeared for a while.

"Because that's not my focus right now, Cashlynn," I say, glaring at her. "My focus is beating my brother, showing him that he isn't the most badass Sheppard sibling, proving to him that I can outsmart him, and…"

Grady leans over to Gage. "You sure you're not rethinking marrying into this family now?"

Gage shakes his head, but his smirk tells me that he knows how I feel about this. This win is for bragging rights. "Not at all. In fact, I hope we wipe the floor with Dallas just so I can watch him pout."

I reach out to high-five him. "That's my fucking husband."

Grady tosses his head back in laughter and then rubs his hands together. "Then let's do this."

Our team lines up along the starting line. I glance over at my brother, glaring at him to make sure he knows that I'm dialed in.

"You ready for this, Hazelnut? This is for all the marbles."

"No. This is about pride, Dallas." I pound a fist to my chest. "Get ready to cry."

He chuckles. "I have tissues in my pocket ready for you when you lose."

"The end of this game will be slightly different than normal," Timothy says, grabbing our attention. "At the end of the race, the last contestant will have to sink three bean bags into the cornhole boards to seal the deal and clench the title.”

I turn to look at Gage. “Shit.”

“Let me go last,” he suggests, turning behind him to consult the team. Everyone nods in agreement.

“Okay. Yeah, I think that’s our best shot.”

Dallas calls out to us as he makes his way to the back of his line as well. “You sure you don’t want Grady to go last?” Grady flips him off as my brother cackles, holding his stomach.

“You afraid you can’t beat me, Dallas?” Gage calls out to my brother, which makes his laughter stop abruptly.

Dallas glares at Gage. “Get ready to lose, Gage. Don’t worry, I have enough tissues for you *and* Hazel.”

Timothy calls out to us. “Teams...are you ready?”

I turn back to him and nod, bracing myself to go first. “Ready!”

Sally calls out from Dallas’s line. “Ready!”

And then the whistle blows, spiking my anxiety even more as I struggle to get the sack on and start hopping across the sand.

Person after person on my team makes their way across, neck and neck with Dallas’s team the entire time. When one person gets ahead, someone else trips, making the lead go back and forth as each person takes their turn.

And then before I know it, Gage is the last person hopping into the sack, leaping across the sand, fighting like hell to beat Dallas to the cornhole board.

The two of them arrive within seconds of each other, sprinting to pick up the bean bags in preparation to throw them.

Dallas tosses his first bag and sinks it right through the hole. “Hell yeah!”

Gage sinks his first as well. “Don’t get cocky, Dallas!”

They both throw their second bag at the same time, but Gage misses as Dallas's slinks through the hole again. "What was that?" Dallas mocks him. "Who's behind now?"

But while Dallas is talking, Gage tosses his third bag and makes it through the hole, tying the score at 2-2.

As if someone is filming them in slow motion, both men prepare to launch their last bean bags in the air, leaving their hands at the same time.

All eyes are on them as they sail through the sky, arching toward the boards and aiming toward their target, making the seconds crawl as we find out who is going to be the champion of the Carrington Cove Games this year.

And when the cheers ring out around me, I don't believe what I just saw.

"Oh my God!"

Timothy bellows out, "Holy moly, folks! The winner of this year's Carrington Cove Games is..."

***

Want to know the winner of the final Carrington Cove Games? Find out who it is in the sneak peek into Hazel and Gage's future!

Scan for
Bonus Epi-
logue

***

My new series, Blossom Peak, features Laney, Hazel's friend from this
book! She's about to be reunited with her brother's best friend who
broke her heart when they were younger.

Want a sneak peek of what's to come? Keep reading

OR you can read All This Time, Blossom Peak Book #1 here.

Sneak Peek at Blossom Peak

"Fuck, it's good to see you, man." Elliot shoves Rhonan and Henley aside to get to me, wrapping me in another hug, this time lifting me from the ground and shaking me up and down a few times before setting me back down.

I fix my shirt as I regain my footing, studying my friend who seems way more cheerful than he typically is. "Jesus, have you been working out?"

Elliot bats his eyelashes at me. "You trying to flatter me already?"

"I mean, as your best man, that's part of my job, right? Motivational speeches and encouragement?"

"Not sure I'll need them." Elliot pulls Tori into his side and kisses the top of her head. "What's the saying? When you know, you know?"

I nod, though I'm still wrapping my head around the fact that this is really happening. When Elliot called and told me he reconnected with Tori and had never felt this strongly for a woman before, I was more than happy for him. The guy's been a workaholic since he graduated from law school, and even before that, his nose was always stuck in a book. He never failed to find time to flirt with women, but marriage was never a goal of his. So, I was shocked when he called to say he was engaged after just six months of dating. Having never been in a serious relationship before, I know I have no room to judge. But anyone would agree that timeline was fast.

Tori rolls her eyes as she giggles. "This guy was adamant about a big wedding too. I said we should elope."

"I mean, I'm always down for a trip to Vegas."

"But if you go to Vegas ,then I can't go!" A tiny voice behind the group of grown men and Tori breaks through our conversation as Ellis pushes her way toward me.

I crouch down to intercept her as she runs into my arms. "Ellis, my girl!" Inhaling deeply, I take a moment to savor seeing this little ray of sunshine again in person instead of through a cell phone, kissing the top of her head through her brown hair as dark as her father's. "How are you, princess?"

"I'm not a princess yet, Uncle Fletcher." She leans back in my arms as I stand to full height again. "But in the wedding, I get to wear a princess dress."

I reach down and toy with the tulle on her dress she's wearing right now. "Then what do you call this thing?"

"A dress, duh." She rolls her eyes.

"Looks like a princess dress to me."

She wriggles in my arms, so I set her down on the floor. "No, this dress is just for twirling." Holding her hands above her head, she proceeds to turn in a circle but loses her balance and falls to the floor.

"Careful, Ellis." Laney pushes her way into our circle, helping her niece stand up again.

Her voice slides across my skin like a memory I can't shake—sharp, warm, and still too goddamn powerful.

Her long brown hair with soft blonde highlights covers her face as she bends down, but when she stands upright again and our eyes meet, a flurry of emotions slam into me all at once.

Laney.

My Laney. Even more beautiful than the last time I saw her.

Fuck. These three weeks are going to be torture.

"I'm okay, Auntie," Ellis says, pushing Laney away before attempting to twirl again and nailing it this time.

We all clap in celebration.

"Finally came over to say hello?" I say, directing my attention to my best friend's little sister.

Laney arches a brow at me. "I was just letting your fan club fawn over you first."

I huff out a laugh, grateful to see that her sass hasn't diminished. "Nice to see you too, Laney."

Rhonan walks back toward the bar in the tasting room, the rest of us following. "Thomas, can you get Fletcher a drink?"

"Just water, Tom," I call out quickly—the last thing I need right now is alcohol.

"Come on, we're celebrating. And it's the offseason, right?" Rhonan pouts amusingly.

"I know, but I just don't feel like drinking tonight, man."

"Save it for the bachelor party then," Elliot says.

Rhonan turns to me, the corner of his mouth turned up. "You're in charge of that, by the way."

I rub the back of my neck, feeling more out of my element and overwhelmed the longer I stand in this room and reality sinks in. "I figured, but..."

Rhonan hands me my glass of water as Elliot slaps me on the back. "Don't worry. Tomorrow, Tori and I are gonna sit down with you and Laney and tell you exactly what we need your help with and what we want as far as wedding stuff goes."

Wincing, I ask, "You sure you don't just want to go to Vegas? I mean, there are strippers there."

"What's a stripper?"

The question comes from about three feet down, where Ellis is tugging on my shirt and looking up at me like I'm some kind of life encyclopedia.

I peer down at her, not sure how to safely answer this question. "Uh, a stripper is a...a dancer," I answer proudly, pleased with my quick response.

Her eyes light up. "Then I want to be a stripper when I grow up," she shouts, catching everyone's attention in the room as she proceeds to twirl around again.

Rhonan glares at me. "Thank you for that."

I put my hands up as I lower my voice and lean toward him. "What was I supposed to say? I mean, technically I told the truth."

Rhonan shakes his head and pinches the bridge of his nose. "I can't wait until I get phone calls from preschool about this."

Patting his shoulder, I say, "I'm sorry. I'll make it up to you while I'm here, all right? Maybe with some babysitting..."

"So you can teach her more about strippers?" He shakes his head. "Nah, I think I'm good."

My eyes dart over to Laney—my partner for the next three weeks apparently—who's standing across the room, laughing at something Dilynne says while Joanne watches Ellis spin in circles.

As if she can sense my staring, Laney looks up and our eyes lock.

Only for a second—but it lands like a punch. And then she looks away, her expression tightening like I'm a bad taste in her mouth.

This woman's irritation toward me hasn't diminished at all in the nearly three years since we've seen each other. The handful of times I came home since the night everything fell apart were Laney-free. She was always conveniently unavailable, busy or out of town. And while I have a pretty good idea as to why she might wish I would fall off the face of the planet, part of me wonders if there's anything I can do to make things right.

Because being near her again has my body reacting to her as if I'm seventeen all over again.

I miss the way things used to be between us—the way I felt like I could tell her anything and she wouldn't judge me, the way I *did* tell her things that no one else knew.

I miss our fucking friendship.

I miss the way she used to smile when she saw me instead of these icy glares that she's downright perfected.

I miss the girl that became the one person I could trust above all others, even more than her own brother and my best fucking friends.

I miss the girl that I grew to want, but knew I could never have.

Pre-Order All This Time TODAY!

Also By Harlow James

***

<u>The Ladies Who Brunch (rom-coms with a ton of spice)</u>
<u>Never Say Never (Charlotte and Damien)</u>
<u>No One Else (Amelia and Ethan)</u>
<u>Now's The Time (Penelope and Maddox)</u>
<u>Not As Planned (Noelle and Grant)</u>
<u>Nice Guys Still Finish (Jeffrey and Ariel)</u>

***

<u>The Newberry Springs (Gibson Brothers) Series</u>
<u>Everything to Lose (Wyatt & Kelsea)</u>
<u>Everything He Couldn't (Walker & Evelyn)</u>
<u>Everything But You (Forrest & Shauna)</u>

***

<u>The California Billionaires Series (rom coms with heart and heat)</u>
<u>My Unexpected Serenity (Wes and Shayla)</u>
<u>My Unexpected Vow (Hayes and Waverly)</u>
<u>My Unexpected Family (Silas and Chloe)</u>

***

<u>The Emerson Falls Series (smalltown romance with a found family friend group)</u>
<u>Tangled (Kane & Olivia)</u>
<u>Enticed (Cooper & Clara)</u>
<u>Captivated (Cash and Piper)</u>
<u>Revived (Luke and Rachel)</u>
<u>Devoted (Brooks and Jess)</u>

***

<u>Lost and Found in Copper Ridge</u>
A holiday romance in which two people book a stay in a cabin for the same amount of time thanks to a serendipitous $5 bill.

<u>Guilty as Charged</u>
An intense opposites attract standalone that will melt your kindle. He's an ex-con construction worker. She's a lawyer looking for passion.

<u>McKenzie's Turn to Fall</u>
A holiday romance where a romance author falls for her neighborhood butcher.

Acknowledgements

It feels AMAZING to finally have this book out in the world, especially after the trouble it caused me.

The first draft of this book was NOT what you just read. LOL But I am beyond thrilled with the final result AND this series. It's fresh, emotional, and steamy. These men are down bad for their girls, and are willing to put in the work to keep them.

With each new series, I pinch myself that I get to write love stories and people read them. It is truly is an honor, and I hope to keep doing this for many years to come.

To my husband: Thank you for believing in me and cheering me on every step of the way. Thank you for traveling with me, investing in my success, and being my person, my best friend, the man that inspires all of my book boyfriends, and my official Book Bitch. I love you.

To my beta readers: Emily, Keely, Carolina, and Kelly: you four are the best voices I have in my corner. Each of you gives me the advice, feedback, and support that I need in your own way. I'm so grateful to have the four of you on my team still after all this time. I love you all and appreciate you more than you'll ever know.

To Kait, my P.A.: Hiring you has been one of the best decisions I've ever made. Your friendship and professional support have helped me so much this year. Thank you for being my newest cheerleader!

To Jess, my social media manager: You have single-handedly made my life better! I have so much more time to focus on writing and other aspects of my business thanks to you. Your time and creativity is appreciated SO much. Thank you from the bottom of my heart for doing what you do for me.

To Kari, my content team leader: I'm SO honored that you agreed to help me with this new aspect of my team! You are such an incredible support and I'm looking forward to how much we can grow this team together.

And to my readers: thank you for supporting me, whether you've been here since the beginning, or you're brand new. I LOVE this hobby turned business of mine. It's an amazing feeling to be able to create art for someone to enjoy and forming a relationship from that. I never take my readers for granted and know that there would be no Harlow James without you.

So thank you for supporting a wife and mom who found a hobby that she loves.
And a future career that I'm working toward with each passing day.

Connect with Harlow James

Follow me on Amazon

Follow me on Instagram

Follow me on Facebook

Join my Facebook Group: https://www.facebook.com/groups/494

991441142710/

Follow me on Goodreads

Follow me on Book Bub

Subscribe to my Newsletter for Updates on New Releases and Give-

aways

Website